I0619566

Finding
Angie

Also by Richard Leighland

House of Fate

Finding Angie

Richard Leighland

Wagoner Oklahoma

Copyright © 2026 Richard Leighland

All rights reserved. No part of this book may be reproduced, transmitted, or stored in any form or by any means—electronic, mechanical, or otherwise—without prior written permission from the publisher, except as authorized by law.

Cover design by AZ Designs
highway photograph by Matheus Bertlli

ISBN: 978-1-947035-66-9
Published by AZ Literary Press
an imprint of AZ Entertainment Group, LLC

For inquiries, including bulk orders, please contact:
AZ Entertainment Group LLC
PO BOX 854
Wagoner, OK 74477-0854

Email: info@az-entertainmentllc.com
Website: www.az-entertainmentllc.com

First Edition

Printed in the United States of America

Love Hurts
—Nazareth

CHAPTER ONE

"I'm going this weekend," I said to Scott. Telling him made me nervous. I gripped the edge of the table to hide it, but we've been best friends for twenty-five years, so it was in vain.

Scott's silence did nothing to soothe my nerves. He stared into his coffee as if he were scrying.

"Well?" I asked.

"What do you think you're going to find?"

I sighed. "I don't know."

"Hell, Ryan. If you don't know, then what's the point?"

I watched the traffic pass by outside the diner window and wondered where all the people were going. What were they thinking? Are they happy? I sipped my coffee. It had grown lukewarm, which made it even more bitter. I pushed the rest of my lunch away. My stomach had been in a constant twist since I'd found her address.

"The point is, if I don't do this now, I'll never do it," I said. "I don't want to spend the rest of my life wondering what if. What if she's been thinking about me this whole time too, and going brings us together in eternal happiness?"

"God, Ryan," Scott laughed. "Nothing's forever."

"How do you know?"

"Name one thing. You gonna eat that?" He nodded toward my plate.

"Go ahead."

"What if she's fat? Gained a couple hundred pounds?"

"I wouldn't care if she weighed a thousand. What she looks like isn't important."

"Yeah, you'd say that. You're in your thirties, thinning hair, and at least an extra twenty pounds. Honestly, you were never great to look at."

"Says you. At least I have most of my hair."

"Yeah, whatever, you can barely notice," he said as he rubbed his balding pate. "What if she's married with five kids?"

"What if she's single?" I countered.

"What if she's forgotten all about you?"

I shrugged.

"I don't think you've thought this through." He shoved a couple of fries into his mouth. "Seriously, what if the girl never gave a shit about you?"

I was taken aback. "That hurts, man."

Scott ate some more fries and winked at the waitress as she refilled his coffee. "Hey, reality hurts, Ryan. The fact remains, she disappeared from your life. Not to mention it was twenty years ago."

"I have to go. Since I found the address, it's been the only thing on my mind. I can't concentrate on anything. Can't even sleep."

"Like you could before?"

"It's something I have to do. Every relationship I have had, I compare them to her. It's not fair to me or them."

Scott pointed a fry at me. "Still think you're making a big mistake."

"Maybe," I conceded.

"What about your job?"

"What about it? It shouldn't take more than a day to get there. Seven or eight hours, give or take. I've got a half-day tomorrow. I'll leave around noon, get a room there and on Saturday, I'll try to see her. Then I'll come back." I leaned back in the booth. "That's it. Monday morning, I'll walk into the office like I do every frigging weekday."

"Sounds like you've got it all planned out," Scott said.

"Yeah. No worries," I said, though I hoped some disaster would strike, so I wouldn't have to make the trip. But I felt I had to do it.

"Why are you still so hung up on her, Ryan?" Scott asked. "Hell, it's not normal."

I shrugged and said, "What's normal?"

"Why now? Why not ten years ago? Twenty years ago, even?"

My feelings for her irritated him; I knew it. "Well, it's something I had always thought about. Last week, I ran into Lissa. I hadn't seen her, Hell, since we were teenagers. She told me Angie had moved to Iowa years ago. So, I got a general area."

"Maybe it was that fucked up school you went to," Scott said. "If you went to a normal school, like normal people, then you wouldn't be all moony right now."

"Oh, come on. It wasn't that bad," I said, but he was right. The school was far from normal.

"She was the only girl in your class," he said. "You should have met more girls, that's all."

"There were two others." I said, though I knew it was a weak defense.

Scott laughed loudly enough to draw attention from other diners. "Exactly. Listen, I still think you're making a mistake. You need to just let it go. I've always thought so, but it's been so long you're in love with an idea, not the real woman. She was what, fourteen? You've built her up in your mind and made her into this mythological goddess. You will be disappointed if you find her."

"Not true," I said.

"Mark my words. People change. They grow up."

I just stared at him.

Scott threw up his hands in resignation. "It doesn't matter. I can't stop you from going if you insist." He leaned toward me. "I just don't want to see you get hurt."

"I understand, but I have to do it."

"All right," Scott tossed a few dollars on the table and stood.

"Y'all come back now," the waitress called from a couple tables down.

"You bet," Scott said with another wink.

I followed him out to the sidewalk and stood there under a tree as he dug the keys to his truck out of his pocket. The breeze brought with it the scent of fall, which I always associated with things coming to an end, but with something new just over the horizon. It made me think about what the Universe had in store for me in the next few days.

"You okay?" Scott asked.

"Yeah, fine. Just thinking."

He looked at me. "Why don't you just call her?"

I smiled and shook my head without speaking.

"All right then. You're going to do whatever you do." He opened his door, then said, "Ryan?"

"Yeah?"

"I don't care for the idea, but I hope you find what you're looking for. I mean that sincerely."

"Okay. Thanks."

As I watched, he pulled into the street, and then I got into my car. The engine cranked, and I listened to the radio DJ. I glanced at my watch and saw it was still early. I headed out just as Mick Jagger sang Angie. His voice seemed more soulful, though I had heard the song hundreds of times. My breath caught in my throat, as it does every time I hear her name pronounced. It seemed to me like an omen. I was meant to do this. I tried not to get my hopes up by imagining the best-case scenario, but if you've ever been in love, especially if you lost it, you know how impossible it can be.

With eagerness and trepidation, I counted the hours until the trip. I spent the evening packing my duffel. I packed little, but it was probably more than I needed to take. Nobody knew I was going to Iowa, except Scott. As I packed, I kept hearing his voice saying, "Bad idea. Let it go." I wasn't concerned about the drive. I just had my car serviced, so barring any major breakdown, I'd be fine. It would not be a long trip, but for me, it was an important one, twenty years in the making.

Finally satisfied, I set the duffel on a chair by the door so I could grab it first thing as I headed out. Then at lunch, I'd call it a day and begin my journey. With my itinerary firmly in mind, I got into bed and attempted to get some sleep.

Six AM came far too soon. Before the incessant beeping could start, I shut off the alarm clock after watching the numbers change. I had hardly slept, and what little sleep I got was troubled. I was too full of memories.

After I forced myself out of bed, I considered calling in sick, but decided against it. All I'd do would be to sit and wait, or leave early. It was best I go to work. At least it would occupy me, and twelve o'clock would come soon enough.

I went to the kitchen and began my daily ritual of coffee and toast. I felt the caffeine work immediately as I watched the weather report. All clear for the trip. I rinsed out my mug, turned off the television and grabbed my duffel. I sat in the driveway and wondered what lay ahead between this moment and when I returned in a couple of days.

☙

"Hey Ryan, you wanna go grab some roast beef sandwiches?" Joe leaned against my cubicle and sipped from the can of Coke that seemed permanently attached to his hand.

I waved a 'give me a moment' gesture as I finished up a call.

"You're on a roll today, huh?" Joe asked.

"Guess so, but Mr. Warner always orders a bunch this time of the month."

"Yeah, I got myself a few monthlies, but I hardly got anything on the board today." He finished his Coke, but held onto the empty can. "How about them sandwiches, huh?"

"I don't know about today, Joe. I'm heading out of town for the weekend and want to get an early start."

"Oh yeah? Where are you going?"

"Heading up to Iowa." I didn't really want to tell him, but it wouldn't hurt. He was just making conversation.

"Iowa, huh? Got some family up there?"

"No, just going to see a friend." I hoped it was true.

"Seems a long way to go just for a friend," Joe said as his eyes moved around my cubicle and took in the pictures and quotes I kept posted. I assumed he was looking to see if there might be a photo of a girlfriend.

"Yep," I said. I didn't mean to be short. I liked Joe. He was a decent family man with a wife, a couple of kids and a dog. There was some comfort in his ordinariness. I decided it wouldn't hurt to grab some lunch with him. I was looking at a long trip, so made sense to start on a full stomach.

"All right, Joe, let's go get a sandwich. You're buying, right?"

"Sure, I got a two for one coupon," he said with a grin.

I laughed. Leave it to Joe the Frugal. "Great. I'll follow you, 'cause I gotta take off right after."

"No problem. Can I use your trashcan?"

"Sure," I said. He pitched in his can as I logged out.

☙

Lunch with Joe was entertaining, as usual. He regaled me with the latest antics of his kids as we ate. I halfway listened, still nervous about the trip. Joe didn't notice. If he did, he didn't let on. I just smiled and nodded at the proper times.

After lunch, I got on the highway, satiated by the sandwich and fries. There was no turning back now. Where would this road lead, and where would it end? Was Scott right? Was I making a huge mistake? Would I only make myself look like a fool?

Maybe, but it was my decision. I had waited far too long to turn back. As I went north, I turned on the radio and cycled through the commercials and chatter until I found some music. I settled back and focused on the drive. I tried not to dwell, but fate wouldn't allow me the luxury.

The song on the radio ended and segued seamlessly into Stevie Wonder's Angie Girl. Everywhere I go, whatever I do, she follows me; always on my mind and in my heart. For twenty years.

Angie.

CHAPTER TWO

Love is a crazy emotion. It does something to a person; it affects his thoughts and actions. It's popular for people to say you always remember your first love, and it's true. Though I probably should have, I never forgot mine. My heart would never let me. As the drive settled into routine, I let my mind wander back in time. So much has happened since, but sometimes, it doesn't feel like a week has passed since the day I first laid eyes on her.

I was starting the ninth grade at New Hope Christian. It was the first year of the church's school. The school was actually just homeschooling in a group setting. It included grades one to twelve, though the freshman class was the highest grade. There were a few first-graders, four fourth-graders and five seventh-graders.

It was small enough so that everyone knew everybody, especially since almost all of us went to church together. My mother had decided I should come here in order to avoid all the immorality and temptations in public schools. I didn't really expect the school to catch on because they only wanted church members' children enrolled, though there were a couple of exceptions.

I was sitting at a table in the fellowship hall with James, another ninth grader. We reminisced about the weekend I spent at his family's ranch, riding horses and camping out like we were a couple of cowboys. He was telling me about something his brother did, but I became distracted, and only half listened.

I saw her.

My first impression was that she was the most beautiful creature I had ever laid eyes on. She had long, wavy strawberry blonde hair that flowed around a flawless face, molded to perfection. She had eyes of the most perfect shade of green. Even from a distance, they glittered and shone. From that day forward, I was a believer in love at first sight.

Many people scoff and say a mere boy of fourteen wouldn't understand anything about love, but who does? Perhaps they don't remember what it was like at that age: those new feelings accompanying the volatile period of life called puberty. Confusing? Yes, of course, but I just knew it was love.

"Ryan!" James shouted. "Earth to Ryan!"

"Huh? What?" I started. The words came out like finger snaps as I returned to my senses.

"You're all spacing out and stuff. What's got you?"

I shrugged, nodded in the girl's direction, and asked, "Who's she?"

James glanced over. In a bored voice, he said, "Her? That's Angie. She's gonna be in our class."

"Oh, yeah?" I wondered why I hadn't seen her before. Surely I'd have noticed. I suspected James didn't know girls existed yet, but I was looking forward to sharing a classroom with this one.

I was about to ask James about her when I felt a heavy hand on my shoulder.

"Now, Ryan, we don't talk like that here."

"Yes, sir," I answered without turning around.

It was Pastor Pemberton, the head pastor of New Hope Christian Church and also acting principal of the attached school. The school, being a part of the church, also followed its rules, and one of the main tenets was that dating, even socializing with the opposite sex, was a big no-no. If God wanted a person to get married, he was going to send that person a mate and tell them they were to marry.

What did a stupid rule like that have to do with a fledgling teenager and his hormones? Ridiculous, yes, but that's what they believed, and I had stepped into forbidden territory when I asked about a person with whom I did not share a common sex organ.

This, of course, intrigued me even more. There's a lot of power in the law of the forbidden, and in this case, it came into play even more strongly. Not only was this girl beautiful, she was also something I wasn't supposed to even think about, much less approach.

I looked around to make sure Pastor Pemberton was nowhere nearby so he wouldn't be able to abort my attempt.

I ignored James, and felt my skin sweat as I approached her. The closer I got, the more nervous I became.

I stood in front of her, and tried to speak. My first attempt came out as a squeak, but I quickly cleared my throat and managed to say, "Hi."

"Hi," she answered, the single word sounding like music.

"I'm Ryan." I extended my hand.

"I'm Angie," she smiled and took my hand.

I held her hand in mine, and noticed how soft it was. It felt right. I attempted to pump a couple of times and let go, but I was lost in her smile and had just plain forgotten. She pulled away without making it awkward, but I could still feel her energy tingle over my skin and up my arm.

"I guess you're going to be in ninth grade?" I asked.

"Yeah, I guess so," she said.

"Cool. It's my first time. Here at this school, I mean."

"Mine too. We just moved here a month ago. Do you go to church here?"

I shrugged and stuffed my hands into my pockets. "My mom makes me come. Why I have to go to school here..." I stopped myself. I didn't want my first conversation with this girl to be a bunch of complaints, so I changed direction. "I haven't seen you before, in church or anything."

"My parents just started. Tina's mom works with mine, and she invited us."

"What do you think about the school so far?"

"Oh, I don't know. I'm not looking forward to it, but my parents don't like public schools."

"Yeah, mine neither."

"It was this or homeschooling." She rolled her eyes and wrapped a loose strand of hair behind her ear.

"At least you can be around people."

She laughed and glanced around the room. "It's a crowd."

I smiled as I studied her every movement and committed it to my memory. I looked away and saw Pastor Pemberton walk back in. He immediately gave me a look that said, 'I know what you're up to, and you're bringing Hell upon yourself.'

"Hey, Pemberton's giving me the evil eye," I said.

"Why?" She smirked and stole a glance toward him.

"We're not supposed to talk to girls," I explained.

"That's just silly."

"It's pretty stupid," I agreed. "I gotta go, but I'll see you in class." I flashed a smile at Pastor Pemberton as I left her and went back to sit with

James.

"Well?" James asked with admiration in his voice as I sat down.

"She seems nice," I said. I tried to be casual, but I was already in love.

"I saw Pemberton looking at you with his 'you're going to burn in H-E-double hockey sticks' look." He whispered the last part as if even spelling the word Hell would send him there.

"Yeah." I couldn't help but chuckle at James' expression.

"Okay, kids, let's all go to our classes now," Ms. Pruitt called over the din of the room.

"Let's get to our classes," I mimicked Ms. Pruitt, and James looked at me with disapproval. Though he sometimes veered a little off the narrow path, he was such a straight arrow. It was probably why we never became good friends. Besides church and the couple of times I went out to his family's ranch, we didn't hang out together.

Marvin was the only other boy in our class, but his personality wasn't very conducive to more than a casual acknowledgement now and then. In a class as small as ours, that was required.

We arrived at the small Sunday school classroom used for our weekday classes. There were only six of us in the class, so we needed nothing big. There were two rows with three desks each, and the teacher's desk was in the corner. A large whiteboard hung on the wall at the front. I took the desk in the back corner, and James grabbed the one beside me. We had timed ourselves so we could get there first and guarantee ourselves a place in the back. I had always hated sitting up close to the front. I felt like it would only lead to more scrutiny, and I didn't want to draw any more attention to myself than necessary. Also, from the back, I could see everything going on, so there were no surprises.

"What do you want to bet Marvin sits in the front right next to Ms.

Samson's desk?" I whispered to James.

"You know we're not supposed to bet," James chided. "Anyway, it would be stupid to bet. We all know he's gonna."

"Yeah," I said. It really was a sucker's bet.

Marvin entered first, followed by the others. He was rather chubby and seemed to roll into the room and squeeze into the very desk I predicted he would take.

Tina came in and headed toward the other desk in the front, her books clutched tightly to her chest. She looked so studious with her hair tied up in a bun and her glasses sliding down the bridge of her nose. Really, she wasn't a bad-looking girl. She kind of reminded me of the stereotypical hot librarian who nobody paid attention to until she threw her glasses off and shook her hair out. Then, every male in sight would start to drool over her. Of course, I never expected it to happen. Tina always took her religion and the church seriously. She abided by all the tenets and never seemed to do anything wrong. I'm sure part of the reason was that her father was a deacon and her mother, our teacher.

Then Angie walked in the room. She smiled and took the desk in front of me. It made me quite happy. To this day, I can describe the back of her head in minute detail. The way it would tilt when she was concentrating on something being said. Her hair was a contradiction of both wild and controlled, and it would fall back smoothly when she leaned back to stretch in her seat. I wanted to take my fingers and run them through her hair, to become lost in it all day long.

Ms. Samson came in, offered a quick good morning as she sat down at her desk.

"You're late," she said as Lissa walked in two minutes behind her.

Lissa just sneered and tossed her jacket over the back of the desk in front of James and dropped into the seat.

James glanced over at me with what I thought was fear.

I didn't know what to make of Lissa. Attitude seemed to ooze out of her. She was nothing like any girl I had met before.

"Miss Davis, we will have respect in this room," Ms. Samson said in a controlled tone, but it was obvious she wasn't happy. "Part of being respectful is being on time. Do you understand me?"

"Yeah," Lissa said as she crossed her arms and slumped in her seat.

"You will answer me with 'yes, ma'am' and you will also sit up straight." Ms. Samson would not take any crap.

Lissa sat up, pushed a strand of her hair behind her ear, and exposed the three piercings she had.

"Yes ma'am." Her voice dripped with sarcasm, which I'm sure Ms. Samson totally missed.

Lissa was so incredibly haughty, and I couldn't help but admire her without knowing why. In our small group of six, we seemed to have the common cliques covered. Lissa was the bad girl, Tina the good, Marvin was the nerd, James the jock. I guess I would say I was kind of the class clown. Angie, however, I couldn't think of what category she fit in. I couldn't put her in a box. She seemed to be above it all. Maybe every group has one of those too.

To be honest, I don't remember most of that year. I couldn't tell you what we did, nor what I learned. I don't even remember offhand what was going on in the world around me. Freshman year at New Hope was the year of Angie and nothing else seemed to matter. Instead of studying academics, I spent the whole time studying her.

Around eleven o'clock, they served something for lunch: some kind of soup or casserole, but several of us had opted to bring our own lunches.

I took my bagged lunch outside to enjoy my ham and cheese sandwich in the fresh air. I thought it would be a refreshing change after being cooped up inside all morning.

As I pushed out the door, I spotted Angie at a picnic table near a big wooden jungle gym. She sat with one of the seventh graders, laughing.

She laughed as if she were actually free. It was pure music and could make you believe in a perfect world. "Hey, Ryan," she called out to me. "Come and sit with us."

In surprise, I looked around and pointed to myself with one hand while the other clutched my brown paper sack.

"Yes, you!" She laughed and shook her head, pushing her hair out of her face when the wind gusted through.

She waved me over when I just stood there like an idiot. I figured since she was with another boy, it might be okay, so I walked over. I was a little nervous. It was a simple hello, but somehow, it felt like destiny.

"Hey," I said and sat down across from them. "What's up?"

"Ryan, this is my brother, Aaron." She lightly touched him on the arm.

"Hey," Aaron said with a bored glance. He didn't seem to care who I was. But Angie did, and it was the only thing that mattered.

"Hey," I answered him just as nonchalantly. I wasn't sure that I wanted a little brother hanging around to spoil anything, as if there would be anything to spoil. However, I realized a brother hanging around would come in handy. I figured I should be nice.

"What did you bring for lunch?" Angie asked as she eyed my sack.

"Um, ham and cheese, some potato chips and oatmeal raisin cookies." Though I liked it fine, it sounded boring when I said it.

"God, I would love ham and cheese." She almost moaned the words. "I'll trade you for my carrot sticks."

"That's okay; you can keep the carrots. I'll split my sandwich with you. If you want some."

"Sure!"

I split the sandwich in half, and she grabbed it out of my hand and bit into it with enthusiasm. She seemed so excited about a simple sandwich; I wondered if she got enough to eat at home.

"It's real ham too," she said after she swallowed her first bite.

"Sure it is," I answered. I never expected to see a girl, especially her, eat a sandwich like that. "I guess you were hungry," I said after she devoured another bite.

"Nah, she's just a pig," Aaron said as he rummaged through his own lunch.

"Shut up," Angie said through a mouthful.

"I'm not all that hungry, so if you want the rest of my sandwich, you can have it," I offered.

"No, it's okay, but thanks. Don't mind my brother; he's a moron."

"Whatever. I'm going to leave you two lovebirds alone," Aaron said with a smirk.

He stuffed the rest of his turkey sandwich in his mouth, then hopped up to find his friends.

I blushed a little. I felt like he had somehow read my mind.

"How do you like school so far?" Angie asked.

"I don't know yet. Ask again in a couple of weeks."

"I don't know either."

The truth was, I was enjoying it. Of course, it was only because she was there, but I didn't want to admit it. "I guess it could be worse."

"I'm bored. I wish my parents would have let us go to a regular school where there's more people and things to do," she said as she watched the younger kids chase each other.

"It isn't much, is it? There's not even enough people to play any sports."

"You like sports?" she said.

"I like hockey and sometimes football, but that's about it," I said. "My dad is into baseball, but I don't like it very much."

"If there were enough people for a baseball team, would you play?"

I shrugged. "Probably. It'd be something to do. I bet they'll start a Bible club though."

She smiled. "They might."

As we talked, I kept an eye out for Pastor Pemberton. I just knew he was lurking and looking to catch me talking to her and actually enjoying myself. It was easy to talk to her, and we found things in common. If we could be friends, I'd consider myself lucky.

We talked until Ms. Pruitt called everyone back into the building to finish our classes for the day. We all filed in and went to our respective rooms and settled into our seats.

James shot me an inquisitive look, and I just smiled and shrugged. I could tell that he wanted to ask where I had been. I figured he had spent the entire lunch period inside, eating whatever they had served. But there wasn't anything for me to tell him. We just talked, though that alone would have been a big deal considering the weird rules about male/female interaction. Merely speaking to a girl alone was something rather scandalous.

Ms. Samson called the class to order. When everyone settled down, she opened up her Bible, a thick, imposing tome, and gave the Bible lesson for the day. Of course, I didn't pay attention to anything but the girl in front of me. Though there were another three hours left in the class, it seemed to pass by in minutes as I floated around in a daydream.

At the end of the day, I walked outside with Angie, careful to keep within earshot of a couple of other kids. My mother was already waiting for me. She waved, and I tried to wave back inconspicuously. Of course, Angie noticed anyway. She missed nothing.

"Is that your mom?" she asked as if it weren't a big deal. It wasn't, but it was also the beginning of ninth grade, and even in a church school with less than twenty students, a boy still wanted to appear cool.

"Yeah," I admitted.

"That's my dad over there." She waved toward a full-size Ford pickup truck and shouted, "Hi, Dad!"

I cringed a little, but couldn't be completely put off by it just because she wasn't as embarrassed about her parents as I was about mine.

"It was nice meeting you, but I've gotta go. I'll see you tomorrow," she said as she threw her bag over her shoulder.

"Yeah, you too," I said, though I didn't want to wait until tomorrow to see her again.

"Come on, Ange, Dad's waiting," Aaron called as he passed us.

I watched until she got into the truck, followed by Aaron. Her father was a rough-looking man with a salt-and-pepper beard. He looked at me and probably wondered what I was doing speaking to his daughter. Even behind the truck's door, he looked imposing. This was saying a lot, since I wasn't a small guy, already six feet tall.

After Aaron closed the door, they pulled out into the street without so much as a look back.

"Come on, Ryan, I haven't got all day," my mother shouted impatiently.

I jogged to the car, tossed my bag into the backseat and slid into the front seat.

"Seat belt," my mother said on reflex. "How was school?"

"It was okay," I answered as I clicked the belt into place.

"Just okay?" she asked, and let a car pass before she pulled out. "Did you make any friends?"

"Come on, Mom. I already know everybody. There's only five other kids in my class," I complained.

I hadn't looked forward to going to school at New Hope. I had wanted to go to the public high school with Scott and maybe even try out for the football team. But I had no choice. I was sure I wouldn't like it, but thought the year would be better because Angie was going to be a part of it.

"Well, that should make it better, if you're already friends with everyone. I would have enjoyed having a smaller class when I was your age."

"It's too much like church," I mumbled.

"Well, church is just as important as school. Maybe even more so." She focused on her driving, though the traffic wasn't very heavy.

I didn't mind the silence so much as I didn't want to argue. Instead, I watched the town pass by as we drove home.

I thought about Angie, and what she might do after she got home. Did she have set routines? Or did she just wing it?

I never thought I'd say it, but I couldn't wait to get to school tomorrow, just to see her again.

CHAPTER THREE

The next morning, the entire school gathered in the sanctuary. Everyone sat in the pews, arranged by classes, with the youngest in front. Everyone was restless and loud. Nobody seemed sure of what was happening, but expected something exciting. Of course, I couldn't imagine anything exciting here.

James, Marvin, and I slipped into a pew behind the girls, since sharing the same pew wasn't allowed in this puritanical system.

"What's going on?" I whispered to James.

"I don't know," he said. "Maybe someone saw you and Angie yesterday, and they're having a meeting about the dangers of talking to girls."

I chuckled. "Stupid, but I wouldn't be surprised."

"Surely not," Marvin butted in. He habitually pushed up his glasses. "They are probably going to do prayers every morning. Why else would we be in the sanctuary?"

"Maybe it's 'cause it's the only place big enough," I said.

"The fellowship hall is big enough," Marvin answered.

"You're such a nerd," I muttered, without a comeback. He was right.

"Nobody cares, okay?" James said. "If you keep arguing, we're gonna get in trouble."

"You care about getting in trouble?" I said and punched him in the arm.

"Cut it out," James hissed.

"I care about getting in trouble," Marvin said.

"Oh, like you ever get in trouble, Marvin," I said. "You're too much of a suck up."

Marvin started to say something, probably that he was going to tell, but James whispered, "Shut up. Ms. Pruitt's going up."

The sanctuary fell silent as Ms. Pruitt walked stiffly to the front and faced the assembly.

"If I can have everybody's attention, please?" She clapped her hands and waited for the kids in front to stop chattering. "We're going to do something different starting this morning. But first, let's start with the pledges and a word of prayer."

Marvin looked over at us with a smug "see, I told you so" look.

Ms. Pruitt led everyone in the pledges to the Bible, the Christian flag, and the American flag. Afterward, she began a prayer that seemed to go on for hours. She had her eyes squinted shut in her fervent prayer, so I used the time to continue my study of the back of Angie's head.

Her hair was several inches past her shoulder and thick with tight waves. Though it was mostly blonde, there were shades of dark brown that made it pop with contrast.

She sat perfectly still, her shoulders rising with the occasional deep breath. I wondered if she felt as bored as I did. I glanced at my watch just as Ms. Pruitt finished with a resounding amen. The whole thing clocked in a few seconds shy of five minutes.

Ms. Pruitt cleared her throat. "You have been called here because starting today, we are going to begin each morning with prayer and exercise!" She clapped and smiled as she scanned the room for anyone who looked remotely excited.

Scattered groans confirmed it wasn't a popular idea.

"Not only do we need to exercise our spirits, but our bodies as well," Ms. Pruitt said. "The Lord Jesus wants us to be healthy in all respects. Now, everyone come closer, but let's give everyone room to stretch. Up, up!" She clapped again and gestured for everyone to stand and spread out.

Everyone stood, most of us reluctantly, and followed Ms. Pruitt's lead in the stretches. The little kids were really into it, but they always seemed to have energy to burn. It made me feel stupid, so I only did it half-assed.

After a few repetitions, Ms. Pruitt encouraged everyone to move forward. Though everyone else obeyed, Angie stayed put, so I did too.

After everyone got settled in their new places, Angie looked back at me, and nodded downward.

"What?" I whispered.

"Come down," she whispered back as she dropped to the floor.

I looked around to see if anyone was watching. There was enough distraction to escape notice.

"What are you doing?" I asked.

"Taking a break," she said as she rested on her elbows. "Not too bad, huh?"

"What if Pruitt notices?" I asked, not really worried.

"I don't think that she can see so good this far anyway. Isn't this silly? Stretching and jumping jacks. I'm not doing that."

"Lying on the floor's silly too, don't you think?"

"Maybe, but not as much as that other stuff. At least down here, you won't sweat."

"You? Afraid of a little sweat?"

"No, but do you want to sweat at the beginning of the day? You'd have to sit in it until you got home."

"Good point," I said. "I guess I wouldn't like it."

I enjoyed lying there with Angie. It felt a little rebellious, but it was normal, and much better than looking stupid. The only problem was I didn't know what to talk about. I just lay there and stole occasional glances at her. She had turned to lie on her back, her hair fanned out on the floor, with a slight smile on her face.

"What are you thinking about?" I asked.

"Listen," she said.

I strained to hear something unusual, but only heard people moving around and the occasional command from Ms. Pruitt. After a moment, I asked, "What am I listening for?"

After a beat, she said, "It's kind of quiet. I like it."

"Yeah, me too," I agreed.

It was rather peaceful. The carpet was soft under my fingers, and there was a hint of lemon-scented furniture polish coming off the wooden pews. In my stolen glances, I noticed little things about her. The sharpness of her cheekbones; the shape of her nose. Every feature was unique and complementary. Nothing about her was out of place.

She folded her hands on her stomach, a simple motion that somehow seemed profound. She sighed softly and asked, "What do you do?"

"About what?" I answered.

"I mean, what do you do after school? When you go home."

"For fun?"

"Yeah."

"I don't know. Hang out with friends, watch TV. Normal stuff, I guess. Why?"

"Just wondering."

"What about you?" It wasn't much, but it was a start. I was curious to know everything about her.

She laughed lightly and said, "Normal stuff."

"Ah," I said. I felt as if I had discovered an important secret of hers.

We spoke occasionally but mostly lay in silence for the half hour everyone else did the exercises.

"Okay, very good," Ms. Pruitt announced loudly. "Doesn't everyone feel better?"

"We better get back up," I said, and we pushed ourselves up from the floor amid the mumbled voices of the assembly.

"Okay, everyone can go to their classes. We'll meet here tomorrow morning and do it all over again." Ms. Pruitt clapped her hands together in dismissal, and everyone filed out of the sanctuary.

James came up beside me and slapped me on the back. "How's that for fun?"

"It was all right," I answered. "Kinda stupid though."

"I didn't see you doing anything."

"Yeah, it's not my kind of thing, so I sort of hid out."

"At least it's better than sitting in class."

I had to agree. It was much more fun hanging out on the floor with Angie. I hoped it would continue without any hindrances.

CHAPTER FOUR

As I drove down a long, lonely stretch of highway, all I could see was the flatness of the landscape. Large, empty fields surrounded me, and the road narrowed to a thin thread until it disappeared into the horizon. It seemed as if it went on forever, leading to parts unknown. I held onto the hope something good would be at the end, just waiting to be discovered.

In youth, we don't think about being afraid, because we had yet to discover anything to fear. It's only when we grow up we realize things might not work out the way we expect.

I probably could have saved myself all kinds of heartache if I had known ahead of time, but then, I wouldn't have learned anything. Angie was my first real lesson, though it would take some time to see and much longer to learn.

Scott knew it long before I did, but wanted to be supportive in his own way. I pined for all kinds of things back then, and he patiently listened to all of it.

From the day I first laid eyes on Angie, I couldn't shut up about her. It's not as bad now. Even after all others have been forsaken, I still do it.

I remember a lot of the conversations Scott and I had, which wasn't difficult. They were very much the same. I could only laugh as I thought about it.

I spent the first weekend after I started New Hope with Scott, and we shared what the first week of school was like.

Scott and I had been best friends since third grade, but that year was the first one we didn't go to the same school. I don't remember the precise moment, but we had been inseparable ever since. We shared everything and knew each other's innermost secrets. We still do today, but now they're more mature. Sometimes.

Back then, Scott's family lived in a small two-bedroom house in the country. Empty fields surrounded their place without a neighbor in sight. For hours, we would explore between the hay bales with only moonlight to guide us. It was a contrast to my house, which was in the middle of town. When Scott came over, we'd still spend hours wandering, but instead of hay and cow pies, we'd roam the neighborhood.

I had always preferred the quiet solitude of the country, so I loved hanging out at Scott's house. It was easier to commune with nature and get lost in the universe's vastness. Scott and I would scan the stars and imagine what life might be like on other planets.

I guess I've always been a kind of romantic. I was always mooning over some girl, so Scott was never a stranger to it. We'd walk those fields as dinner settled. Scott would prattle on about things I had no concern for. My mind never strayed far from Angie.

"What's wrong with you?" Scott asked when he realized I wasn't paying attention.

"Nothing," I answered, and continued to watch the sky with my hands shoved in my pockets.

"Bullshit. You're acting weird." He eyed me suspiciously. "Aw shit. You've gone goo goo over some girl again."

"No." I tried to deny it, but he wasn't convinced. "Yeah, so what if I am?"

"Dude, when are you gonna learn? I didn't even think that there would be any girls at that stupid school your mom got you going to."

"There's girls."

"Yeah? She's probably some sort of nut."

"She's not a nut."

Scott blew a raspberry.

"Really, she's not. She's cool."

"I bet. You gonna ask her out this time, or are you just gonna dream about it and bother me like you did with Laura?"

"I can't ask her out."

"Why not?"

"We're not allowed to."

"Oh yeah. God hasn't told you to marry her yet, huh?"

I regretted telling him about the stupid rule the church had about dating.

"It sucks, 'cause I like her a lot. We've been kind of hanging out a little."

"You get to do that?" he asked.

I shrugged.

Scott laughed and shook his head. "Does she like you at least?"

"I don't know. I think so, but I can't really tell. She's the most beautiful girl I've ever seen."

"Shit, you say that about all of them. Have you ever seen an ugly girl?"

"Yeah, but this time it's true."

"You say that all the time too, but whatever, man. Just forget about it and keep looking out for UFOs. I got a good feeling about tonight."

"Yeah, sure," I said, but she wasn't something I could forget about.

I knew my infatuation annoyed Scott. I seemed to always have one girl or another in mind, but with Angie, it really was different. Most of the time, it was mere adolescent lust, but this time, it was a budding friendship I wanted to grow into more. The obstacles, though, were overwhelming.

Angie had shown no interest in more than a friendship, but to be fair, neither had I. Even a simple friendship had to be hidden because of the church's ludicrous rules. It wasn't realistic, but that's how it was.

If I really wanted to know, I'd have to come out and ask.

Scott listened, but I kept in mind that his situation differed from mine. He went to the public high school. There, interaction between the sexes was actually encouraged. In many ways, I was stunted and never truly had a proper channel for my emotions. I had only Scott to talk to, and though he got irritated, he was always a good sport.

Little did I know, I would have another ally.

☺

"So, do you like my sister?" Aaron wasted no time asking as he slid across from me at the picnic table.

"What?" I looked around and wondered who had put him up to it.

"Do you like my sister?" he repeated with a tinge of impatience and leaned forward on the rough wood, chin in his hands, with a stupid grin on his face.

"Why are you asking me this?" The grin made me nervous. I bit into my ham and cheese sandwich and tried to focus on that instead.

"I don't know. Just wondered. It's okay if you do."

I swallowed the bite of sandwich and washed down with some soda before answering, "Yeah, I guess I do. Angie's okay."

"That's not what I meant. I mean, do you like her, like her?"

"What, like a girlfriend?"

"Yeah, like a girlfriend!" Aaron slapped his hand against the tabletop while his stupid grin grew even bigger. "Do you?"

"We're not supposed to think like that." I felt like an idiot. What did I care? "Why are you asking?"

"Just wondering, geez. She likes you."

"She tell you that?" I perked up a little, but felt certain he was bull-shitting me.

"Nah, she don't talk about that kind of stuff, but I can tell she does."

"Yeah?"

He nodded.

"That's crap. You can't tell that sort of thing," I said nonchalantly. The truth? There was nothing I wanted more, but I didn't want to let on how much. Aaron was likely saying it so he could make fun of me. Or run off and tell her.

"It's true, but you don't have to believe me."

"I'm not saying I do or don't."

"I think you like her too." He pointed at my apple. "You gonna eat that?"

"No, you can have it," I said and pushed it toward him.

"Thanks." He took the apple and fisted it into his mouth, biting into it with a loud crunch.

It could have been sharing my fruit with him, or the intimacy of his inquiry into what I felt about his sister, but I felt a kind of kinship with Aaron at that moment. Though he was only a seventh grader and Angie's brother, I thought we could become good friends and that he might be a useful way to delve more into Angie's world. It was selfish, but it didn't matter. My mind was teeming with possibilities.

"Okay, so let's say that maybe I do like her," I muttered as I fiddled with my empty soda can. As soon as the words left my mouth, I considered the repercussions.

Aaron smiled, a piece of apple skin jutted out from between his teeth. "I thought so, but I don't know what you see in her."

"You're her brother," I said. "You got a piece of apple in your teeth, by the way."

"I also live with her. I know all the dirt." He picked at his teeth with his fingernail.

"Maybe," I said. I didn't want to taint the idea of perfection I had built up.

"All the dirt," Aaron repeated and waggled his eyebrows as Ms. Pruitt rang the bell to call us all back to class. "See ya around. Thanks for the apple."

"No problem," I said, but he had already gone. I got up and made my way back to class.

I thought about what he had said, and considered the possibility he would tell her, and I'd look like a groveling moron. If he did, I had some confidence she wouldn't believe it. We had spent enough time just talking in the mornings, when we were supposed to be up and exercising with everyone else. The time had become a kind of ritual for us. I knew we were friends, but Aaron had put into my mind the possibility there might be more. Did he really think she liked me, as in more than just friends? If so, how could it work here, with all the restrictions?

I got to the classroom and slid into my desk. Ms. Samson gave me the "you're late" look, though I wasn't. Angie glanced at me and smiled. I smiled back before I pulled my book from under the chair. I opened it, a mere prop, while I proceeded to study the back of Angie's head and the way her hair lay across her shoulders and fell down her back. Just another typical afternoon.

⚉

"Are you dressed?" my mother said through my door.

"Almost," I answered.

She came into the room, licked her finger and ran it through my unruly hair.

"Mom!" I protested. "That's gross!"

"You need a haircut." She continued to fuss with my hair. "Where's your tie?"

"I don't want to wear a tie."

"You want to look good, don't you?"

"No," I answered stubbornly.

"Put on a tie."

"Fine," I grumbled and grabbed a random one from the closet, a red clip-on with blue stripes.

"Don't wear a clip-on."

"Why not? Nobody can tell the difference."

"I can tell the difference," she said, then picked one more to her liking.

"Mom," I groaned as she looped the tie around my neck.

"Hush, I'm your mother. I'm allowed."

I gave up and let her knot the tie and smooth out the collar of my shirt, thankful we were at least in the privacy of our home.

"I don't want to go to church today," I feebly protested.

"You're going to church."

"Isn't it enough that I have to go there every day for school?"

"That's different," she said. "Stop arguing with me. When you get out on your own, then you can go to whatever church you want."

"What if I don't want to go to church at all?"

She said nothing. She tightened my tie a little too tight, I thought, and brushed off my sleeves. Then she narrowed her eyes and said, "That will be your choice. But until then, you're going to church. Understood?"

"Understood." I resigned myself to my fate.

"Good. Now get in the car."

"Yes, ma'am." There was no sense in arguing with her. Maybe Angie would be there. At least it would be some consolation.

☙

We got to church in plenty of time, so I wondered why she was in such a rush. She said hello to a few of her friends, and we sat in a pew in the middle of the sanctuary.

I looked around for Angie, but didn't see her. I glanced at my watch and figured her family was a bit more sensible about the time to arrive at church. As I looked, I saw a few new faces, but most were familiar.

Angie and her family showed up about ten minutes later. I watched her subtly. She didn't look happy. It was probably because she was wearing a dress. The dress was simple, but I thought it looked good on her, especially with her hair loosely tied back with a ribbon.

With Angie and her mother side by side, I saw the similarities. Her mother's figure was fuller, but they had the same bone structure and hair color. It was easy to imagine what Angie might look like when she got to her age.

"Hey Ryan," Aaron said as they approached.

"Hey," I answered him, then said, "Hi Angie."

She smiled, but her father glared at me. He wasn't even discreet. He gripped his wife's arm a little more tightly and sped up his steps, pushing his family toward their seats.

I looked away and grabbed a Bible. I needed something to get my mind off his intimidating look. It puzzled me how he could dislike me without knowing me. Maybe because I said hi to his daughter. He probably had the mindset that a boy who said hello to a girl had some ulterior motive. He'd fit into the church fine.

"Is she one of your classmates?" my mother whispered.

"Yeah," I mumbled as I randomly flipped through pages.

"She's pretty." It was all she said, but there was a lot more behind the words.

"Whatever," I said under my breath.

She smiled knowingly.

I stared at the words of the Bible without seeing them and felt a surprised relief when the musicians began the first song of the service.

I tried to follow the song lyrics thrown onto the screen by the overhead projector, but couldn't. Instead, I watched the people. Some had their hands raised, as if trying to reach heaven. Others clapped along with the music.

Some of the younger girls danced in the front. It was a strange dance, but they looked happy. They held their hands stiffly to their sides, modestly keeping their skirts from flying high enough to expose too much knee. Tina was with them and twirled a long white ribbon as she danced. She looked ecstatic, her head thrown back and her hair loose and floating as she spun. Her eyes were closed, and her face shone as the ribbon circled her in a wild, random pattern. I thought it strange that she was dancing in front of everyone. She always seemed so reserved. The other girls were different. They were only eight or nine years old and having a good time. They didn't care what people thought.

Maybe there was something to the idea of being moved by the spirit, because during the praise and worship time, Tina seemed to lose her inhibitions. She wasn't someone I would normally be into, but she wasn't hard on the eyes. And seeing her dancing with such abandon, I had to admit I found it attractive.

I glanced over at Angie and her family, sitting a few pews ahead. I wondered what she was thinking about. She looked so proper, standing straight with her head up and hands folded chastely in front of her. I knew she wouldn't consider dancing in the front, but I imagined what she would look like if she did. She'd look good, I thought, and wished she would do it at least once.

Aaron looked over at me and flashed a grin. His mother grabbed his arm and whispered something in his ear. He rolled his eyes and turned around. I understood he found the dancing girls amusing. I was sure he had seen nothing like it before.

The dancing didn't happen every week, but it was often enough to make it a normal occurrence. Plenty of strange things happened at the church. People passed out for no reason; they would roll around on the floor and cackle. It was guaranteed that every week there would be people babbling in "tongues." The dancing was probably the most normal thing that happened during the service. I always found it amusing, but still couldn't wait for it to be over.

CHAPTER FIVE

I had been on the road for several hours straight and was growing tired of the monotony of the drive. Somewhere in northern Missouri, I looked for a place to stop and have a bite to eat. The roast beef sandwiches I had with Joe seemed ages ago. I spotted a truck stop and pulled in to gas up my car and fill up my other tank in the diner.

"Just sit anywhere you want, Hon, and someone will be right with you," said a woman as soon as I walked through the door. She wore a pair of jeans that looked painted on. The logo tee she wore was so tight across her ample breasts, her nipples threatened to tear through the fabric. She looked to be about my age, but must have lived some rough years.

I nodded and found a table off in a corner where I could have some privacy. It wasn't very crowded, just a few truckers at the counter eating greasy food and drinking coffee as they chatted. A couple of families sat in booths upholstered in worn, red vinyl.

I picked up a menu from behind the napkin dispenser and looked it over. Nothing I had to have stood out, but none of it seemed unappetizing.

"Can I get you something to drink?" asked the waitress. She looked like she was pushing sixty.

"A cup of coffee and some ice water," I said.

"Sure thing, Hon. Do you know what you want?"

"Not yet."

"Take your time, hon. I'll be right back with your coffee."

"Thanks," I said as she hurried off. She moved pretty good for someone her age.

No matter where I go, waitresses seem to call me "hon," or some variation. I wasn't sure I liked it, but it's not a big deal. Maybe they didn't realize they were doing it.

She came back shortly with my water and a pot of coffee and poured it expertly into my cup. I had seen a cheeseburger and onion rings delivered to another table. It looked good, so I ordered it.

I waited for my food and watched the other customers. A family came into the restaurant with a little girl, about four years old, and an infant asleep in a carrier. They were an attractive all-American family, and I imagined they were probably on their way to visit relatives somewhere.

They placed the carrier on a flipped-over high chair and settled into the booth in front of me. The waitress came by and gushed over the baby like a grandmother. The little girl stood in her seat and looked at me with big, curious eyes. Her hair was full of thick curls, tied up with a bright pink ribbon. I smiled and waved at her.

She didn't wave back. Instead, she put her fingers in her mouth, as if unsure of what to do. Her mother whispered in her ear. She giggled and slid into a booster seat. The mother, noticeably worn out, muttered apologies. I just smiled and shrugged it off. She was just being a kid. At least she wasn't misbehaving like I had seen so many children do in public places.

After a while, the waitress came with my food and set it down. It looked better than I had imagined. Maybe because I was hungry.

"Anything else, hon?" she asked.

"No, this is good. Thanks," I said, and she smiled and went on to other diners.

I ate and watched the family interact in the next booth. If Angie and I had married and started a family, I wondered what it would have been like. I thought it might look much the same, and I let myself daydream a bit.

I asked myself again whether I was doing the right thing. Who was I to drive hundreds of miles to a town I had never been to before, much less heard of, to see a woman I didn't really know? Perhaps Scott was right, and this was a fool's errand. I had no right to disrupt the life of a grown woman, just because I was in love with a perpetual fourteen-year-old girl. She probably had a family. A life she had built. It had been twenty years.

I finished my meal, and the waitress checked in and tempted me with hot apple pie. I wasn't in the mood and slipped her a five-dollar bill. She called me 'hon,' again before she moved on. I glanced over at the family as I left. They were oblivious to everything, busy trying to get their daughter to eat her food rather than play with it. I paid the bill and got back on the road.

I drove and thought about whether I would ever have a wife. Maybe a couple of kids to call me Daddy. There had been opportunities, but I never took them. It wasn't too late, though. Despite being a little over-weight, I was fairly healthy. I'd still be able to play with my kids. It wasn't out of reach, though being over thirty made the possibility dimmer.

I knew if I turned around now and went back to my life and my job and compared every girl I dated to what I remembered of Angie, I would only regret it. The thought pulled me forward.

I needed to do this. To know for sure. I could never live a full life if I didn't. My gas tank was full. I had a chance to eat and rest some, so I had no excuse not to continue.

To get my mind off it, I hit the scan button on the radio. It stopped at a station just as Chuck Berry was starting his rendition of *South of the Border*. I recalled memories of Mexico and the first expressions of a love in bloom.

☺

At the end of class in October, Ms. Samson rapped on her desk. "I have an announcement." She looked around the room. Satisfied she had everyone's attention, she continued, "The church is planning a mission trip. I'll send permission slips home, and you can discuss it with your parents. If you'd like to take part, have them sign your slips and bring them to me by the end of the week."

"Where is it to?" Marvin asked.

"Monterrey, Mexico," she answered. "We'll spend two weeks there building a church, as well as share the gospel of Jesus with the people."

"Oh, that's wonderful!" Tina clapped. "I'll be able to work on my Spanish!"

Lissa snorted and muttered something under her breath. I couldn't make it out, but it was certainly something crude.

"That will be enough, Lissa," Ms. Samson scolded.

She folded her arms and slouched while a secret smirk curled her lip. She awed me, though I never considered anything more than an amiable friendship with her during school.

Marvin raised his hand and patiently waited until Ms. Samson acknowledged him and asked, "What if we don't know how to speak Spanish?"

"Then you'll be locked up in Taco Bell until you learn," I blurted.

Everyone laughed. Except, of course Marvin and Tina.

"Ryan, that is uncalled for," Ms. Samson said. Her nose twitched like it did whenever she got really irritated. "That is a good question, Marvin. There will be interpreters available, but it won't hurt to learn a few words and phrases." She passed out the slips and continued, "We will leave at the end of next week. Along with the slips is some information that will tell you and your parents what you need to know. Also, it lists things to bring and not to bring."

I looked at the papers handed to me. I wasn't sure I wanted to go, but thought I'd wait and see if Angie would. If she did, then it was definite.

As usual, I didn't pay attention during the rest of class. I wasn't excited about the idea of going to another country to build a church. I knew only a few words of Spanish, almost all food related. But it would be a chance to experience another culture. It might be interesting, especially if Angie went. I thought about it until the end of class.

☺

"Mexico, dude," James said as soon as we stepped outside.

"Yep." I didn't share his enthusiasm.

"Are you going?"

"I don't know," I said. "It depends."

"I'm gonna." James was giddy. "I bet my parents'll be all for it because it's a mission trip. Think about it; we could get real tacos."

"I'm sure there's more than food," I said.

I spotted my mom waiting in the car. I looked for Angie and saw her talking to Tina.

"My mom's here. Gotta go," I said and left him with his visions of Mexican food and sombreros.

"How was school?" Mom asked as I got in the car.

"Fine," I said. "Ms. Samson said they're planning a trip for the school to Mexico."

"I see." She glanced over at me. "Do you want to go?"

"Maybe, but I don't know. It's to build a church, she said."

"I think it would be a wonderful experience."

"You'd let me go?"

"Of course. It would be a chance for you to see how other people live. It's also good to do at least one mission trip in your lifetime, to take time to help those less fortunate than you are. You'd be going with the church, so I can't imagine you being able to get into much trouble."

"Yeah, I guess." I looked out the window; familiar sights passed by as I thought about it.

The next morning, Angie and I took our usual place on the floor. Over the last several weeks, our friendship had grown as much as it could. It was a wonder we hadn't been discovered yet, especially since we took to holding hands. It was a forbidden pleasure we shared when we were certain no one would see. Only James and Aaron knew we took to the floor to talk during exercise time. I didn't think either of them thought anything more went on under those pews.

"Are you going to go to Mexico?" I asked as I lazily traced her fingers with mine.

"I want to, but my dad doesn't want me to go."

"Why not? It's a church thing," I said.

"Probably because I'm a girl."

"Are you? I haven't noticed." I grinned.

"Shut up." She pulled her hand away and rolled over onto her stomach and propped herself on her elbows. "He's letting Aaron go. He's already signed his permission slip. It's not fair."

Her long hair brushed the floor as she picked at the carpet.

I understood she was upset, and rightfully so. It was unfair. "What about your mom?"

Angie looked up at me. Her green eyes flashed as she shrugged. She acted as if she didn't care, but I knew better.

She sighed. "She said that she'll talk to him about it, but I don't know."

She looked so beautiful, even when she felt the injustice. The fire flared from within her and made her aura shine brighter. Beautiful, yes, but I never wanted to be on the wrong side of it. I reached out and brushed my fingers through her hair.

"If you're not going then I don't want to," I said.

"Don't stay because of me," she said. "It'll only make me feel bad."

"It wouldn't be any fun without you."

"Anyway, it's to build a church, not to have fun. We wouldn't get any time together."

"We don't now, so what's the difference?"

She shrugged. "Go. You won't even notice I'm not there."

"I'll definitely notice," I said.

"You're just saying that."

"No," I asserted.

"Their rules are stupid," she said. "I wish we could be somewhere else. Anywhere but here."

She took my hand and ran her fingers over mine. It made me feel better.

"If we were somewhere else, like at a regular school, would you have even noticed me?" I asked.

She smiled. "Yeah, but you wouldn't even know I existed. You'd probably be on the football team and chasing after the cheerleaders."

I shook my head. "No way. You're the prettiest girl in the world."

"Am not." She tucked her head as color rose in her cheeks.

"No—"

I started to argue, but Ms. Pruitt called the end of the exercise period and began another epic closing prayer. Angie and I pushed ourselves off the floor and rejoined their world.

I hadn't told her, but my mother had already signed my permission slip. If she ended up not going, I would not turn it in. Really, it wouldn't make much difference, because they would separate the boys and girls, but it was the principle.

If everyone went, there would only be six boys and five girls. Four adults would chaperone, so actually getting any alone time would be almost impossible. But all I needed was an opportunity just to see her, and the trip would be worthwhile. If she didn't go, I wouldn't even have a chance.

Why her father didn't want her to go was incomprehensible to me. I didn't understand why he was so controlling. Now that I'm an adult, I understand he was kind of chauvinistic. He thought he was protecting her. Though I don't have kids of my own, I can sort of understand.

Back then, we were innocent and unknowing of the ways of the world. We didn't understand our own feelings, and it was an unpredictable time in our lives. Discussions about sex and relationships were confined to the realm of sin. Angie and I hadn't ventured past simple hand-holding, but according to the powers that be, it was a mere step away from intercourse.

Her father was highly suspicious of me. I could tell by the way he answered the phone when I called, or how he looked at me when he saw me at the school or church. I never had bad intentions; in fact, I didn't know how to have them. But though it wasn't something I understood fully, I was hopelessly in love with Angie and would do, or give up anything for her. Even a trip to Mexico.

☙

On Friday, we had to turn in the permission slips. I had been carrying mine the entire week, and it showed signs of wear.

I was sitting in the fellowship hall with James when I saw Angie come in. She wore a huge smile as she waved at me.

"You going?" I mouthed to her.

She nodded and flashed her permission slip.

I smiled and involuntarily touched the pocket where I kept mine.

James glanced at Angie, then eyed me. "What's going on?"

"Nothing," I said.

"You guys are gonna get in trouble. You know that, right?"

"How?" I asked. "We're not doing anything."

"You're getting obvious," James said. He leaned in and dropped his voice. "Someone's gonna notice. You know how they are."

"But we're not doing anything," I repeated, though I wondered how anyone could know, or what they might have seen. Angie and I had been careful. Maybe someone had finally noticed we weren't up and doing exercises, or something.

James shook his head. "You know we're not even supposed to talk to the girls, much less lay on the floor holding hands and making smoochy faces."

I laughed. "We're not."

I realized the observations of our peers were more astute than those of the adults. I wasn't sure who knew what, and whether it would end up getting us in trouble.

James looked around again before he said, "I'm not gonna say anything. I can't promise everyone else won't."

I nodded. "Who else knows?"

"I think Tina suspects it. If she knows for sure, she's gonna squeal."

"Yeah, I know," I said. The last thing I wanted was to hurt my and Angie's relationship. I didn't know how it could be done, but I wanted to move forward somehow. In my heart, I had already decided I was going to marry her. Of course, I didn't dare mention it. I did not know how she felt, and it wasn't a conversation we had. A lot of it had to do with the circumstances, but there was a lot I kept to myself. Looking back now, I wonder what might have happened if I had been forthcoming.

After my conversation with James, I tried to avoid her the rest of the day. I didn't want to give anyone ideas. We saw each other; it couldn't be avoided, but she said nothing. I think she understood.

Though I tried, I couldn't keep myself away from her for long. I called her later that evening. The phone rang several times, and I almost hung up. She answered with a breathy, "Hello?"

"It's me," I said.

"Hey," she said, then covered the receiver. I couldn't make out the muffled conversation, but I caught my name.

"Sorry, it was my dad," she explained. "I can't talk long."

"Okay," I said. "You going for sure?"

"Yeah. My mom talked to him. He made a big deal about it, though.

He acts like I'll get in trouble."

"How?"

"That's what I said!" she said. "What can I do when those church people are going to be there for the entire time?"

"Yeah. I'm glad you get to go. I'm going too."

"You'd better. I'd be mad if you didn't." She sighed, and I could almost see her eyes roll. "My dad's giving me the eye, so I gotta go."

"Okay. I'll see you at school?"

"Yeah," she said and hung up abruptly.

I noticed our phone calls had become very short. If I didn't see and talk to her regularly at school, I'd have different ideas. I called only occasionally because I knew, though didn't understand why, her father did not approve of us talking. Sometimes, if it seemed iffy, I'd talk to Aaron, but even this seemed frowned upon. Though I only saw him and Angie together, I had grown to like him, and we had become friends in our own right.

I shrugged it off and went to my room. At least she got to go, and I daydreamed about what it might be like if we somehow managed to get some time alone.

☙

"All right, boys, let's load up into the van and get going," said Mr. Samson.

We all started to move toward the van, when he held up a hand.

"Hold up, boys. Does anybody need to make a last-minute trip to the restroom?" He looked at each of us, and when nobody answered, said, "I'm not going to be stopping every hour. If you need to go, you better do it now. We have a long trip ahead of us."

Marvin lowered his head and ran inside.

"There's always one," Mr. Samson said, and we all had a chuckle. "Okay, if there's nobody else, let's get in the van."

We clambered into one of the Econolines the church purchased for the trip. I got in first and made my way to the back. The new-car smell was overpowering, but I knew it wouldn't last long. Especially not with six boys and two grown men riding in it for many hours. Aaron came in behind me and grabbed the seat next to me. James and his brother John took the middle. Marvin finally showed up, out of breath from running. He looked relieved the front seat wasn't full and sat down next to Matthew, the only eighth grader.

"You don't mind it if I sit back here?" Aaron asked before fully settling in.

"As long as you don't fart like James," I said loud enough for James to hear.

"Shut up," James said, and bounced in his seat to test the cushion's suitability for a nap.

"You planning on sleeping the whole way there?" I asked.

"Yeah, genius. That's exactly what I'm gonna do." He held up a small pillow, slipped it behind his head, and settled back in his seat.

James really slept during most of the trip. So did his brother, which was fine by me, but I couldn't. I had never slept well in a moving vehicle.

Mr. Samson and Mr. Cole, our chaperones, paid little attention to us, but I'm sure they knew what everyone was doing at any given moment.

For a group of teenage boys, we were fairly well behaved, though we were all excited and full of high expectations. Our chaperones drove in the fact that the trip would not be all fun and games, but a lot of work.

They gave the "you're not just representing your country, but the church and, most importantly, Jesus Christ" speech more than once. Though we didn't plan on getting into any trouble, only Marvin and Tina took the "mission" part of the trip seriously.

When the trip was underway, Aaron and I talked. Though we were friendly with each other, it was the first time we had the chance to really get to know each other, since Angie was always there. We talked about the normal stuff boys talked about: sports and video games. I knew he played guitar, and I played drums, so we talked about how cool it would be to start a band. We tossed names around without thought of it ever coming to fruition.

Of course, we talked about Angie. I guess he thought he could turn me off of her with some of his revelations, and he shared a few choice things, but all it did was make her human and therefore, more accessible.

It was true; his father didn't care for me at all. Aaron said it was because he thought I spent too much time with them. This seemed strange to me, as I only saw them at school and church. If I spoke to them, I had always been respectful of his parents. I didn't understand then, but now, I realize a father knows when a boy has more than just friendly feeling toward his daughter. I admit I had those feelings, but I never even imagined anything untoward or hurtful to her. The things I learned on that ride, I didn't bargain for, but should have expected they would come up at some point.

After what seemed an unbearably long time on the road, we pulled into a burger joint. The sudden silence roused the nappers. The girl's van pulled in next to us, and I waved at Angie. She had also taken the back bench. She looked like she had just awakened. Her hair was a little mussed, but she was still beautiful.

"Break time, boys," Mr. Samson announced. "We'll get some food and stretch our legs a while."

We stumbled out of the van and felt the pull of muscles as we stretched the kinks from the long trip. We got half an hour to eat and use the restroom before we continued.

Aaron and I went in and ordered burgers, fries, and chocolate shakes, then found a corner booth where we could watch everything around us. Not wanting to lose our prime location, we took turns using the restroom.

"Can I sit with you guys?" Angie asked in a tired voice.

I had my mouth full of food, so I could only nod.

She sat across from me and asked, "Where's Aaron?"

I thumbed toward the restroom as I attempted to swallow the oversized bite I had taken of my hamburger.

"Oh. You okay?" she asked.

I choked down the rest of my bite. "Fine. You sure you're allowed to sit with us?"

She shrugged. "Sure. My brother will protect my virtue."

"Yeah?"

"He won't let you look at me too long." The corner of her mouth twitched. "Or try to hold my hand."

I snorted. "Yeah, whatever. How was your ride?"

"Horrible." She stole a fry from my tray and popped it into her mouth.

Aaron returned and took the seat next to his sister. "Hey Ange. How's your ride?"

"I already asked that," I told him.

"So?"

"Not as good as yours, I bet," she complained.

"We're having a blast, aren't we, Ryan?" he said with a grin. He seemed to take a morbid pleasure in his sister's discomfort.

"Don't listen to him," I said. "It's not bad, but not fun either." Angie being miserable made me feel bad. Tina was the only other girl in our class going, since Lissa opted out. The other three were seventh graders. She had little in common with them, and Tina was probably not good company. She only wanted to talk about Jesus and frowned upon everything else. Even if she had wanted to, her parents were chaperones, which would have ruined any worthwhile conversation. I wouldn't have wanted to ride in the same vehicle with her either.

"I wish I could ride with you guys," Angie said.

"That bad?" I asked.

Her shoulders sagged as she blew a gust of air. "Tina and her mother started singing those stupid Sunday school songs. For at least two hours. And when they weren't singing, those little brats made noise. I wish I could have brought my Walkman."

"Or earplugs," I interjected. Her outburst surprised me. It wasn't a side I was used to, or even knew. But I understood.

She laughed. "Sorry."

"It's okay."

"Earplugs would be great," she said as she grabbed a cheeseburger off Aaron's tray and took a bite.

"Hey!" he protested. "Get your own!"

"Don't be a glutton. You've had three already. We're supposed to share." She pointedly grabbed his chocolate shake and finished it.

Aaron pouted, and I had to laugh. He glared at me and muttered, "traitor."

"I'm always on her side, man." My laugh turned into a grin.

"Thank you." She smirked at him. "At least somebody is."

"It's only 'cause you're in love with her," Aaron fired back.

"Shut up." I felt heat rise.

"Of course he loves me," Angie flashed me a smile. "Supposed to love everybody. I bet he loves you too."

"Gross," Aaron said.

"Let's not get weird," I said.

I was sure my feelings for her were obvious. I hoped only she felt the same way. Though there were no big declarations, we expressed them in small, concrete ways.

I noticed the adults clear their area and said, "I think they're ready to leave."

As if on cue, Mr. Samson said, "Come on, kids. Time to get rolling. If you need to go, better do it now."

The kids dumped their trash and made for the restrooms.

"Back to the torture chamber," Angie moaned and trudged forward, as if it would prolong the inevitable.

"It'll be okay," I tried to assure her, but it didn't seem to take.

"You have any earplugs?" she asked hopefully.

"No, sorry."

"Just as well. Maybe I can find some later, somewhere."

"Maybe."

Aaron came up behind us, slung his arms around our shoulders and laughed.

"Don't be a brat, Aaron."

"Never!" Aaron shouted as he pushed between us and climbed into the van.

"He can be such a brat," Angie said. "Bye."

"See ya," I said and watched her get in the girl's van.

Ms. Pruitt shot me a suspicious look as if I had been doing something contrary to the teachings of the church. In a sense, I had been. I ate lunch at the same table as a girl. It didn't matter whether her brother was there. I smiled at her as if I hadn't done, or thought, anything wrong and got into the van.

"How much longer before we get there?" Aaron asked. He had already settled into his seat and patted his stomach as if thoroughly pleased with himself.

"I don't know. Ten hours? Maybe more."

"This is taking forever."

"It is a whole other country," I said and subtly waved at Angie through the window. We pulled out and drove a short distance to a gas station.

"Hey, Mr. Samson?" I called out as he started to get out of the van.

"What is it, Ryan?"

"Can I go in and use the restroom?"

"Didn't you just go?"

"I forgot," I answered in a small voice.

"Fine, but make it quick." He sounded annoyed. "I don't want to be waiting on you all day."

"Come with," I whispered to Aaron, and he followed me out.

"Where are you going?" Mr. Samson asked him.

"I gotta go too, sir," Aaron said with a guilty smile.

Mr. Samson let out a heavy sigh. "Be quick about it. Both of you."

"Thank you," we said.

"You gotta go for real?" Aaron asked as we neared the door.

"No, I want to get something, and I need you to give it to Angie."

"Okay, I guess."

We walked into the store, and I asked the clerk where I could find some earplugs. He pointed toward an aisle. I picked them up and paid for them. Then I handed them off to Aaron and got back in the van.

I watched as he spoke to Ms. Samson. She nodded and he handed it off to Angie. She looked at me through the window and mouthed, "Thank you."

Mr. Samson gave Aaron a look when he got back in the van, but didn't mention it. He turned and said, "Okay, boys. This is your last chance. We've got a long drive ahead, and I do not want to stop unless necessary."

James and Marvin jumped out and followed Mr. Cole as he went in to pay for the gas.

We got back on the road where, shortly after, James and John had fallen asleep again. Aaron looked like he wanted a nap himself, but I was in the mood to talk.

"Hey, Aaron," I whispered.

"What?" Aaron turned from the window, where he had been watching the passing scenery.

"Nothing, just wanted to talk."

"About?"

"You looking forward to this?"

Aaron narrowed his eyes at me. "Really? That's what you want to talk about?"

"No, I..." I hesitated. I knew what I wanted to say, but was nervous about saying it.

"I'm taking a nap, Man."

"I'm in love with your sister." I said it quickly, then looked around and hoped no one else had heard.

"Is that it?"

"Yeah."

"Dude, I know."

"That obvious?" I asked. The fact he knew it worried me, but he was casual enough to negate it. However, if he knew, I wondered who else might, and what problems might come from it.

Aaron shrugged. "It is to me. She is my sister."

"Oh," I said and fell silent.

"We talk sometimes," Aaron said after a while.

"About me?"

"Yeah. She loves you too, you know."

"She does?" I felt elated by the revelation. It was different hearing it from someone else.

"Don't know why, but she does."

"Anyone else know?" I asked.

He shook his head. "Not for sure, but they think it. Especially my dad."

I slumped in my seat. "That sucks."

"I don't know what you see in her, but whatever."

"Does it bother you?" I asked. Aaron was two grades behind me, and it wasn't really his business, but I found I cared what he thought and wanted his approval.

"Nah. You're okay."

"Thanks." I tried to hide my relief by studying the passing scenery.

"The rules are stupid."

I looked over at him and nodded.

"I like Katie," he confessed.

"Yeah?" I was a little surprised.

"It's stupid we can't talk to the girls. Everywhere else it's normal, so why does it have to be so weird?"

"Wait, you like Katie?" I didn't think she was Aaron's type, but who can really tell? Katie was in his class. She was a nice girl: quiet and smart.

Physically, she was a skinny little thing with mousy hair and a light sprinkling of freckles.

"So?" he said defensively.

"No, man." I raised a hand to him, as if I would need to hold him off. "She's cute. I just didn't think you'd be into her."

"She's great, but hung up on the rules." He sighed. "They all are."

"Yeah, what can you do?"

He shook his head. "Don't know. You're lucky, Ryan."

"Why?"

"We're not like that. Angie and me. All this stuff? It's not the same. My dad, he's totally into it, because he likes being the boss."

"He doesn't need church rules for that."

"It makes it more okay," he said. "Just be careful. I don't want Angie, or you, to get in trouble."

"Yeah."

I had nothing else to say. I turned to look out the window and watched the Texas landscape pass by. Aaron turned his head on the seat and began to nap. I stayed quiet and got lost in my own thoughts.

In San Antonio, we stopped for the night, settled into our motel rooms, and ordered pizzas. After we ate, Mr. Cole led a devotional and talked about the importance of missionary work and how we should consider the firsthand experience a blessing. We were all restless after being on the road for over eight hours, but grateful for the food and a chance to stretch. It was to be the last relative comfort we'd have for the next couple of weeks.

We finally arrived in Monterrey the next afternoon. We drove along the pothole-filled streets until we reached a house built with concrete blocks on a nearly grassless lot with a single, sickly-looking tree.

"Here we are," Mr. Samson said. He turned and, with a somber expression, continued, "Mr. and Mrs. Gomez have opened their home to us. It's not what you're used to, but it is one of the nicer homes. I expect you all to treat them with the utmost respect while here. I don't want to hear any complaining. We'll have dinner with them and then you boys rest up. We begin work on the church tomorrow."

"Do they speak English?" Marvin asked.

"They both speak a little, so we'll get by," said Mr. Samson. "Any more questions?"

"Are we going to get to do anything besides build a church?" James asked as he rubbed his eyes. Everyone else wondered the same thing, but James was the only one brave enough to ask. Probably because he had just woken up.

Mr. Cole laughed. "Don't y'all worry now; we'll have some free time before heading back. Though we want you to learn something about missions and sharing Jesus Christ with other cultures. They don't have the same opportunities to hear the gospel as you do. But we want y'all to have fun and see the country."

"That's right. We're going to have fun. Make sure that you thank our hosts and," Mr. Samson added, "don't drink the water. Drinks will be available to you. We don't want anyone getting sick."

We piled out of the vans and took in the surroundings. The air felt heavy and thick. Though the house wasn't in great shape, it was solid. Inside, the floors were concrete, with a few worn rugs covering them. There wasn't much furniture, but the place was clean. The Gomezes obviously took pride in their home. Compared to the other houses in the area, this was luxurious and had mostly reliable electricity and running water.

We met our hosts, and they showed us our room. We stowed our bags and gathered outside. They had set up tables and chairs and strung lights around the yard. Even for this meal, boys and girls sat at different tables. Mrs. Gomez brought out pans of homemade enchiladas, corn, beans, and rice. It looked and smelled delicious. Mr. Gomez offered a prayer in broken English. His heavy accent was hard to understand at first, but we got used to it. As soon as he said, "Amen," we dug in and practiced what little Spanish we knew with our hosts. I had never eaten better enchiladas. Mrs. Gomez beamed with pride as she watched us enjoy the food she had worked hard to prepare.

After dinner, we went to our rooms and staked out spots on the floor. Our room was quite large, but with six boys and two adults, it seemed small. I had chosen a spot against the wall underneath a window, where I hoped to catch a breeze, and laid down.

Eventually everyone settled, and the room became quiet. I lay on top of my blanket, my hands behind my head, and listened to the sounds of the outdoors drifting in through the open window. It felt strange being in another country, but in the night, it felt much the same as it did at home.

I thought about what the next couple of weeks might bring. I thought the idea of a mission trip was silly. None of us, except for Tina and her parents, spoke passable Spanish. Our interactions with the people wouldn't be easy. I was just a kid along for the ride to a strange land. What I hoped for was the chance to spend time with Angie, even if only for a minute. I didn't care about building a church or evangelizing. Angie was the only reason I went on the trip.

Was I wrong to not care? Was I selfish to come, just so I wouldn't be apart from a girl I loved, but couldn't even court properly? I tried to put it out of my mind and drifted into a fitful sleep, very aware the only thing separating Angie and me as we slept was a thin wall. I envisioned a future of impossible possibilities.

A few days later, Angie and I had sneaked out during a church service. The people inside were busy jumping and shouting "in the spirit," so there was enough distraction for us not to be missed. I wanted to tell Angie how I felt, but even after what Aaron had told me, I was afraid to. The sun was disappearing below the horizon, and it felt otherworldly. It gave me some courage.

"What do you think so far?" Angie asked.

"I thought it would be weird," I said. "But it's not very different, really."

"I thought it would be."

"Yeah. I like working on the church," I said.

"You do?"

I was as surprised as Angie. "Yeah. It's kind of cool to make something from nothing."

"I enjoy the kids. We can't really talk, but it feels like we understand each other," she said. "Kind of makes me want to be a teacher."

"I thought you wanted to be a vet?"

"I do, but...is that weird?" It almost sounded like she wanted validation.

"No," I shook my head. "I like the kids too. Sometimes I think people and animals are the same. Animals might be easier to get along with, though."

She laughed. "Sometimes."

We fell into silence as twilight came upon us. I knew we had little time left.

"It's nice out here," I said, unsure of what to say.

"I thought it would be warmer." Her arm brushed against mine as we walked.

We stopped at a low concrete wall. In the sky, the stars twinkled.

I took a deep breath. "Angie...I like you a lot. Maybe—"

"Ryan," she interrupted.

"No, I get it. It's supposed to be wrong, but I can't help it." It wasn't what I imagined I would say, but it was enough.

"I do too," she whispered. "I like being friends."

"I don't want us to just be friends."

She looked away from me. I could see only her profile.

"I can't stop thinking about you," I saw she was thinking, though I couldn't tell what about.

She whispered, "I don't think we can even have what we have now."

"Why not?"

She turned to me; her eyes said she wanted more, but something held her back from saying it.

"Because, Ryan..." She leaned against the wall for support. "How can we?"

"Maybe God is telling me," I said, but didn't believe it.

We stood there while the statement hung in the air. Short of divine intervention, I couldn't think of anything. I could tell she struggled with the same desire. We were in a strange position. Another time, another place, we could develop a relationship like normal teenagers, and have a chance to grow into each other, to discover. But our situation wasn't normal.

As we gazed into each other's eyes, something seemed to take control, and I suddenly leaned in and kissed her. She gasped, but didn't pull away. As far as kisses go, it was chaste and a bit awkward, but in it was every emotion, and it felt, the entire universe.

I felt heat radiate from her as she placed her hands on my chest and gently pushed to break the kiss, as if she didn't want to stop, but had to.

She quickly pulled her hands away. "Someone might see."

"Geez, I'm sorry." I realized fully what I had done. I could still feel her on my lips and knew I would carry that briefest of moments with me for the rest of my life.

"It's okay."

"Is it?" I grew paranoid and looked around for anyone who might have seen our moment that shouldn't have been.

"We can't be together, Ryan," she said. "If we try, they won't even let us be friends."

"They won't let us be friends anyway," I said bitterly.

She sighed and nodded.

"Why does it have to be this way?" I asked.

She shrugged. "I don't know, but it is."

"Really, I can say God said we're supposed to be together," I said again. It was all I had.

"It won't work."

"Why not?"

"We're not old enough," she said. "We couldn't get away with it."

"Is that all?" I shoved my hands in my pockets, turned toward the empty street, and muttered, "I'm in love with you."

"I love you too, Ryan, but..."

I turned back to her. As I looked into her eyes, I understood. I hoped what we had was strong enough to last forever, but it was something neither of us could know. I thought that maybe in a few years the shackles of our age could be broken. However, a few years seemed so far away, and it would be fraught with difficulty. Age wasn't the only thing that stood in the way.

"Do you want to get a soda?" I asked before the silence became too awkward.

"Sure," she answered, then laughed. "I have never drunk so much of that stuff in my life."

I smiled. "Me neither."

"But we can't drink the water."

"Nope," I said. "James showed us why."

Though we laughed, the kiss hung heavy in the air.

We walked to the little market between the church's meeting place and the house. We bought orange sodas and sipped them on the way back to the meeting. In case we were missed, we could say we wanted something to drink, and have evidence. But this was something we hoped to avoid. We walked in silence; words were unnecessary. There was no bitterness between us, but a kind of sadness. We had lost our innocence that night, but not in the way people imagine.

To understand, one would have to know the church's position on the concept of love and relationships. The church not only discouraged dating but actively prevented it. Natural emotions ranked among the highest sins that would send you directly to Hell. The church taught God would provide a spouse if they were meant to marry, even though celibacy was highly encouraged. God would only tell men if he intended them to marry. He never said a thing to women. Nobody dated, at least not openly. It was all up to divine revelation. If a man received this revelation, he reported it to Pastor Pemberton, who either approved or rejected it. He performed the wedding within a month, if he approved.

If one developed feelings for someone outside these parameters, they would trip you up with guilt and make you feel dirty until you broke and gave up the relationship. Some had committed suicide because of this, but this was a route I never considered taking.

The dynamics had changed now that we had expressed our feelings tangibly. We not only had to hide them from everyone else, but also from each other. Nothing would be the same, and would only become more difficult. I still held hope that we would persevere and come out not only together but stronger.

"I guess I'll go in first," Angie said as we neared the meeting.

"Okay. I want to stay out here a little longer anyway."

"Ryan," she looked at me so sadly. "I'm sorry."

I knew she meant it. I was too.

"It's okay, Angie. I'll always love you." I felt a heaviness bearing down on me. "Still friends?"

"Always and forever." She reached out and let her fingers brush against my arm. It was the most intimate gesture I had ever felt, then or since.

I watched her go inside. After the door closed, I remembered to breathe. It was bittersweet, and I held on to those three words, spoken in her voice, close to my heart and fervently hoped they would always be true.

On the last weekend, they took us into Monterrey as a reward for our hard work. The congregation was thankful for the building and had taken up an offering for us. They had little to give, but it was enough to get us back home.

We explored the city and the sights together. After a while, they let us wander on our own and told us to meet them at a predetermined spot in an hour. Aaron and I were almost giddy with freedom, and we tried to take in everything we could. Before long, Aaron spotted a street vendor hawking fresh tacos.

"Dude!" he shouted and pulled me toward the cart. "Let's get some tacos!"

"Do we have to?" I wasn't really in the mood for tacos.

"Uh, yeah, we have to. We're in Mexico. What's more Mexican than tacos?"

"Pesos?" I said.

"No," he answered. "Tacos."

"Fine, we'll get tacos," I acquiesced.

I actually just wanted a simple burger. We had spent the past couple of weeks eating the local cuisine, and I missed my normal fare. But I figured there would be plenty when I got home. After all, where else would I get authentic Mexican tacos? The food was nothing like what we thought of as Mexican food, and once home, it would all pale in comparison.

With our minimal Spanish and some finger pointing, we got a dozen tacos and bottles of pineapple soda and took our meal to a nearby bench.

"I thought I loved tacos before, but I was wrong," Aaron said after he inhaled his first taco.

I agreed; they tasted incredible. I couldn't place the flavor of the meat. It wasn't quite like beef or chicken. I thought maybe it was the spices, but whatever it was, it was delicious.

"What do you think is in it?" I asked.

"Meat," he mumbled through a mouthful of taco.

"I had no idea," my voice dripped with sarcasm.

"Why don't you go ask?"

"Okay," I said as I got up.

The vendor smiled as I approached, and I asked, "What kind of meat do you have?"

He held his smile, but I could tell he didn't understand.

"¿Qué?" I asked and pointed at the meat.

"Sí, sí," his grin grew wider as he nodded. "Es cabra."

I shrugged and shook my head.

He thought a moment, then said, "Goat."

"Goat?"

"Sí, sí! Cabra. Goat." His head bobbed up and down enthusiastically.

"Oh." I thought a moment, then said, "Gracias."

Goat. I ate goat. I didn't think anyone ate goat, and if I had known that's what it was, I probably wouldn't have tried it.

"What is it?" Aaron asked when I got back.

"Goat," I said as I plopped back down on the bench and looked at my remaining meal.

"What?"

"The meat. It's goat."

Aaron had already polished off his tacos, but after hearing what it was, I wasn't sure I wanted to finish. I ate them anyway. They were good, and I was already invested.

"What do you think of me and Angie together?" I asked as I finished my last bite.

He rolled his eyes. "What do you mean?"

"Well, like if she were my girlfriend."

"I thought she already was."

70

"Yeah, but what do you think?"

"I don't know."

I wadded up my paper tray and tossed it into a wastebasket. Like an afterthought, I said, "I kissed her last night."

He laughed. "That's gross."

I shrugged. "It was weird."

"I bet it was. It's my sister."

"I'm serious, Aaron."

"Me too."

"They won't allow it," I said. "They don't even like us being friends."

"Everyone already knows," he said.

My heart dropped. "Knows what?"

"Nobody thinks you're kissing or anything, but they know you like each other."

"Who?"

"The guys. My dad. But he thinks that of everybody. Come on, we already talked about it."

"Yeah," I said. "Should worry?"

"Nah, just don't get caught smooching or anything really bad, like holding her hand."

"Yeah," I said. "That's the worst."

Aaron sighed and turned to me. "What's your deal with my sister?"

"I don't know." I shook my head, then said, "Forget it."

Aaron shrugged, then hopped off the bench. "Let's check out stuff. We still have a half hour."

"Sure." I pushed myself up. I couldn't help but wonder, with everything that had happened, how it would end up when we got home, where things would go back to normal, though it was anything but.

CHAPTER SIX

When we returned home, preparations for Christmas were in full swing, with New Hope planning the annual Christmas pageant. Like every other church across America, it would culminate in a nativity scene. Though things had changed between me and Angie, we still held onto our little rituals. We were more careful when there were people around, which was almost always. It felt as if time alone was a rarer luxury, and if we had some, it was only for a moment. Angie consumed my every thought, and even my dreams.

About once a week we talked by telephone, but even then, we were careful about what we said. We never knew if someone might be listening on an extension. We were able to remain friends through it, but our relationship was stunted, and it made my heart heavy.

On many nights, I hung out with Scott and talked about Angie incessantly. I would play certain songs on repeat and find deep meaning in a lyric, or the sound of a note. Even in the blatantly Christian lyrics of Stryper, I found words that described in perfect clarity my feelings, or Angie herself.

"Let it go, man," Scott said one night as we wandered the fields behind his house.

"Why?" I would not let it go, and we both knew it.

"It won't work out; that's why."

I shrugged. "I think it can."

"Look, man." He stepped in front of me and stopped. "It's not meant to be."

"But it is," I said. "If it's not, then why do I feel this way?"

"You're just horny." He walked away, and I caught up with him.

I shook my head and sighed. "No."

"Yes. Just go choke the chicken."

"Come on!" I couldn't help but laugh.

"Yeah, man!" He grabbed me by the shoulders and shook me. "Choke the shit out of it until you get it out of your system."

I pushed him off. "It's not about that."

"Yeah, it is. I can get you one of my dad's magazines, if you want. He won't miss it. He's got tons in the shed."

Scott started to make me mad. "What me and Angie have, it's pure."

"Bullshit," Scott said with a snort and laughed uncontrollably.

"It's not bullshit. You don't get it," I said over his laughter. Nobody could understand, and I had to find a way to make it work. Alone.

Scott finally calmed, then said, "Man, just come out with it. Or drop it. What's the worst that can happen? God strikes you dead? Won't happen. Not over some girl."

"I could lose her," I stated. It was simple, but the most devastating thing I could think of in my young life.

"There's plenty of chicks out there. You just haven't met any yet."

"I don't want to meet any."

"You'll forget about her eventually," he said. "Twenty years from now, you'll say, 'Angie who?' and that's only if you remember her name."

I disagreed, but didn't say it. We continued our walk, and I let the conversation make a natural turn to more important things like aliens and monsters.

After Wednesday evening service, Angie and I ventured outside and walked around the church. It was cold. Angie had worn her coat, but I had left mine at home. I didn't think about the unpredictable Oklahoma weather. The chill didn't bother me. I enjoyed the bite as the wind blew against my skin.

We had a rare ten minutes to ourselves, and we enjoyed the fact we were alone. I sensed something was going on; it brought a sense of dread, and I didn't want to know.

"Ready for the pageant?" I asked to break the silence.

She shrugged. "What's to get ready? It's just standing around in bathrobes and looking at a doll. A couple of songs."

"Yeah," I said. "It's the same every year, I guess."

She didn't seem like her normal self. I could feel the tension emanating from her. Finally, I asked, "Is something wrong?"

She bit her lip and glanced at me.

"What is it?"

"My dad doesn't want me to talk to you anymore." Her voice was a whisper.

"Oh." I shoved my hands into my pockets. I had already known it, but something must have happened. "Why?" I asked. "What did I do?"

"He says you want to be more than just friends."

I smiled. "I do."

"He thinks I'm encouraging it."

"Talking to me encourages it?"

She didn't answer straightaway; she pulled her coat tighter and watched a car pass by.

She sighed and shook her head. "I don't know."

"But we don't go to each other's houses. Our parents don't hang out." I tried to understand, but couldn't.

"Ryan..."

"Everyone else goes out and does things. Why can't we?" I said.

"I don't know." The inflection of her voice told me it was hard for her too.

"This is bullshit," I huffed. It was the first time I had ever used a curse with her, but she didn't seem to notice. "What does your mom say?"

"It doesn't matter."

"Yes, it does," I argued.

She shook her head. "No. She has to do what my dad says. He's the man." Bitterness crept into her voice. "She's a woman. It does no good."

I didn't know what to say. I didn't really know what her situation at home was like, just what I heard from her and Aaron. My own parents had divorced. My dad lived in Texas, and I hadn't seen him in a couple of years.

"What are we going to do?" I asked.

She shrugged.

We came to the bench near the front door and sat down. I looked at the moon as if it could give guidance. Unnaturally full and bright, it glowed reddish-orange as it hugged the horizon.

"I don't know if I can give you up," I said.

The lonely sound of a train whistle broke the silence.

"No matter what, Angie, you'll always have my heart."

"Don't say that." Her voice was thick with emotion.

"It's true," I said. "You're the best thing that's happened to me. I wish it were different. I'd give anything for it."

"Me too." She looked away.

I took her hand, a simple intimacy. She squeezed once and let go. We didn't know how long this would last. In another place, maybe, but fate dealt us a cruel hand. It allowed us to experience this, but withheld a proper outlet.

"Angie!" Aaron's voice shattered the moment. "We're leaving. Dad's looking for you."

"Okay," she said as she stood.

"Hey, Ryan," Aaron said.

"Hey," I said. "I'll see you later." I offered my hand, and she reached so only our fingers touched.

"Thank you," she said with sad eyes and walked away.

"See ya, Ryan." Aaron contradicted the solemnity.

"Yeah, see ya," I said.

I watched them get into their father's truck. I tried to understand what was happening and wondered how much longer it would last.

☙

Thursday morning I woke up feverish, and didn't go to school. I actually begged my mom to let me go, but she said my health was more important.

I couldn't care less about school, but since it was the only time I saw Angie, I wanted to be there every day. With the prospect of not seeing her for four days, I even hoped I'd be better by Sunday, so I could at least catch a glimpse of her in church.

I tried to call her Friday evening, but my phone number had been blocked. I set the handset back in the cradle and stared at it as if it were my worst enemy. In a sense, it was. Part of me knew the end was coming, and this was just the beginning.

On Saturday, I had recovered, and my mom let me go to Scott's house. I convinced him to let me call Angie. Reluctantly, he did, and I got through.

Aaron answered the phone, and I said, "What's going on?"

"Um, hey." He sounded surprised to hear from me. "You wanna talk to Angie?"

"Yeah, if I can," I said.

"Hold on."

He set down the phone, and a couple of minutes later, Angie picked up and asked, "Where are you?"

"I'm at Scott's house," I said. "I tried to call yesterday, but couldn't get through."

"Yeah," she whispered. "My dad had your number blocked."

"Why?" My shoulders slumped. I expected it, but hoped I was wrong.

"He said you call too much."

"But I don't. Why does he think that?"

"He's being weird," she said. "I didn't see you at school. I would have told you. Where've you been?"

"Home. I was sick."

"I'm sorry, Ryan. I wish that we..." She went silent for a second, then whispered, "Gotta go," and hung up the phone.

"She hung up on you?" Scott eyed me from where he sprawled in an easy chair.

I stared at the receiver, then said, "Yeah. I don't know what's going on."

"It's that weird school. How come you don't go to a normal one?"

"Man, I've told you this already," I said.

He swung his legs onto the floor and rested his elbows on his knees. "If you had gone with me, like we always did, this wouldn't be happening."

"We didn't go to school together until third grade," I said.

"Whatever. You'd have a girl you could go with and maybe get some wang dang sweet poontang." He grinned and played air guitar.

I shook my head and laughed. "You've been listening to your dad's Ted Nugent record again?"

"You're avoiding the issue."

"No. Anyway, I don't want 'poontang.'"

"Yes you do." He hopped up.

I ignored him. If I said anything, he'd just keep at it.

"School sucks, but yours is fucking nuts." He glanced around to make sure his mom didn't hear him say the F-word. "I'm bored. Let's go for a walk."

"No, I think I'll go home," I said.

He rolled his eyes. "You're not gonna get weird, are you?"

"No, just don't want to get sick again. I want to go to school Monday."

"Shit," he muttered and turned on the TV. "Got weird, but whatever. Want to stay and watch *You're On*."

"It's okay."

"Come on," he said. "We can call in and mess with the old guy."

"Maybe next weekend."

"Yeah, all right then." He sulked, but tried to hide it.

Normally, I would be enthusiastic about doing it, but I felt depressed and sensed my world was heading towards an inevitable end.

༄

The next few weeks were a blur. Angie and I tried to be discreet when we spent any time together, but it became awkward. People noticed, especially the ones we didn't want to.

"Ryan, Pastor Pemberton wants to see you in his office," Ms. Samson said as she came into the classroom.

"What for?" I asked, but I knew what it was about.

"You have to see him to find out," she answered.

Everyone watched as I got up and left. I felt as if I dragged a body with every step. At his door, I knocked.

"Come in," Pastor Pemberton called.

I opened the door and stood with my hand on the knob.

"Come in. Have a seat." He motioned toward the wooden chair in front of his desk.

I sat and tried to get comfortable as I waited for him to speak.

He jotted a few lines on a pad and acted as if I weren't there. Finally, he set down the pen with a flourish and looked at me. "How are you doing?"

"Okay," I said. I was wary of the false friendliness.

He folded his hands on top of the desk and leaned forward. "I called you in to discuss your behavior."

"My behavior?" I focused on the widow's peak of his otherwise thick red hair.

He nodded and drummed his fingers on the desk. "You are aware of the rules here, aren't you?"

"Yes, sir."

The leather of his chair creaked loudly as he leaned back. He tented his long manicured fingers under his chin.

I sat there without a word.

Finally, he said, "Let me ask in a different way, Ryan." His adam's apple bobbed with each word. "What is the nature of your relationship with Miss Kempker?"

I didn't like how he said our names; it was a mixture of disgust and malice.

"We're friends." I let defiance come through my voice.

"Is it not more than 'being friends?'" His mustache formed a line under his bright red nose as he smiled. It made me like him even less.

"No," I said and focused on the wall of pictures and certificates. Anything to avoid looking at him.

"I was your age once, Ryan. Whether you believe it or not," he said.

I didn't reply, but wondered what he would have been like then.

"I understand. Miss Kempker is a lovely young woman. However, it is not your place to usurp God by pursuing her."

"But I'm not pursuing her," I nearly shouted.

Pastor Pemberton held up his hand to quiet me. "Of course, you are a young man, and as such, being in a fallen, sinful condition, it's difficult to exert self-control." He rested his hand on the Bible. "You need to pray to Jesus for the strength to avoid temptation."

"But I'm not—"

"Son, if God intends for you and Miss Kempker to be friends, he will let you know in due time."

"We're already friends," I said. "What's wrong with that?"

"Because, my son," he answered. "It leads to temptation, and young men are very susceptible to the fiery darts of Satan, and we must do everything we can to avoid them. Therefore, we have rules. They help you do just that."

"But how is being friends with someone wrong?" I would not let it go.

He leaned toward me. "Ryan, let's just make it easier and not put yourself in a position you cannot control." He leaned back and smiled slightly. "If we need to, we can call in your mother."

"This is stupid," I muttered under my breath and shifted in the chair.

Pastor Pemberton did not appear fazed.

"Do we have an understanding?" His eyes regarded me as if he overlooked sin in his great benevolence.

"Yeah." I tried not to let my anger show. He tried to make Angie and me feel guilty, though we had done nothing wrong.

"You can go back to your class," he said. "Do remember what we discussed." He nodded toward the door dismissively and went back to his notes.

I got up but stood there for a moment. He stayed focused on his notes, so I left.

Instead of going back to class, I went to the bathroom. I wasn't sure what to do. Everything seemed to work against us, and I wasn't sure Angie and I would make it.

I didn't know it then, but within a couple of weeks, it would be over. The only thing left now was a tiny sliver of hope.

CHAPTER SEVEN

Just after ten o'clock at night, I passed a big wooden "Welcome to Chester, Iowa" sign. A motel with a vacancy caught my eye, so I pulled in. I was tired, not just from the trip, but from the memories. I wanted to rest and think about what would come next.

The lobby was stuffy, but clean. The floor had worn linoleum, and fake greenery and cheap prints decorated the room. A plate-glass window looked onto the highway. I went to the counter and pressed the call button. A dull buzz came from behind a door along with a dog's frantic bark.

A sign taped behind the counter read, "Pets Welcome," and I hoped my room wouldn't smell of dog, or worse.

A large woman in a muumuu waddled toward the counter. She looked to be late fifties. She turned to the open door, shouted, "Get back!" then shut the door quickly.

"I'd like a room," I said. "Until Sunday." I felt a little bad because it looked like I had woken her.

"Okay, just fill this out." Her voice had a roughness to it, which indicated she was, or had been, a smoker.

I quickly filled out the card and slid it toward her.

"Smoking or non?" she asked.

"Non," I said, though I wasn't picky.

"Where you coming from?" she asked with a yawn.

"Oklahoma," I answered, and dug out my wallet.

"Quite a way from home, aren't you?"

"I am indeed."

"I've got family in Tulsa. You from around there?"

"I work in Tulsa," I said, though I hoped she wouldn't want to chat much longer. I appreciated the friendliness, but was ready to sleep.

"Here I am, just talking your ear off." She laughed. "You probably want to get some rest."

"It's fine," I said and handed her my credit card.

"Well, you're nice for saying so." She took a key from the rack. "Here's your key. Room 212. It's in the back, right next to the vending machine."

"Thanks," I said.

"You let me know if you need anything."

I nodded. "I will. Thanks again."

She gave a closed-lip smile, probably to hide bad teeth. I left and drove to the back. I locked my doors, though I didn't think it necessary, and looked over the vending machine. I found it lacking, but there was a small diner across the street.

The room looked comfortable, and more importantly, clean. I tossed my bag onto a chair next to a small table and checked out the room. There was a kitchenette, and the bathroom had a tub. I flopped onto the bed and turned on the TV, but found nothing interesting.

I felt conflicted about tomorrow, but had waited so long, and traveled too far to turn back. What would I find? Why didn't I just write or call instead? What if I had the wrong address? What if she didn't want to see me? What if, Hell forbid, she was dead? Mainly, I worried this entire trip would be for nothing.

From my wallet, I took out and unfolded the lavender notepaper I had written the address on. I stared at it for a moment, then took out her faded photograph and let it take me back.

I had carried the photo for twenty years. From the first day she gave it to me, it lived with me. In a sense, she had been with me through it all. I always saw the photo as an icon of love, hope, and perseverance. It had blemishes from time, and a trip through a wash cycle, which it miraculously survived with her features untouched. As soon as it dried, I laminated it. I didn't want to leave to chance another mishap.

It was my only photo of her. I regretted never taking any, or asking her for more. It was a school photo, where she wore a floral print dress and rested her hands in her lap. She hated wearing dresses, and it was the only time, outside of church, I had seen her in one. Though she had her crooked smile, I could tell she wasn't happy wearing the dress. Her blonde hair hung loose down her back; a simple headband kept it from falling over her eyes. It wasn't how I always pictured Angie in my mind, but when I looked at it, I felt her eyes bore into my soul, and it was like being with her again. There was a thin veil between this world and that one, and the photo was the portal between them.

I turned it over and reread the now illegible note written in the green ink from her favorite pen. Though the message had faded away, I knew exactly what it said. The only thing that remained was her signature.

"Love, Angie."

It read like a command, and I had followed it willingly for two decades.

I wondered what she would look like now, if time had been kind, and if she had kept the same spirit. How had life changed her? I turned the photo back around to the image of the fourteen-year-old girl and tried to see the woman I hoped to find tomorrow. I clasped it to my chest, closed my eyes, and drifted away on hope and memories and let go of the fear.

The next morning I awoke on top of the covers with the photograph still clutched to my chest. I smoothed out the photo and slipped it back in my wallet before getting out of bed.

I stepped outside. The warm sun on my face contradicted the chill. I hadn't thought about the difference in weather, and realized I should have brought a jacket. I was sure I'd manage for a couple of days and walked to the diner. A cup of coffee would warm and wake me up.

The café was busy, but not crowded. I sat at a table near the window and watched the traffic. I tried to imagine what it might be like to live here. It seemed okay, but then my experience was limited.

"What can I get for you?" asked the waitress. She was slightly overweight, middle-aged, and her accent was distinctly Midwestern.

"Just a cup of coffee," I said, then added, "maybe some toast."

She smiled and moved gracefully among the customers and chatted with them familiarly.

A few people glanced at me. They probably wondered who I was, and where I came from. I realized this was a place with regulars. They had their own coffee mugs and sat at the same table every morning. Any outsiders became objects of scrutiny, never mind the diner was next to a motel.

I smiled and nodded at the most obvious and turned back to the window. The brief glimpses of small-town life in Iowa weren't much different from anywhere else on a Saturday morning.

"Here you go, Hon." The waitress set a steaming cup of coffee and a plate of toast on the table.

"Thank you," I said.

"You from around here?" she asked, which only confirmed my suspicions.

"No," I said. "I'm up here from Oklahoma." I didn't want to seem unfriendly. She was just doing her job. It didn't escape my notice she called me Hon.

"Oklahoma?" She grinned. "Guess you got a lot of cowboys and indians there, huh?"

I laughed. "We have a few."

"I've always wanted to go, but the closest I got was seeing the movie."

"It's close enough for most people," I said.

I found it funny how many people thought Oklahoma was littered with teepees and cowboys and indians were always at war with all the scalping and shooting, just like in the westerns. I didn't quell the misconceptions. People could think whatever they wanted.

"Now you let me know if you need anything else, okay, Hon?"

"Sure thing," I said and sipped my coffee as she moved on.

The coffee was strong, and the caffeine hit quickly. I spread butter on the toast and after taking a bite realized how hungry I was, but I was so nervous, I could barely eat.

I wondered what Angie was doing now, and about her reaction when I showed up unannounced. If I stayed here and wondered, I'd end up too nervous. It was time. I couldn't afford to not follow through.

The waitress returned, but I declined a refill. The cup I had contained enough caffeine for three normal cups, anyway. I left a generous tip and paid my bill.

Back at my motel room, I took a shower. I imagined the hot water washed away all the negative feelings and poured on positive energy. I stayed a few minutes longer than necessary, then brushed my teeth, combed my hair, and studied the result in the mirror.

I wasn't a fifteen-year-old boy anymore. My hair had thinned, and I had a couple of gray hairs. There were some lines around my eyes, but there was enough of the boy I was, so I thought she would recognize me. He was still a part of me. Though I had more experience now, our souls were the same.

"Well, here goes," I said to my reflection and took a deep breath.

I stepped outside, looked back into the room, and wondered what kind of man would return.

❧

I parked across the street from a red brick house trimmed in white. I glanced at the number written on my heavily creased paper, then at the numbers over the garage. It was the same. For a moment, I sat and looked at the place: a manicured lawn, picket fence along the sidewalk, and the porch had a couple of padded rocking chairs with a small table between them. The house wasn't extravagant, but it had personality. It was the embodiment of the quintessential American dream: a house suited for a family. It was a potential outcome I had to prepare for.

"No backing out now," I muttered as I got out of my car and went through the gate. My stomach twisted, and my hands shook while I forced myself forward. I sort of hoped no one was home, or someone else lived there so I would have a legitimate excuse. When I reached the door,

I took a deep breath and pushed the doorbell. A soft chime sounded from inside. I stood there for what seemed an eternity and wondered if I should push it again.

The doorknob turned, and I stepped back as the door opened.

After twenty years of wondering and loving, I was once again face to face with Angie.

Though she had filled out a little and her face had matured, she looked exactly the same. Her hair was the same wavy blonde, pulled back in a loose ponytail. The same shining green eyes, and the same crooked smile that seemed to always play on the corner of her mouth.

She looked at me quizzically. "Can I help you?" she asked, a hand on the doorknob. Even her voice sounded the same.

I couldn't speak straightaway. "Angie," I finally said, her name catching in my throat.

She leaned toward me. Her eyebrows creased a little, just as I remembered them doing when she considered something. Her mouth widened. "Oh, my god. Ryan?"

I nodded, whispered, "Yeah."

"Ryan? Is it really you?" She threw open the door and wrapped her arms around me. "God, I can't believe it's really you!"

"Really me," I said and returned the embrace. I marveled at how natural it felt. How it seemed only days since we had seen each other, and the last twenty years had never existed.

She broke the embrace and said, "Do you want to come in?"

"Sure," I said.

"Come in," she held the door open, and I went in. "Wow, I just can't believe you're here."

"Yeah, me too. You have a nice place." I was just beginning to feel the reality of it myself.

The front entrance led to a small foyer that opened to a dining room and a living room with a stone fireplace. She had simply decorated her home, and it felt inviting.

"Do you want a cup of coffee?" she asked. "It's still fresh."

"Sure," I said, though I wasn't sure I needed more caffeine.

"I'm sorry about the mess, but I never expected—"

"It's neater than my place, so no worries."

She smiled. "Make yourself comfortable, and I'll get the coffee."

She smiled and looked me over. "What on earth are you doing here?"

"I was in the neighborhood," I said, unable to take my eyes off her. "You haven't changed."

"I've changed plenty. What has it been, twenty years?" she said.

"About that."

She shook her head. "So, where are you living now?"

"Same town, if you can believe it," I said.

"And you came all this way—"

"To see you," I finished. "Maybe it was a bad idea, but I wanted to."

"No...how did you find me?" She sounded more curious than suspicious.

"I ran into Lissa. She said something about you moving up here, so I looked you up."

"You know you could have just called, don't you?"

I shrugged. "My weekend was free."

She laughed. "What have you been up to?"

"Not much. I'm an account manager for a chemical company in Tulsa," I said. "About seven years now."

"That's interesting."

"Not really," I said. "What about you?" I asked, then heard the front door open.

"Angela, I'm home." A baritone voice came from the foyer, followed by a tall, classically handsome man carrying a grocery bag. Broad-shouldered and about six foot four, he filled the doorway. "I thought we had company." He glanced at me, then at Angie.

"Angela," I mouthed at her.

She smiled demurely and shrugged.

I had never heard anyone call her Angela. Not even her parents, as far as I knew. Everyone had always called her Angie. She had hated the name, so it was weird to hear it come from, in my perspective, a stranger.

I stood up and offered my hand. "I'm Ryan."

"Pleased to meet you, Ryan," he said with a toothy smile. "I'm Bill, Angela's husband."

"Ryan's an old friend from back home," she said easily but seemed to watch me for my reaction.

"So, you got married," I said to Angie.

"She sure did," Bill said. "Though I can't understand how she let me talk her into it."

Angie rolled her eyes. "Bill, stop that."

Bill laughed and held up the bag. "I'm gonna get this stuff put away."

He took the groceries to the kitchen. I heard two small voices shout, "Daddy!"

"You have kids too?" I asked.

"Oh God, I was so shocked at seeing you; it slipped my mind."

"I can have that effect on people," I said. "So, two?"

"Yep. Girls," she said with pride. "Eva is six, and Lily will be four in a couple of months. They're in the back watching a video for probably the thousandth time."

I shook my head. "It's hard to wrap my mind around you being married with kids and living in a house with a picket fence."

"Yeah, but it makes me happy."

"I'm glad," I said. "At least you stay busy."

She laughed. "Oh yeah. Between the kids, school, and the house, I don't get a lot of free time."

"You're going to school?"

She nodded and sighed. "I teach fourth grade, so I take care of kids seven days a week."

"It doesn't surprise me," I said. "You being a teacher."

"It doesn't?"

"No, it's what you wanted to do."

"I wanted to be a veterinarian," she corrected.

"At one point you said you thought about being a teacher, and I said there wasn't much difference between kids and animals."

"I think you may be right." She grinned and said, "Would you like to meet my litter?"

"That would be great," I said, though a part of me wanted to say no. Still, I followed her through the doorway to a kitchen opening to a breakfast nook and a family room. A little alcove housed a well-used office space. Two little girls, still dressed in their pajamas, lay sprawled out on a large area rug, watching a cartoon on the television. I saw they both had their mother's hair.

"Hey girls, I'd like you to meet someone." Angie clapped to get their attention.

Both girls rolled over and sat up.

"This is Mommy's friend Ryan," she said.

They looked at me with curiosity.

"Hello, Mommy's friend," the older girl giggled.

"Hi," the younger one said shyly, and focused on a small rag doll lying next to her.

"It's nice to meet you," I said in the tone that people often reserved for small children—or animals. "What are your names?"

"Eva," the older girl said, proudly pointing at herself before turning her finger to her sister. "That's Lily."

"Those are pretty names. Did you make them up yourselves?"

Eva giggled. "No, my mommy made them up."

"I don't believe you. Did your mommy make up your name, Lily?"

Lily clutched her doll to her chest and nodded at me with wide eyes, unsure of how to regard me.

"I guess it must be true if you both say it," I said, and scratched my head.

Angie laughed. "Why don't you girls go get dressed? You don't want to be in your pajamas all day, do you?"

"But it's almost over," Eva said with a whine.

"Okay, but as soon as it's over, I want you to get out of those pajamas."

"Okay, Mommy," Eva said for both of them, and they returned to their show.

"They're beautiful, Angie. They look just like you."

"Thank you." She smiled. "Though I think Lily takes after her father. They're both my little angels."

"Angela," Bill said as he came into the kitchen. "I got a call, so I have to go. It shouldn't take more than a couple of hours."

"Then you'd better hurry," she answered.

"I hate to run, but you know how it is."

"I know." She sighed.

He looked at me and said, "Are you going to stick around for supper,

Ryan?"

"I don't know," I answered. I felt nervous at being asked.

"I'd like to get to know you, so I hope you don't have to run."

"Yeah, sure. I've got a room until tomorrow, so I'm not in a hurry," I said.

"Great. Goodbye, girls!"

"Bye, Daddy," they called.

"Gotta go," he said and rushed out the door.

"Doesn't it bother him I'm here? A stranger?" I asked Angie.

"No, he's fine."

"Oh." I thought it was strange. Most guys would be wary. "Why did he have to leave?"

"Probably got a call. He's with the fire department."

"That's cool. He's a fireman?"

"Well, a volunteer. By day, he's an electrician. Both make me nervous."

I nodded. "He seems like a nice guy."

"He is." She sat at the table and looked out the bay window into the backyard. "It's nice outside today."

"A little cold," I said and took a chair on the other side.

"You get used to it. It still gets hot in the summer."

"I think I could. I always liked it chilly. So, how long have you been married?" I couldn't help but feel jealous of Bill, but I tried not to.

"Almost ten years," she said. "It doesn't seem very long, but when I say it out loud..."

"These days, it is a long time. How did you meet?"

She smiled. "If you can believe it, a blind date."

"You're kidding."

She shook her head. "Nope. He's the brother of a teacher I worked with. She thought we'd be perfect. So far, seems she was right."

"That's great." I had hoped for another outcome, but I could tell she was happy, and that was what mattered.

"What about you, Ryan? Did you ever get married?"

"No, never did." I looked out the window into their backyard; the toys scattered across it told the world a family lived there.

"Why not?"

"I don't know. Just haven't found anyone I wanted to settle down with, I guess." I didn't want to tell her there was no one I could love more than I loved her. "You're happy?" I said to turn the conversation from me.

Her eyes glittered. "Yes."

"You must be. I noticed he calls you Angela. You must really love him if you let him do that. I called you that once, and you about took my head off."

She laughed loudly. "I still hate it. But he refuses to call me Angie. He says it reminds him of the Rolling Stones song."

"Yeah? I can't help but think of you when I hear it."

"Bill can't stand them."

"Can't stand the Stones? Blasphemy!"

"It's forgivable. He's a good husband and father, so he can call me whatever he wants."

"He seems to be a nice guy," I said.

"He is." She glanced at me. "He reminded me a lot of you, actually."

I said nothing, because how could I? Part of me was happy for her, but another was sad it wasn't me who was married to her, and the father of her children. I had come all this way to find answers two decades old.

"Angie, what happened?" The question came without my realizing it, and I immediately regretted the way it sounded.

"It was so long ago, Ryan," she whispered. "We were young."

"You disappeared. I never got a chance to say goodbye or anything."

"I'm sorry, Ryan. Truly, I am."

"Where did you go?"

"My dad moved us here a few months after you went to live with your dad. My uncle had started a construction business and wanted my dad to come. He used it as an excuse to leave Oklahoma."

"Did you stay in touch with anybody?"

She shook her head. "No. We didn't really know anyone, except from church. He didn't want us staying in touch with anybody there."

"Didn't you ever get my letters? I wrote you a lot."

"Did you?"

"Yeah."

"I remember getting one. You had just gotten to your dad's place in Denison. I wrote you back, but I don't remember more."

"I remember the letter." What I didn't say was, I still had the letter. I had it tucked away at home, in my desk. Over the years, I had read it thousands of times.

"You talked about going to your cousin's wedding and being a bridesmaid. You hated the dress."

"I remember it. It was a hideous shade of pink, and it fit weird. Totally uncomfortable."

"Maybe because you weren't used to wearing them."

"Yeah, sure. I couldn't wait to get out of it, then vowed I'd never wear a dress again."

"Obviously, you didn't keep the vow."

She shrugged. "Well, a girl's wedding is special. I got to pick the dress, so it was okay."

We were silent for a moment and watched the girls.

"You really never got my letters?" I asked again. I didn't really know what to say.

She shook her head. "I'm sorry. My dad probably got them. I would have written back if I'd known."

"Always thought you would," I said.

"Sometimes, I thought you forgot about me."

I never had, but I didn't say it. Instead, I said, "He never liked me, your dad."

"No." She sighed. "I wouldn't let it bother you, Ryan."

"Hard to not let it." It had always bothered me; I never understood why.

"I know, but he never liked anybody. He thought he was protecting me. He wouldn't have liked Bill either," she said, a touch of sadness in her voice.

"Did he change his mind?"

"He never met him," she said. "He had an aneurysm a couple of months before I met Bill."

"I'm sorry."

"Yeah, that's life. At least he got to see both me and Aaron finish college. He would have liked Bill eventually, I think. He would have adored Eva and Lily."

"I'm sure. Grandkids usually bring them around. They'd have to. How else would they get to have the grandparent experience?"

"True." She smiled as the girls ran past us without even a glance. "He would have had to tolerate him."

"Indeed," I said.

"I miss my dad. He was a hard man sometimes, but he meant well.

He was just doing what he thought was right. I think he would have been proud of how things turned out."

"I'm sure," I said. "What about your mom?"

"My mom spoils them, so I guess it makes up for it."

"It's a grandmother's job," I said. "How is she? And Aaron? Do they live around here?"

She nodded. "My mom's doing well. Aaron lives in Des Moines. He's trying to make it with his band."

"That's cool. I remember we talked about playing music together. Glad he's trying. Is he any good?"

"Yeah, I think they're good. He's not making much money, but he loves it. I think they can make it someday."

"I'd like to hear them sometime," I said, and wondered if I would ever get the chance.

"You know, my mom always liked you."

"Did she?" I was surprised, but remembered she had always been nice to me.

"Mm-hmm. She used to say you were like a puppy. You'd follow me everywhere if you could."

"She's right. I would have." I didn't have to say it; the fact I was here sort of verified it.

"Mommy, Mommy!" Eva ran into the room with Lily at her heels. "Can we go outside and play?"

She shook with anticipation, like a little dog. Lily stood behind her, a doll clutched close while she sucked her fingers. I caught her looking at me from the corner of my eye, but when I looked back and waved, she ducked her head, though she continued watching me from under her brow.

"Lily, did you dress yourself?" Angie asked.

Lily nodded shyly.

"Come here," Angie waved her forward.

Lily shuffled over, and Angie deftly got Lily's shirt turned around the right way. "You can go play if you put on your jackets."

The kids cheered and rushed to throw on jackets, then ran to the backyard to play on a big wooden contraption.

"They really look a lot like you," I said, then chuckled. "I can't believe that you're a mom."

"Sometimes I can't either," she said. "They're good girls. I couldn't ask for better."

We watched the girls play on the swings.

I turned to her. "Can I ask something without you getting upset?"

She raised an eyebrow. "You can ask, but I can't promise I won't be upset."

"Fair enough," I said. "Why didn't you try to get in touch with me? You knew how."

She looked away. "Ryan..."

"I'm sorry, Angie." I regretted asking, but I wanted to understand.

"No, it's okay," she said. "It's just...it broke my heart, Ryan, but my dad. He didn't want..." she sighed heavily. "I think you're the main reason he moved us here. He didn't say it, but I know it."

"Oh, I see."

She let out a short, bitter laugh. "I never even had a proper date until I was in college."

"Seriously?" I asked. It was ridiculous, but I believed her.

"Yeah, but I wasn't interested in dating. I focused on classes. He had nothing to worry about, but it didn't stop him."

"Did you ever think about me?"

"Yes," she admitted. "All the time, at first. But I guess life took over."

I felt like I had been dismissed.

"I did think about getting in touch, after I was in college," she said. "But I figured you'd moved on. Forgot about me. I didn't want to bother you."

I shook my head. "Why would you think I'd forget you? You could never bother me."

"Oh, Ryan." She tugged at a strand of hair. "We were young, and our lives were different. I guess I focused on other things and then I met Bill."

"I never stopped thinking about you." I grinned. "It sounds creepy, I guess."

She smiled. "No. Well, maybe a little. I've wondered what might have happened if things were normal. That school, the church. It was crazy."

"Oh yeah," I said. "Very."

"Did you ever stay in touch with anyone?"

"Some. Ms. Samson died of cancer a few years ago."

"I'm sorry to hear that. How did Tina take it?"

"She took it well. She still goes to the church, and she married James."

"You're kidding."

"Serious. They have three kids."

"I thought she'd become a nun, or something."

"Scott, remember him?" I asked and she nodded. "She used to go into his store. He liked her, even after I told him about her. He tried to ask her out, and after, she wouldn't go there."

She laughed. "Oh my god, that's funny."

"She couldn't stand the thought of someone being interested without God saying it was okay."

"She was weird, but a nice girl. Still can't imagine her marrying James, of all people."

"They got a sign, I guess, but I don't really keep up with any of them. You hear things, though. And, of course, I ran into Lissa recently."

"I remember her. None of the other girls liked her, but I did. There was something about her. How is she?"

"Fine. She hasn't changed. She still looks fifteen, though she's had a baby."

Her eyes widened. "A baby?"

"Yep, a boy. Not married," I said. "I didn't talk to her for long. Just bumped into her and chatted a couple of minutes."

"I used to talk to her at school. I told her about us."

"Yeah?" I was, and wasn't surprised.

"She was the type you could," she said with a shrug. "My parents hated her. Said she was a bad influence."

"Nah, she was her own person," I said. "I kind of had a crush on her."

She gave a mock gasp. "I'm shocked."

"Not a normal one," I said. "I wouldn't have ever dated her. It's hard to explain."

"I get it. In a way, I did too. I wanted to be like her, but was afraid to be." She blushed. "It was stupid."

"Well, I'm glad you stayed you. I'm glad you're happy."

"I am, but are you, Ryan?"

I smiled and watched Angie's two little girls playing and laughing. I looked at her, still so beautiful, and it hurt a little to have feelings come back, and know it could never be. To realize after twenty years of longing, she had a life. She had found her happiness. She was exactly where she should be, and it was what I really wanted all along. For her to be happy.

"Yes, I'm happy," I answered.

I thought: Am I, really? Could I move on after this? Would I continue to reach for an ideal? I had no clue, so all I could do was wait and see.

CHAPTER EIGHT

I spent the rest of the day with Angie, and got to know her again. I watched her with her girls and thought she was a wonderful mother. With a career and a family, she had done well for herself. It wasn't perfect, but what is? She didn't let negative things get her down. She had a good life.

A normal life.

Around two in the afternoon, Bill came home and smelled of smoke. He didn't seem bothered I was still there. After he cleaned up, I spent some time with him and realized we had a lot in common. He was easy to like. I understood how Angie could have fallen in love with him.

We talked about our work, and he regaled me with firefighter stories. A part of me wanted to hate him, but it was impossible. Bill was intelligent, hard-working, and genuine. He placed his family above everything else, and though he and Angie had been married for so long, he was still completely in love with her. He devoted himself to his daughters, and they worshiped him.

It would be dishonest for me to say my heart wasn't a little broken, since she was now out of reach, but I sincerely was happy for her. She was healthy and secure. It was more than I had hoped for her, outside of a life with me.

Later in the evening, we had dinner and visited until it got late. Eva and Lily seemed attached to me and insisted they had to tell me good night a dozen times. I wanted to think they couldn't resist my company, but knew it was just an attempt to stay out of bed for as long as possible. Angie finally got them to bed, and I turned to Bill.

"How can you do this?" I asked.

He raised an eyebrow. "Do what?"

"I'm a virtual stranger," I said and held out my hands.

He grinned. "Not anymore, you're not."

"Come on. I was a stranger who drove hundreds of miles to your house. A guy who'd been involved with your wife, and you don't seem the least bit jealous."

"I'm not jealous, Ryan."

"It's like it doesn't bother you at all."

"Why should it bother me?"

"Look, I'm not saying there's anything to worry about, but I'm curious. Most guys wouldn't come in, see a strange guy, and then invite him to hang out with his family and stay for dinner before taking off for several hours."

"Ryan," he chuckled as his large hand gripped my shoulder. "I've known about you for ten years."

"Yeah?"

"Yeah. A strange car in front of my house? I wondered about it, but when I saw the Oklahoma plate, I figured it out. There wasn't a surprise. Actually, I'm happy to finally meet you."

"It's a strange thing to say." I wasn't sure what to think, but I felt relieved.

"Maybe, but I knew it would happen, eventually. What you and her had was special. Most people never have it, and if they do, it's once in a lifetime. When you love like that, it doesn't stop."

I just nodded.

"From what she's said, I gathered you had loved her so much you wouldn't do anything to hurt her, then or now."

"That's true," I said.

"If it's true, my friend, what is there for me to worry about?"

I chewed on his words and concluded he was right. I gained more respect for him because he understood, and it was a relief.

"Bill, she's lucky to have you," I said. "I'm truly happy to have the chance to meet you and the kids. Thanks for taking care of her."

He laughed, "Oh, she can take care of herself well enough. Always has."

I laughed with him. "Oh yeah, she has."

"Ryan, it was great to meet the man behind the legend. Please keep in touch."

"I will."

"I know you probably won't make it up often, but if you ever do, you're welcome in my home anytime."

"Thanks. I appreciate it."

"Don't forget to say goodbye to Angela."

"If I didn't, she'd never forgive either of us." I paused and said, "It blows me away she lets you call her Angela. She almost ripped out my tongue once when I did."

He let out a deep belly laugh. "Oh, she has to put up with it."

"Yeah?"

"Don't like the Stones, and I especially don't like that song. I use the name?" He tapped his head. "It'd get in there."

"Must be love," I said.

"Oh, she still hates it, but she's used to it now. Marriage gives you some privileges. Not many, mind you, but that's one of 'em."

"Makes sense. Guess I can't get you to a Stones show when they're in town, huh?"

He shook his head. "Not for a million dollars."

"Ah, that's a shame. I guess you're a Beatles guy."

"Nope. I'm a country boy," he said with a grin. "Give me Willie and Waylon anytime."

"You boys talking about me?" Angie asked as she came into the room.

"Of course not. We're talking about the superiority of country music," Bill said.

"Sure you were." She glanced at both of us as if she would find the truth. "The kids are in bed, but they want their daddy to come read to them."

"Ah, well, duty calls." Bill got up from his chair and shook my hand. "Ryan, it's been great getting to know you. Drive careful now, okay?"

"Sure, Bill," I said. "It's been a pleasure."

He went to read to the girls and left me and Angie alone.

"You've got a great family, Angie. I'm glad I got to meet them."

"They're great," she beamed. "I really am happy to see you again, Ryan. It's been a long time."

"It doesn't seem to have been so long now," I said.

"True." She looked toward the hallway, then said, "I know it probably isn't what you expected—"

I held up my hand. "I'll be honest: it wasn't. But it's better. Yeah, I hoped for the chance we could be together again, but I also knew it would be a long shot."

I sighed. This is what I had come for. I had closure. "Angie, you are a beautiful, vibrant woman. You always were. It wouldn't be fair to expect it. Twenty years is a long time to wait."

"Have you been waiting, Ryan?" she asked.

I let the silence hang for a moment. "In a way, yes. I always will be, but it's okay."

"I want you to be happy too." She rested a hand on mine. It still felt electric. "Don't keep yourself from possibilities. There's so much out there. You should be open to them."

I cleared my throat. "I am, but you're tough to top."

She rolled her eyes. "I'm not."

"You are. I'm not the only one. There's a man and two little girls who think so too."

"You're sweet to say it."

"Nah, it's just the truth." I finally removed my hand. "We're not going to lose touch again, are we?" I wanted to hear her say it before I left. At least I would have it to hold on to.

"No, Ryan," she said. "We won't. It's too bad you're so far away."

"It's not too far," I said.

"I guess not." She lowered her head and fingered her wedding ring.

"Time's been good to you, Angie. I wouldn't want to change it." I stood up. "I should go."

She stood and hugged me tight and whispered in my ear, "Goodbye, Ryan. You're still my friend; you always will be. Don't forget it."

"No, I won't forget," I whispered back. I felt her against me and I transported back two decades. She was a woman now. A wife. A mother. Underneath it, though, she would forever be the girl I had loved.

I returned to the motel, took a shower and let the hot water wash away the day. My emotions were mixed. Though Angie was happy and had her family, I still wanted her. Bill was right; I would never jeopardize the happiness she found, and had fulfilled her.

My trip served its purpose. Could I have gotten closure with a phone call? Sure, but I thought coming here was the best thing to do. To see it with my own eyes, I couldn't deny it, whereas over the phone, there would always be room for doubt. Now that I had my closure, what would I do? I wondered what fate might have in store for me after I returned home.

I got out of the shower and dried myself off. The towel was thick, which seemed a luxury in a cheap motel. I crawled under the covers, pulled her picture out of my wallet, and compared it to the woman I met today. Though she was older now, with more life behind her, the essence was still the same. I had found her, but I also felt I had lost her again. I decided I would hold on to my memories and take solace she had built a happy life for herself.

I decided I was happy after all. Everything was going to be fine. Even after all these years, she was still my friend, and I fell asleep with this small comfort in mind.

The next morning I finished packing, then drove to the front to drop off the key. The same woman was sitting at the front desk, watching a game show on a small television. She looked rested this time.

"Good morning," she said. "Did you have everything you needed?"

"I did, thank you," I said. "I have to say, this is one of the best places I've stayed. Comfortable and clean. You do a good job."

She beamed. "Thank you. We try our best. Stop by when you're up this way again, okay?"

"I will," I said, then wondered where I could go with this. "Listen, I work for a chemical company in Tulsa, and we deal with a lot of motels."

"Oh," she said with a chuckle. "You're a salesman."

"Well, I don't like to think of myself as one." I took a card from my wallet. "I thought I'd leave my card, in case you have a question, you can call."

She batted her eyes with comedic effect. "Is this how people flirt nowadays?"

"Yes," I laughed. "Handing out cards shows you have a job. Is it working?"

"Come now," she giggled and took the card. "Well, it won't hurt to look. In this business, we're always looking for those types of things."

"Great," I said. "My name's Ryan Logan. You call that number, you'll get me directly."

"It's nice to meet you, Ryan." She smiled. "I'm Barbara Kenyon, though I don't have a card."

"Oh, I couldn't forget you, Ms. Kenyon. If I make it up this way again, I'll stop by."

She laughed deeply. "You are a salesman."

"Maybe so," I said.

Though I meant it, I wasn't sure I'd ever come back. I left Barbara to her show and stopped at the diner to have breakfast before heading home. It would be a long trip, and I needed the fuel. I sat at the same table, and ordered a full breakfast and coffee.

While eating, I half-listened to the conversations. I made little of it, but found solace in the sounds of life. I finished and got a cup of coffee to go, then pointed my car toward home.

I wasn't sure what I would do now. Until this point, Angie had always been on my mind. She always would be, but now that I had seen her again, what would change? By pulling this door closed, did I open others? Could I finally move on and find someone to fall in love with, maybe even start a family?

I was thirty-five years old. Most guys I knew had married, divorced, and some had married a second time. Had I kept myself from love by comparing everyone with an ideal?

No, I was still young. It wasn't beyond my reach. Now, perhaps it would be easier to discover. I had a decent job and had some money saved. Life was open, and best of all, she was still my friend. It was something I could find comfort in.

CHAPTER NINE

It was strange going back home, almost like a dream. Everything seemed different, though nothing changed. Only I had changed. When that happens, the world takes on a new perspective.

Even at work, my performance improved. It could have been because it was the week of Thanksgiving. Everyone anticipated a couple of days off to spend with their families around the dinner table. I wasn't an exception.

I arrived at my mother's house at about one o'clock and let myself in. She never locked her door, despite my warnings. She was in the kitchen, taking the pie out of the oven. It was the only traditional part of our Thanksgiving dinner. Neither of us were crazy about turkey, and since it was just the two of us, we were having steak and potatoes, with blueberry pie instead.

"Ryan, you're early." My mom wiped her hands on a towel and gave me a hug.

"Never too early to visit my mother," I said.

"In that case, you're late," she said in mock indignation. "Let me look at you."

"I'm fine, Mom," I said, and resisted the urge to roll my eyes.

"Well, I'm about to put on the steaks. I don't think you're eating enough."

"I eat plenty." Exasperation colored my voice. "I could stand to lose ten or twenty pounds."

"There's nothing wrong with a little extra."

"Right, Mom," I said. "Do you need help?"

"I have it all taken care of. You can set the table if you like."

"Okay, Mom." I set the table and sat down to watch her work. It was the same routine we'd had since I went to college.

When everything was finished, we sat down to eat.

"It's delicious, Mom," I said. "I'm glad we do this instead of turkey."

"Well, you always like to be different," she said. "When are you going to bring someone with you?"

It was her not so subtle way of asking when she'd get some grandbabies.

"Mom, don't start."

"Well, why not? If you'd find a good church, you could meet a nice girl and settle down."

"Mom," I said, not hiding my irritation.

"You won't be young forever, Ryan."

I stabbed my fork into my steak. I decided to tell her.

"I saw Angie last weekend."

She sipped her tea, trying to place the name, then smiled. "The Kempker girl?"

I nodded.

"Did you see her in town?"

"No, in Iowa."

"You went to Iowa?"

"Yes." I shoveled a spoonful of potato into my mouth. It probably wasn't smart to tell my mother.

"Well, I'm not surprised," she said. "You were always smitten with her."

"How do you know?"

"Oh, Honey, a mother always knows." She smiled knowingly. "She was a nice girl. How is she?"

"Fine."

"How are her parents?"

I shrugged. "Her dad's dead. She says her mom's doing good."

"Oh, that's a shame about her father," she said. "What is she doing now?"

I knew it wasn't the real question.

"She's a teacher."

"Oh, well, that's nice."

I took a bite, chewed for a while.

"She's married. Has two kids."

"I'm sorry, Ryan."

"What is there to be sorry about?"

She shook her head. "Honey, you've always been crazy about that girl. Maybe now, you can move on."

"Mom, I moved on a long time ago. I just haven't found the right person yet."

"Would you like some pie now?" she changed the subject and got up from the table.

"Sure, Mom." I didn't want to pursue it further. We both knew I hadn't moved on. I hoped she would forget it and followed her into the kitchen for a slice of pie.

I spent the day after Thanksgiving with Scott. We sat by his fire pit, smoked cigars, and sipped brandy. The setting sun behind the trees enhanced the solitude.

"So you found her," he said.

I nodded. "Yeah. I kind of feel like I can move forward now."

"You always could, Ryan. You just have a bad habit of getting hung up on things."

I dipped my cigar into my brandy. "Maybe you're right."

He shrugged. "So, how did it go? You haven't said anything yet."

I took my time with a pull on my cigar.

"Well?"

"She's married," I finally said.

He gave a short laugh. "That figures."

"She's got two kids. Girls."

"It's a natural byproduct of marriage."

"Yeah. She's happy, Scott."

"So she forgot all about you, huh?" He gave me a see-I-told-you-so grin.

If I were in his shoes, I would think the same thing, so I dismissed it.

"Funny, she never did. She even said her husband reminded her of me."

"And you believed her?"

I shrugged. "She's got no reason to lie to me."

"Women do strange things."

"He's a decent guy. They seem happy. I'm happy for her."

"Really?"

"I asked myself the same question." I sighed and sipped my drink.

I spent the entire trip back asking it, but we don't always say out loud what's in our hearts. There was disappointment, yes, but I had no bitterness.

I had a fantasy where she would be single. She would have pined for me until I showed up; we'd be madly in love and start a perfect life. It was a fantasy I quickly gave up. The girl I knew wouldn't have done it. If she were, we'd be miserable. Not every fantasy should become reality.

I had expected it to turn out this way, even if remotely, and I knew it was actually what I wanted for her.

"You know, Scott, it isn't the happiness I wanted, but I am happy."

"Maybe you've grown up a little."

I grunted. "I grew up a long time ago. I didn't stay a child, just because I still love her."

Scott finished the rest of his brandy and sighed. "Doesn't matter anymore."

We sat in silence for a while, the tendrils of our cigars floating away on the breeze. In the distance, an owl hooted.

Scott stubbed out his cigar. "Hey, Ryan?"

"Yeah?"

"What if I said I'm setting you up with a girl?"

"As opposed to a guy?"

He laughed. "I wouldn't do that to you."

"You might," I said with a smirk.

"Get real. What would you say?"

"I'd say you're fucking crazy."

"What if I said she's perfect for you?" He grinned stupidly.

I stared at him. I wasn't in the mood for jokes.

"You've got to be kidding me. No."

"Not kidding. You interested? Say the word and I'll give you her number."

"I said no, Scott. You deaf?"

"You'd like her."

"No, Scott."

"She's a nice girl."

I sighed in frustration. "I said no. What part of no don't you get?"

Scott shook his head sadly. "I thought so."

"You thought what?"

"You're still hung up on her." He leaned forward in his chair and looked me in the eye with a stern gaze. "Move on, Ryan. She's got a life. You saw it for yourself. Move on with your own."

Moving on seemed to be the theme this week.

"Okay, Scott, you win. Give me her number and I'll call her."

"Will you?"

"I might even invite her out."

"Awesome," he said and relished the victory. "Take her somewhere you'll actually interact. No fair taking her to a movie or some play."

"Fine, Scott."

"Dinner's fine. Amusement park, mini-golf—"

"I said fine. No movie, and I'll even speak to her."

"Great!" He pulled a card out of his pocket and waved it at me.

"You had this shit planned, didn't you?" I asked and reached for the card.

"Maybe." He pulled it away, just out of my reach. "You gotta promise."

"Don't be stupid, or I'll change my mind," I growled at him. "What's her name, anyway?"

"Angie," he said with relish.

"Oh, Hell no. Absolutely not." I jerked back as if the card were diseased. "Forget it."

He laughed. "Relax. I'm just kidding."

"You're not funny."

"I think I am."

"What's her name, really?"

"Her name's Brooke," he said with a sigh. "She's a receptionist, twenty-seven, lives in Tulsa, and best of all, she's single."

"What's wrong with her?"

"Nothing."

"You're too excited."

"Trust me."

I didn't. "Why?"

"I'm your friend, that's why."

"She fat?"

"Nope."

"I bet she's a frigging manatee."

He shook his head. "She's cute."

I chuffed. "Bet she's got prop marks on her back."

"Come on, man, give it a chance."

"She's probably a fucked up, insecure, neurotic, emotional mess."

"Give me some credit," Scott said.

"Why don't you ask her out?"

"I work with her," he said with a shrug. "Look, if you don't like her, no harm."

"I don't know, man."

"Give it a chance." He waved the card under my nose.

I grabbed it. "I'm holding you responsible if she's a psycho manatee."

He grinned. "Sure."

"Why are you doing this?" I asked. It felt like he was up to something, but he seemed sincere.

"I just want to help you be normal for once," he said. "Now that you've got this ridiculousness out of your system."

I glanced at the card. It was one of Scott's with her name and number written on the back. The handwriting was nice, unlike Scott's illegible scrawl. I could see him chatting up some poor girl and could only imagine what he said about me. If she willingly gave her number, it couldn't have been too bad. I decided I would call her, but with no expectations.

"I'll probably regret this, but I'll do it for you," I said.

"No, you're doing it for you, and you won't regret it," he said assuredly. "I bet you'll ask me to be best man at the wedding."

"Let's not get ahead of ourselves." I wished I could share his confidence.

I had called Brooke, and we got to know each other a little. Her voice was pleasant, and she didn't sound fat. Then again, a voice doesn't always indicate body mass. As we talked, she admitted to some of the same reservations I had. We were comfortable with each other on the phone and decided to meet.

Freshly showered and shaved, I examined my reflection. I considered changing shirts, but decided it was fine and ran a comb through my hair.

I was nervous.

I glanced at my watch. If I wanted to be on time, I'd need to leave. It was a forty-five-minute drive to her place, and I wanted some wiggle room. I did a final check in the mirror and grabbed my keys. Nervousness aside, I looked forward to it.

I pulled into a space in front of her building, grabbed the bouquet, bought on a whim, and headed to her door. I looked around the place and was relieved it didn't look like a ghetto. The place was nice. There was a pool, covered for the season, and a playground where a few kids chased each other in a late game of tag.

I pressed the doorbell and waited. So far, so good, but I'd yet to meet the girl.

The deadbolt clicked, the door opened, and there she was. She was short, hovering around five feet, and petite with pale skin and coppery red hair. I'm not usually attracted to redheads, but she was cute, in the girl-next-door way. Definitely not a manatee.

"Ryan?" She looked a little flustered.

"These are for you," I said and handed her the flowers.

"Wow!" She laughed and took them. "I didn't know people did flowers anymore. They're beautiful. Thank you."

I grinned sheepishly. "I guess I'm old-fashioned."

"Do you want to come in? I'm not quite ready yet."

"Sure." She started up a set of stairs and I followed her.

"I won't be long. Promise."

"I'm not in a hurry," I said. As she went up the stairs, I couldn't help but check out her backside. I thought it was cute too.

"Make yourself comfortable." She waved toward a futon against the wall and left to get ready.

I looked around. Her apartment was plain, but cozy. I found it refreshing. A small kitchen and dining area was just off the living room, and a short hallway led to a bedroom and bath. The furniture was mismatched, and a small TV stand was against the stairwell wall. A well-stocked bookcase sat next to a sliding glass door leading to a small terrace. I went to check out her bookcase. A mixture of fiction and nonfiction showed her eclectic taste. The shelves included a copy of Atlas Shrugged and a volume of Nietzsche, so I knew she wasn't afraid of philosophical reading. A couple of Nora Roberts novels showed a romantic side. What I didn't see was a selection of "self-help" books, which was telling. From her shelves, I could tell she was an intelligent girl, which I liked. She was also attractive; I liked that too.

"How long have you lived here?" I asked.

"In this apartment? Six months," she said as she walked in the room. She had on black jeans and a white blouse and just enough makeup to accentuate her features.

"You look nice," I said and glanced at my watch. "You made good time."

"If you think three hours is good time, we'll get along."

"Three hours?"

She laughed. "Not really. There's not enough of me to take that long."

"So you ready?"

"Whenever you are." She grabbed her purse from the table, and we headed down the stairs.

"Plenty of exercise, going up and down those steps all the time," I said as she locked the door.

"It was awful when I moved in, but I like it. I can leave the door open on the terrace and not worry about people just walking in."

We got to the car, and I opened the door for her.

"A gentleman," she said. "I'm impressed."

"Don't get too excited. Next time, I'll just honk my horn. If I'm in a good mood, I won't yell at you to hurry."

"Well, maybe we'll see about that," she said.

I liked this girl. Even if it didn't turn into something serious, I thought we could be friends.

"So, where are we going?" she asked as I started the car.

"McDonald's," I answered.

"McDonald's?"

"They have a two for one special on Big Macs. I thought we'd split one and save the other for a second date."

"Scott warned me about your sense of humor."

"I'm serious," I deadpanned.

She rolled her eyes. "Fast food is for high school dates and married couples with kids. We are neither."

"Guess I'll have to change plans, then," I said. "I was looking forward to a Big Mac."

"I'm sorry." She patted my shoulder in mock consolation.

"Do you like Thai?"

She shook her head. "I heard it was really spicy."

"It can be, but we can ask them to hold off on the spice. I think you'll like it."

"I can give it a try."

"Adventurous," I said. "I like that."

I glanced over, and she smiled. Scott was right about her.

We ate at my favorite Thai place, and after sampling a dish I suggested, she loved it. Afterward, we took a walk in the park and talked as we enjoyed the crisp evening air. I took her home, and the moon hung fuller and brighter than I had ever seen it. We got to her door, and she turned to me, with the breeze dancing through her hair.

"I had a good time tonight," she said.

"Me too." I hesitated, then said, "To be honest, when Scott told me about you, I almost didn't bother."

"Really?"

I nodded. "He likes to screw with me, but I'm glad I did."

She grinned. "You thought I'd be fat and ugly, didn't you?"

"Well..."

"It's okay. I thought the same thing, but Scott's not always wrong."

"True." It was a relief to get it out and learn I wasn't the only one with reservations.

"At least I'm not fat," she said as she patted her stomach. "But that might change with Thai food."

"You're not ugly either," I said and felt heat rise in my cheeks.

"You're blushing," she laughed. "That's too cute."

"It's just the air," I said and felt warmer.

"It is not. Look at you."

I turned away. "Oh, stop."

"You want to come up for coffee?"

I hesitated.

"I mean actual coffee. I'm not going to have sex with you."

"Well, damn it," I muttered, then grinned.

She laughed. "Sorry, but I'm not the kind of girl that goes to bed on the first date, no matter how much fun I had."

"Okay, as long as I'm not under any pressure to perform."

"Great," she said as she opened the door.

I followed, once again appreciating the view.

I sat at the table, and she started the pot. Soon, the smell of strong coffee filled the air.

"This was the best blind date I've been on."

She smiled. "For me too. Most of the time, it's a disaster."

"So true," I said. I was relieved it went well, for both of us.

"It's the first time someone brought me flowers." She adjusted the water glass she had requisitioned as a vase. "They're really pretty."

"Maybe we can do it again, if you're not averse to it."

"I would love to."

I finished my coffee, then rinsed the mug out in the sink.

"So, I should go. I'll call you?"

"Yeah, that would be good."

As we faced each other, I considered whether I should kiss her good night.

"Well, good night," I said, and she nodded her head. I leaned in, hesitated, then went for it. She kissed back. I pulled away, not wanting to seem pushy.

"That was nice."

"I thought so too. I'll call you."

"Okay, drive safe."

"Good night, Brooke."

I let myself out and walked to my car, with a little spring in my step.

The evening, especially the kiss, stayed on my mind as I drove home. Brooke was great, and I wondered where it might lead. I'd have to thank Scott, but then, he'd probably remind me of it all the time.

Angie crossed my mind a few times, but not as often. I couldn't re-member a time when I didn't make comparisons; I saw Brooke as her own person.

Maybe this was what I needed. I would just take it as it comes, and not rush anything. There was nothing for me to lose.

CHAPTER TEN

Things fell into perspective over the next few weeks, especially after I spent the holidays with family and friends. For New Year, I took an inventory of my life. It wasn't bad, though I had the normal roller-coaster trajectory most people ride occasionally. Being able to see Angie again helped more than I imagined it would. I was glad we reestablished our friendship and stayed in touch. I liked Bill and talked with him often. We had become friends as well. Brooke and I saw each other regularly, and our relationship was developing nicely.

I felt satisfied.

Angie thought it curious I had met Brooke the same way she and Bill did. She thought she was the one. Especially because of how I spoke of her. It was too soon to tell, I thought, but she might be right. Scott thought the same, and didn't let an opportunity pass to let me know he was responsible, just like I knew he would.

The annoyance was worth it. I was happy.

"Hey, Ryan," Joe leaned against my cubicle and sipped a Coke.

"Hello Joe, whaddya know?" I asked as I finished an email.

"Heard you just got back from a Bloodhound show," he returned with a laugh. "I'm okay. What are you doing for lunch?"

"Thought I might stay in and get something out of the vending machine. Catch up on some work. Those burritos are to die for."

"Ah." He swirled his can. "You don't really want that, do you?"

I didn't. I probably could have used a break.

"We can go grab something," Joe said.

"Let me guess, roast beef sandwiches?" It was a safe bet. He loved those things.

"Not for me. It's Friday, but you can have one if you'd like."

"That's right." I had forgotten Joe was Catholic. On Fridays, he usually had fish.

I had asked him once whether Catholics could eat meat on Fridays now. Joe affirmed Catholics could eat meat except during Lent, but he was used to the rule because he had grown up with it.

"They have good fish sandwiches, so we can go."

"Sure," I said. "Just let me know when you are ready."

"Okay. Use your wastebasket?"

I nodded and he tossed his can and went back to his cubicle.

I glanced at my watch and saw I had an hour before lunch. My stomach rumbled in anticipation as I scrolled through my accounts.

"You ready?" Joe asked.

I glanced at my watch. It seemed only minutes passed, but it had been an hour.

"Yeah, give me a minute," I said. "You want me to drive?"

"You want to?"

I shook my head. "Not really."

He waited as I finished up, and we went out to his car. He had a ten-year-old Buick, but it looked new.

"How do you keep your car this nice with kids?"

"Easy," Joe answered. "I don't let them ride in it. You should take a gander at my wife's car, and it's newer." He patted the dashboard with sincere affection. "She's an old lady, but she's been good to me. It's funny. I don't even like Buicks."

"So why did you get one?"

"When you don't have money, you can't be choosy. There's a big difference between fifteen hundred and fifteen thousand."

"Just one zero."

"But it's a big zero."

"True. Sometimes what you end up with turns out to be the best thing for you."

"Never thought about that. Roast beef? Tell me now," he said as we approached the sandwich shop.

"Fine with me," I said.

He turned into the parking lot. "This place has the best fish sandwiches. I have coupons."

"You always have coupons."

"When it's your favorite place, it only makes sense."

"Does that mean you're picking up the tab?"

"Only if you like fish sandwiches. I've got a buy-one-get-one-free coupon."

"Big difference between free and six bucks," I said with a grin.

"It's settled then." Joe dug around the center console for his coupon.

The restaurant was full of people grabbing a quick bite during their lunch hour. I tried to guess their professions based on their attire or belongings, but I gave up after a few people. How was I going to know if I was right?

"Come on, let's find a seat," Joe said.

We took our trays and took a table next to a window. Joe wasted no time tearing into his sandwich.

"So good," he mumbled through a mouthful.

"What about Catholics who can't eat fish because they're allergic?" I asked.

He shrugged. "They'd be stuck eating beans or salad."

"That would suck."

"Well, we can eat meat now, if we want."

"That's right," I said.

"Diane with that one customer." He chuckled. "Is Jesus there?"

"Yeah, but an understandable mistake. She just didn't know English and Spanish say it differently. Can't give her too hard a time about it," I said, though I'd ribbed her about it myself.

"Well, it deserves some." He nodded toward my sandwich. "You going to eat that?"

"Yes, I was just working on the fries first." Truth was, I wasn't a fan of fish. I unwrapped the sandwich and took a bite. I didn't expect to like it. "Wow, these are good. Usually, places like this, the fish is crappy."

Joe regarded his sandwich. "I'd say it's sophisticated, but really it's still fast food."

"No fast food is sophisticated. It's just fuel. A lot of places try for atmosphere so more people will come in. It's a great marketing ploy."

Joe nodded and stirred a fry in the ketchup. He looked troubled, so I asked, "What's on your mind?"

"Oh, that rumor is still bugging me."

"What rumor?" I wasn't aware of any rumors.

"The one where they're shutting down the office?"

I shook my head and shrugged. "When did that start?" I hoped there wasn't any truth to it. I didn't want to look for another job.

"That's right. You left for Iowa that afternoon."

"Hell, Joe. That was a couple of months ago."

"Maybe it's blown over."

"Well, did anyone say when?" I asked.

Joe shrugged. "Maggie's the one that brought it up. Said that the home office thinks we aren't bringing in enough, but didn't give a date."

"No one mentioned it to me."

"I'm sorry, Ryan. I should have thought to tell you."

I sighed. "We have only nine people. We do okay, so I don't see a problem."

"I think I'll look for another job. If it's true, I want a head start. At least now I can be choosy."

"No, Joe, it's probably not true. If it were, she would have said something to me."

"I think she just let it slip. You know how she is. She gets emotional about things and doesn't always think."

"Yeah, so don't worry about it, Joe."

We finished up our meal and headed back to the office.

"Do you think I should ask Maggie?" I asked as we pulled into the lot. Though I had heard nothing, Joe's concern had me a little worried.

"It's up to you. If you do, I'd like to know if I need to start job hunting."

"Sure. What are friends for?"

☺

Instead of going to speak to Maggie straightaway, I worked a few accounts. I did well that afternoon and even landed a good motel account. I decided then it would be a good time to talk to Maggie about the rumor.

"Wow, Ryan!" Maggie nearly shouted as she clapped her hands. "You're on a roll today. What is it, eight thousand so far? Wow!"

"Just one of those days, Maggie. I'll probably be dry for the next couple of days." Even though I was used to it by then, Maggie's enthusiasm always made me uncomfortable. "Listen, Maggie, can I talk to you in private?"

"Sure. Why don't we go to the back?" She stood with effort, but I knew it couldn't be easy to carry around three hundred pounds.

"What did you need to discuss?" Maggie asked as she shut the door behind her.

I leaned against the table and was straightforward. "I heard a rumor the home office was shutting us down. Apparently, I wasn't here for the meeting. Is it true?"

Maggie blew a gust of air. "They discussed it. I shouldn't have said anything. If they do, I don't know when. I planned on letting you all know if there are developments."

I digested the information. "Can you tell me whether I need to look for another job?"

"I can't be sure, Ryan. I think they're seriously considering it, but will try to have some options if it happens."

128

"What options?"

She fiddled with a bottle of cleaner. "I don't know, but they would apply to those who have been with the company for at least a year. You shouldn't have to worry."

"Yeah, it's kind of hard not to," I said.

"I understand. You're one of our best people. I'm sure there'll be a place for you if you want it."

"I enjoy working here. With you and everyone."

"It's a wonderful group, but they'll do what they think is best for the company," she said with a hint of bitterness. "Just keep it to yourself, okay? I don't want anyone to worry. If something happens, we'll have a meeting."

"I understand, but I will tell Joe. Nobody else."

"Okay, but don't let him worry. He does it too much already."

"True, but it'll be fine. Thanks for being honest with me."

"No problem, Ryan." She clapped her hands and said, "Now go get more on the board!"

"I'll do my best."

I stopped by Joe's cubicle.

"Hey, Ryan. Did you talk to her?"

"Yeah. I don't think there's anything to worry about. Things will probably work out."

"That's good." He looked relieved.

"We can talk more later."

"Sure thing, Ryan. Thanks," he said, then went back to his work.

I sat at my desk and checked the time. It was too close to quitting time to do any substantial work, so I just shut down my computer and got ready to go home.

CHAPTER ELEVEN

I walked the aisles of the liquor store and felt completely lost. I wasn't a connoisseur, but Brooke invited me to dinner at her place, and I thought I ought to bring a bottle of wine. I had no idea what to choose. In my limited knowledge, it was something you drank, and sometimes people cooked with it. When I asked Scott, all he said was to stay away from boxes and screw-on caps. Finally, I grabbed a bottle of red wine with a cork and called it good. I also picked up a six-pack of hard lemon-ade. I knew that was good and might be a suitable alternative if the wine was a bust.

The relationship between Brooke and me had grown comfortable. We were probably at a point where we should think about where we were going. I enjoyed being with her, but wasn't sure I wanted to be very serious. She gave out "serious" vibes, though she wasn't pushy. She let me know her feelings in her unique way.

I could see being with her long term. She was fun, smart, easy to talk to, and over time, she'd become more beautiful to me. I caught myself now and then comparing her to Angie, and it bothered me. Angie was not in my future beyond friendship, and I knew it. She and Bill were in it for the long haul.

For me and Brooke to move forward, I would need to put all of it behind me. I didn't want to screw things up with her, and it could be my last chance at starting a family; I wasn't getting any younger. No kid wanted to play with an old man hobbling along on a cane.

I got to Brooke's place a little early and did a quick check in the mirror. After brushing my hair back, I grabbed the bottle of wine from the back seat, but left the hard lemonade. I didn't want to look like I was trying to get her drunk.

I found the door unlocked, so let myself in.

"Is that you, Ryan?" Brooke called out.

"No, it's the ol' big bad wolf," I answered with a growl.

"Please don't eat me!" she cried as she peeked from behind the wall.

"You made this too easy." I grabbed her and nibbled her neck.

"Stop!" She laughed and pushed me away. "I don't want to burn the food."

"Maybe I'll save it for dessert."

"Don't count on it," she said.

I sulked. "Denied."

"You're early, but it's almost done. Hope you like chicken."

"Love chicken. I brought wine." I held up the bottle. "Don't know if it'll go with chicken, though."

"As long as we like it, it doesn't matter."

"I like your practicality."

"I'll need a corkscrew." I put the wine on the counter and checked out the food. "Looks good."

"Go, get out of my kitchen. Sit in the living room like a good boy until I call you."

"Yes, Mother," I said. I went over to the stereo and glanced through her CD collection. I saw a couple I liked, but settled on the couch instead.

"Sorry if I'm too early." The smell from the kitchen made my mouth water.

"Better than being late."

"Agree. Being early's a habit." I picked up a magazine from the end table and flipped through it without reading.

"It's ready," Brooke called out.

"You want me to do anything?"

"Nope, just sit down," she said.

The food was already on the table, and it smelled delicious.

"I haven't eaten all day, so I'm starving," I said. "What is it?"

"Chicken meatballs with peanut sauce," she said as she set down glass tumblers filled with the wine. "I found the recipe in a magazine."

"An Asian influence, huh?"

"Yeah."

"It looks interesting."

"I thought I'd use you as a test subject."

"I've never thought of putting peanut sauce on meatballs," I said. "Never thought to use chicken for meatballs either."

"It's meat, so why not?"

"Makes sense. So, this is it? No candles?"

"Do you think this is supposed to be some storybook dinner? I suppose you want soft music playing too."

"Well ..." I started, but she gave me the look. "No, it's fine. Anyway, we're just going to wolf it down, then have wild, crazy monkey sex on the floor because you couldn't wait for a bed. Who needs music and candles for that?"

"You think so?" Her eyes twinkled as she pointed. "Be happy you're getting dinner, because that's all you're getting, mister."

"Yes, ma'am." I took a bite of a meatball. It was good, and the flavors came together, though it seemed an odd pairing. "This is incredible. If you keep cooking like this, I'm going to get fatter."

"You're lucky. I don't normally cook for people."

"I feel privileged."

"I'm glad you like it. You're a good test subject."

"For this, you can use me any way you want."

"Now that's a double entendre if there ever was one," she said with a smile.

"Just one of my many talents. Your picking up on it? I think I like."

She sighed and shook her head.

Why was I fighting with myself over this relationship? So far, it was as close to perfect as I've ever had. We had only known each other a couple of months, and though I was happy, I felt I was holding back. I felt guilty for comparing her to the past, though she compared very well.

I was thirty-five and hadn't had a serious relationship. There had been one or two that could have ended up in marriage and family. I could have been happy, but my stupid hang-up over Angie kept me from it. I saw it only after the fact.

Would I let it happen with Brooke, too? The whole point of going to Iowa was for closure. I got it, but I couldn't figure out what held me back from moving on to something new.

Angie had always been a big part of my life, but it was the girl, not the woman, who was always on my mind and heart. She was married. She had children. It was long past the time for me to move on. Everyone had been saying it for years, so why couldn't I make up my damn mind?

"A penny for your thoughts," Brooke said. Her expression made me think she already knew.

"You'll be cheated. I'm just concentrating on the food."

She raised her eyebrows as her grin widened. "Your plate's empty."

I looked down, and sure enough, it was clean. "So it is. Is there more wine?"

"A little."

"More wine would be fantastic."

She poured more into my glass and then added to hers. "For a guy who knows nothing about wine, you made a good choice."

"I used the spin around and take the one you point at when you stop method."

"I'll have to remember that. You want to take a walk? It's a little chilly, but it's a nice night."

"Sure. It'll give the food a chance to settle."

The night was crisp and quiet as we strolled through a grove of trees behind the apartments. I reached out for her hand. She wove her fingers into mine and smiled. It felt right.

"This is probably going to sound stupid," she said, "but I feel like I'm sixteen again."

"It doesn't. I sometimes feel like I'm ten, and have been told I act it."

"I don't think so. Fourteen maybe."

"Thanks," I said. "When I was a kid, I used to go out and wander like this. I miss it."

"What, being a kid?"

"That too." I was sensuously aware of her smooth skin. There was a contradiction between the strength of her grip and the delicacy of her bones. "I like being a grown-up. We get special privileges."

"Such as?"

"This." I pulled her to me and brought my mouth to hers and let myself get lost in the sensation as we explored each other through a kiss that melded body and spirit.

"What's gotten into you?" she said breathlessly.

"Just wanted to thank you for the lovely dinner," I answered.

"Wow, if that was for dinner, what was dessert?"

"Dessert?" I said. "I should have waited."

"No dessert," she said with faux sadness.

"There can be. I have hard lemonade in my car. It's not food, but a nice alternative," the suggestion popped out unexpectedly. I'd forgotten I bought it.

"Wine, hard lemonade," she looked at me askance. "Are you trying to get me drunk?"

"It's only a six-pack," I said as if it were something I did all the time.

"I think we can handle it," she said as we headed back to her apartment.

Our kiss had awakened my senses, and I realized she was what I wanted. Nothing so simple had ever said so much. Though my reservations were fading, some remained.

I glanced at her profile in the dim lighting along the sidewalk. I thought she was pretty, but she was very different from the women I've dated. Her red hair was smooth and straight, with a subtle curl just above her shoulders. With her petite frame, the light sprinkling of freckles across her cheekbones, and her small upturned nose, she could pass for sixteen without trying, but she was definitely a woman who could handle herself. There was a lot I liked about her, and that I enjoyed kissing her didn't hurt. I found myself wondering what she'd be like in bed, and why I hadn't tried to find out.

"Do you want a lemonade?" I asked as we neared my car.

"Sure. I've never had one," she said.

"They're probably warm now."

"Not the only thing," she said with a wink. "But that's what ice is for."

Well, I could definitely find out, I thought.

We stopped at my car to grab the lemonade from my back seat, then went inside.

We cracked open a couple bottles and found they were still chilled. We got buzzed enough to loosen inhibitions and what started as a simple kiss turned into a whole lot more.

☺

"Where are we going with this?" Brooke asked as we lay in bed. The morning sun had begun to stream in through the window.

"I don't know," I answered. I wanted to be honest, but didn't want to say something I wasn't sure of, or didn't mean. Especially now. Whether or not we wanted to admit it, we were vulnerable.

"I like you a lot, Brooke, and I enjoy spending time with you. It's more than I've had in a long time."

She laid her head on my shoulder. "I don't want you to think I'm trying to pressure you into anything."

"I don't think you are, but I won't lie to you," I said. "Let's just see what happens and enjoy the ride."

"I'm not normally like this, but I feel a connection with you." She kissed me, her pert breasts pressed against my chest. "I'm enjoying the ride so far. Very much."

"Me too." I ran my hand down her back and cupped her swells.

She let loose a girlish giggle, and I pulled her on top of me and slid into her, our bodies melding perfectly into one. She arched her back and moaned, low and primal, as I grasped her hips and felt her move us both back over the edge.

CHAPTER TWELVE

"Absolutely, Ms. Kenyon," I said into the phone and noticed Maggie hovering over me.

"Ryan, do you have a moment?" she whispered.

I held up a finger and mouthed, "One moment."

Maggie nodded and looked around my cubicle. She chuckled when she spotted my Carl Jung action figure.

I continued my phone call. "Of course, I'll stay with you next time I'm up…" I grinned at Maggie and gave her a thumbs up. "Okay then, let me know if you need anything…you too," I finished and hung up the phone. "What's up, Maggie?" She looked so confused, it was difficult not to laugh.

"What was that all about, or should I be afraid to ask?"

I glanced at the phone. "Just setting up a liaison with one of my female customers."

She gasped. "Oh my god, Ryan! You better not be."

I couldn't hold it in anymore. I laughed. "Don't worry, Maggie. Ms. Kenyon owns the motel I stayed at when I was in Iowa. I gave her my card, and she just made an order."

She sighed with relief. "Well, that's good."

"Indeed. Check it out." I turned my screen toward her.

"Wow!" She clapped. "You're on fire!"

"Thanks," I said. "Did you need to speak to me?"

She nodded. "Can we talk in the conference room?"

"Sure." I wasn't sure what she wanted to talk about, and the look on her face wasn't giving it away. I just hoped it wasn't something bad, because the new account had me riding high. I had expected nothing to come of it when I handed her my card, but my whim had paid off.

Maggie closed the door and stood there as if guarding it. I leaned against the table with my arms crossed.

"You're not in trouble, Ryan," Maggie said. "It's probably good news."

"What's up?" I wasn't sure I believed her.

Maggie sighed. "I just heard they're closing our office."

"That's not good. It sucks," I said. "When?"

"It'll be official on Friday."

"This Friday?" I nearly shouted. "That's only three days' notice."

"They're just officially announcing it Friday," Maggie clarified and began to tear up.

I had been in awe of Maggie's open emotions for seven years. I realized her penchant for easy tears was likely why this office hadn't been as successful as it could have been. How she managed to stay on was anybody's guess. Diane, Joe, and I were the ones who held things together whenever they got critical. I wondered why she hadn't included them in this meeting and imagined what our fates would be.

"So, what's going to happen to us? To Diane and Joe?" I asked.

She grabbed a tissue and dabbed her eyes. "I don't know."

"Come on, Maggie," I said. "You've got to know something."

"They might let them work from home. They'll be able to keep their accounts. The company will probably let go the employees who've been here for under two years. At least that's what I understand."

"So some of us are screwed out of a job," I said.

Her tears ran freely. "I know it's not fair."

I noticed she didn't really include me in this, but I thought of places to send my résumé.

"Why aren't Diane and Joe here? Joe's been here as long as I have, Diane longer. Don't you think they should know?"

Maggie crumpled the tissue in her hand. "Yes, but I wanted to speak with you first."

"Okay. What for?"

"I think they'll make you an offer. I wanted to tell you, so you'd have a chance to think about it."

I shrugged. "Wouldn't it just be working from home?"

"I may be wrong, but I think they want you to run another office."

"Really?" I wasn't sure what to think. I had done nothing to be considered.

"Maybe. You could do it. It'd be a good promotion if you want it."

"But if they did offer, and I accepted, I'd have to move." I didn't like the idea of moving somewhere new.

"Most likely."

"But why not just keep this office open? I don't understand. Anyway, I like Tulsa."

"I understand, but this office has been the lowest producing for several years."

"I can't see how that makes a difference," I said. "Are they coming here for the meeting?"

"No, it'll be via video conference from the home office," she said. "I'll learn everything at the same time as you guys."

"This is crap, Maggie."

"I know, but if they offer you the promotion, it could be good for you."

"I'm not sure if I like it. Where would they want me to go?"

"They have several offices, but I don't know which one. It's not a guarantee, though."

"Yeah, I know. I'll think about it. Will you tell the others?"

"I will shortly."

"Okay." I straightened and smoothed my shirt. "I need to finish up some stuff, so..."

"Okay. Do think about it."

"Sure, thanks," I said and headed back to my cubicle.

I thought about it. The home office was in Arizona, and I knew they had offices in New Jersey and Washington State. I couldn't recall where the others might be, but I didn't care. They would have to offer me a lot more than a promotion to make me pull up roots and plant myself so far away. My mother, my friends, and the familiar places I loved were here. And there was Brooke. I wanted to stay here, and would rather take a work-from-home job than a promotion.

There was no reason to decide anything until Friday, when I would know more. In my life, I had learned it was best to keep your mouth shut and let the other side show their hand first.

☙

Wednesday night, Brooke and I sat on the floor of her terrace and watched some of the neighborhood kids playing. I hadn't told her about what was happening at work yet. I still wasn't sure what I wanted. The possible promotion would be a chance to solidify my career, but it wasn't what I envisioned doing with my life. Though I enjoyed my work, the idea of having to move held me back. My relationship with Brooke had grown enough that I would need to talk to her before I decided. No matter what happened, she was a part of it.

"You've been quiet all evening," she said.

"I know. Just thinking about work."

"Something wrong?"

"There's some stuff going on. I'm wondering if I'll have to find another job."

"Why?"

I sighed. "They're closing the office."

"Well, that sucks." Brooke rested her head on my shoulder and took my hand.

"Yeah." I ran my thumb over her fingers. "Next week. Everyone will have to find another job."

"Maybe Scott can put in a good word for you," she said. "We could work together, have lunch together. Or we could have lunch." She waggled her eyebrows.

I chuckled. "Tempting, but Maggie said they might let some of us work from home."

"That'd be nice. You could work naked."

"I could."

"I wish I could work naked."

"Me too, but if you did, I'd get nothing done."

"Yeah, because you'd be too busy throwing up."

"Not true. You're beautiful," I said and pulled her in for a kiss. "I love looking at you."

She blushed. "You're so full of it. I'm all pale, and my boobs are too small."

"Nuh-uh. Your boobs are perfect. They stand right up and say, 'Hey there! How are ya?'" I gave one a squeeze and said, "I'm fine, and so are you!"

"Stop that!" she laughed and slapped my hand. "Maybe you shouldn't get to work at home if you'll act like that."

"Maybe not." I sighed. The next part would be hard. "Maggie said they might offer me a management position."

"Yeah?"

"It'd mean a raise and more benefits," I said, though I wasn't sure who I was trying to convince.

"I sense a 'but' in there somewhere," she said.

I nodded. "If I take it, I'd have to move."

"I see." If she felt anything, she didn't show it. "Are you going to take it?"

"I don't know. Home is here. What do you think?"

"It's up to you, Ryan," she said. "What do you want?"

"What about us?" I looked away and focused on a woman walking her dog.

She didn't answer.

"If I move, what happens to us?" I asked. "I like where we're going."

She shrugged. "Long-distance relationships can work."

"Can they?"

"People do it all the time," she said. "I guess I could move too."

"You'd do that?"

"If it comes to it, yeah," she said.

I thought I could detect hesitation in her voice. "What if we don't work out?"

"There's always a chance," she said with a shrug. "But I don't want to hold you back."

"I don't want you to do that either."

"Why don't you find out what they say first?" she asked. "Whatever you decide, I'll support you."

"Really?"

She nodded. "I want you to be happy."

"It's a shame it took so long to find you. You're smart. Beautiful." I kissed her cheek and smelled her hair as I nipped her neck. "You smell good. Taste good."

"Stop." She pushed me away playfully. "People are going to see."

"I don't care," I said.

"Take it inside, you bad boy."

I jumped up and swooped her into my arms. "Whatever you say!"

"What are you doing?" she squealed. "Put me down!"

"Taking it inside, as you commanded," I said and didn't put her down until we got to the bedroom.

Friday morning, Maggie announced the meeting would be that afternoon, and the office buzzed with tension. People questioned her, but she deferred them to the meeting. She mentioned nothing from our conversation last week, so I wondered if she had accurate information then.

"I'm so nervous," Diane said as we got our coffee. "I can't stand it. What about you?"

"I'm sure there's nothing to worry about," I answered.

"I'm an old lady, Ryan. If I lose my job, no one is going to hire me."

"You've been here eight years," I said. "You, me, and Joe? I think we'll be fine."

She grew somber. "These days, none of that matters."

Diane was in her late fifties, so I understood how she felt, but she had a good record, which ought to help her. Though I had some idea of what might happen, I didn't want to get anyone's hopes up. If my information was wrong, I didn't want to be the bad guy.

"Well, I think it's crap we're getting closed down, but I honestly think they won't leave us cold."

She eyed me warily, as if she could tell I had insider info.

"Hey guys," Joe said as he walked up. He wore a smile, but his eyes betrayed him.

"Hey, Joe," we said.

He surprised us by pouring himself a cup of coffee.

"I thought you hated coffee?" I asked.

He shook his head. "I just don't drink it often."

"I've never seen you touch the stuff."

"I only drink it when I'm really nervous."

"Seems counterproductive."

He shrugged as he took a slow sip, wincing as it went down. "Looks like everyone's anticipating the meeting."

"I know I am," Diane answered.

"Yeah, but you can't blame us," I said. "We've all just been told we're losing jobs. Amber's already packed up her desk."

"She's always kept a nice space," Diane mumbled, more to herself.

Everyone felt the change in the room's energy that week.

We took our coffees back to our desks and tried to act as if it were just another day, where we would come back on Monday as if staying or leaving was our choice.

☺

After lunch, Maggie called the meeting. We all headed to the conference room and took places around the table. A large monitor sat at the head. Maggie closed the door behind her and clapped her hands.

"Okay, we'll start in a couple of minutes. I want to remind you to be respectful and save any questions for afterward." Though she tried to sound strong, I heard the emotion in her voice. "Do you understand?"

"Well, let's go nip this in the butt!" Joe said in his Don Knotts impression.

There were a few light chuckles. Joe's impressions were a favorite in the office, and they lightened the mood, but today? Not so much.

"Yeah, Joe, let's," I said and patted him on the back.

I never had the heart to tell Joe it wasn't nip it in the butt. His misquote hurt no one, and I found it endearing. Joe's impressions would always be a pleasant memory of his unique character.

The screen flickered to life and several men and women, upper management from the home office, appeared. They looked at us from the screen as if witnesses to an execution. It felt like they were in the room, their own table an extension of ours. It was a little spooky.

Everyone quickly settled down and the meeting began. It seemed to go on for hours and confirmed mostly what we had all feared. After we had been dismissed, I stood along with the others and wished I had the foresight to go ahead and pack up my desk earlier.

"Mr. Logan?"

I stopped and turned toward the monitor.

"Would you stay here with us a moment?" asked Mr. Beyer, the senior manager.

"Yes, sir," I replied and sat back down.

Maggie gave me a thumbs-up as she left the room and closed the door.

The room was silent. I assumed Maggie would stay. Alone in the room, I felt more nervous. We had all lost our jobs, though we who had been there at least a year were given the weekend to consider working from home. It was a job, but it wouldn't be the same. Only half of us met the requirement. I knew Diane and Joe would take it, but I wasn't sure of the others.

I was curious what would happen, though I had decided I wouldn't take a position somewhere else. It was a promotion, I didn't want to move, especially since things had started to look up for me. I was prepared to turn it down and ask to work from home. There wouldn't be a raise, but I didn't care. At least I'd still have a job.

Mr. Beyer shuffled some papers and took a sip of water. "How are you doing, Mr. Logan?"

"I'm good, sir," I answered. "And you?"

"Fine, just fine, Mr. Logan," he said with a grunt. "We are impressed with your work."

"Thank you very much, sir," I replied.

"As you are now aware, we will keep some of you, in some capacity, with the company," he said.

I nodded.

"We would like to offer you a management position with one of our other offices. How does that sound to you?"

"I'd like some time to consider," I said. "It's a big step."

"Of course, Mr. Logan." He tapped a pen on his paperwork. "We're prepared to offer a starting salary of sixty thousand a year, with benefits."

He leaned back in his chair, and I tried to keep a poker face. The offer was at least thirty thousand more than what I was making now. It was tempting, but I wasn't sure I really wanted it.

"It's very generous, Mr. Beyer. I'd have to find a place, and, well, it can get expensive." I knew it was a weak excuse, but it was all I could think of.

"I understand." He scratched his chin. "We'll cover your moving expenses and give you a per diem, so you can book a hotel for a couple of weeks until you find a place. We'd really like to have you stay on our team, Mr. Logan."

"I appreciate that, sir." I still thought it would be better to stay in Tulsa, but realized I hadn't asked where they wanted me to go. If it were close, like Oklahoma City, or somewhere within a couple hundred miles, I'd be more apt to take it.

"Out of curiosity, Mr. Beyer, where would I be going?"

"Yes, we haven't discussed location, have we?"

I shook my head.

He looked over his paperwork and said, "It'll be the Des Moines office."

I perked up. "Iowa?" I hadn't known there was an office there. Des Moines wasn't but thirty miles from Chester. From Angie.

"That's right," said Mr. Beyer. "It's a fairly new office, but productive. We have fifteen employees there, and it has brought in seven figures the past couple of years." He leaned back in his chair and grinned proudly.

"If you don't mind my asking, why me?"

"Good question, Mr. Logan," said Mr. Beyer. "We believe you have a lot to offer the office, and with your performance here, we wanted to give you the opportunity. I think you would do very well."

148

For the first time, I seriously considered it. Though the salary and their confidence in me were impressive, it wasn't what was on my mind. "Could I have some time to think about it?" I asked.

"Of course, Mr. Logan. Take the weekend to consider and call me on Monday morning. If you still have concerns, we can discuss them then."

"Yes, sir. I appreciate the opportunity," I said. "I'll call you on Monday."

"Great!" Mr. Beyer clapped his hands together once. "I'll look forward to it."

The screen went blank, and I was left alone with my reflection. My mind was reeling. The office location changed everything, but part of me thought it wasn't a good idea.

I got up and went back to my cubicle. Maggie looked at me questioningly. I flashed her a covert thumbs-up; she beamed. Joe and Diane looked at me, and I shrugged, as if it weren't a big deal. I didn't want to cause any contention, so I wasn't sure if I should say anything, but if they asked, I wouldn't lie.

I sat at my desk, checked my voicemail and returned calls as I scanned my email. I found it difficult to concentrate. What would happen if I took the offer? What if I didn't?

One thing was for sure; it was going to be a very long weekend.

CHAPTER THIRTEEN

That evening, Scott and I sat on the edge of the lake and sipped on Rolling Rock. I had told him about the meeting, but I kept the location to myself. It wasn't something he needed to know straightaway, and I wanted it to be as neutral as possible.

"What am I going to do?" I asked.

"Up to you, my friend," he answered.

"I'm tired of people saying that."

"What, you want people to decide for you? That'll make you happy," he said with a touch of sarcasm.

I shook my head. "No, but some advice would be nice. It's why people ask."

"Sure, but I think you already know what you want. You just want to be validated." He dropped his empty bottle and grabbed another.

"Maybe," I said. "I'm just not sure."

"Okay, so what is it you want? No bullshit."

I sighed and picked at the label on my half-drunk bottle. "It's better money. That's a plus. But money's not really important."

"It doesn't hurt," Scott said. He pulled cigars from his pocket and offered me one.

I lighted it and took a few puffs. "Brooke and I are onto something good here. If I move, it'll get fucked up."

"Sounds like you're still trying to talk yourself out of it. What's the problem?"

"I don't know."

"Before today, you were dead set against the idea. You were going to turn it down, but now you're fighting with yourself over it. Why?"

A fish splashed nearby.

"Sixty's a lot of money. With the benefits, it would probably be smart to take it," I said, but my heart wasn't in it.

"Bullshit, Ryan." Scott drained the rest of the beer and leaned forward in his chair. "What aren't you telling me?"

I looked away.

"Come on. What else is there?" he insisted.

I sighed heavily. He was right. I had prepared fully to turn it down. I knew even if I didn't get the work at home job, I would be able to get something comparable, maybe even better. But they had mentioned the location.

"It's in Iowa," I finally said.

"What?"

"The office. If I take it, I'll have to move to Iowa."

He laughed. "Oh, goddammit, Ryan. Let it go. You have to let it go."

"I have let it go," I said. I really wasn't in the mood to get into this again.

He shook his head. "She's married. She has children. Two of them. Don't take this job over some idea in your head. You've got nothing coming. Stay friends, exchange Christmas cards, call now and then, maybe visit when you take a vacation, but that's it."

"That's not what it's about, Scott."

"Yeah, it is. Don't bullshit me. I've known you too long." Scott looked at his beer. "Brooke really likes you. Hell, she can't seem to shut up about you. You've done the unskinny bop. You're not getting any younger, and Brooke makes you happy; I can tell. Don't throw it away on something twenty years old."

"You're right."

"Of course I'm right."

"You have to admit, the money is good."

"Oh, bloody Hell. If you're doing it for the right reasons, Ryan, then take the damn offer. Go to Iowa and freeze your ass off. You know how cold it gets up there?"

"Yeah, I was there. It wasn't bad."

"A couple of days doesn't count. It gets really fucking cold there."

"I like cold."

He sighed and finished his beer like a man who needed it. "Look, talk to Brooke. She's the one you need to be having this discussion with. We'll always be friends, but I'm not going to sleep with you."

I frowned. "You're breaking my heart."

"Whatever, man," he said with a laugh. "Hey, maybe she'll go with you."

"Maybe she won't."

"Yeah, something you'll have to consider. Can't expect her to give up her life to follow you. It's a big step, considering you haven't been to-gether that long."

"I know."

"Look, man, you have all weekend. Talk to her, and get your priori-ties straight. For now, just relax and have another beer."

He grabbed one from the cooler and tossed it to me. As I caught it, he said, "Get drunk. I'll drive you home."

"I don't think you should."

"Then stay here."

"Maybe I will," I said, and swallowed half the bottle at once.

"One last thing to consider, Ryan, and then I'll drop it. It is good money, and for some reason, you like your job. How often do people get to do work they enjoy and make a good living besides?"

"Not often," I answered.

"Damn right. And you might be able to talk them up another five grand."

"True."

It was like Scott to lay out all the options, but I needed to examine my own reasons and sort out my priorities.

☙

On Saturday, I had fully made my decision. Perhaps it was stupid, but I felt there was a reason the opportunity came along. How the Universe works is beyond my explanation, so I can only go with my gut feeling. However, I also knew I'd have to accept the consequences of my choices, for good or ill.

I had tossed and turned all night with my thoughts. I dreaded talking to Brooke about it, though I knew I should. Things would work out if it was meant to be. Though I wanted us to work, I also wanted other things. Impossible things.

It wasn't something I wanted to discuss over the phone, so without telling her I was coming, I drove to Brooke's apartment. This was definitely a face-to-face conversation. I put on some music to distract me, so

I wouldn't overthink everything before I got there and make it harder.

Brooke had given me a key, so I let myself in and slowly went up the stairs. It was as if I was trying to stop the inevitable.

"Hey, you," Brooke said as my head poked over the wall. She was curled on the couch, flipping through a magazine. Enya played softly on the stereo.

"Hey," I answered.

She got up and kissed me. "What are you doing here?"

"I missed you." I brushed a loose strand of hair behind her ear. "What are you up to?"

"I'm just by the phone, waiting for you to call." She slipped her arms around my waist and laid her head on my shoulder.

"All in vain," I said. "I'm out with this smokin' hot redhead."

She scowled at me. "I'm jealous."

"You should be. She's amazing." I kissed her, relishing the softness of her lips.

"I'll bet." She pulled away. "You want something to drink?"

"No, I'm okay." I hesitated. "I actually wanted to talk to you about the offer."

"Oh?" She sat on the couch and folded her legs under her.

"Yeah." I sat down with her. I had told her everything, but hadn't indicated I had decided.

"You're taking it, aren't you?"

I nodded and sighed. "Yeah. It wasn't easy, but it's really too good of an opportunity to pass up."

"That's great. I'm happy for you."

She said it, but her manner betrayed her. She wasn't happy. I moved closer and took her hands in mine.

"I want you to know, no matter what, I want us to work. I'm happy with you, Brooke. You make me happy. I don't want this to affect us."

"But it does, Ryan," she said. "How are we going to work if you're hundreds of miles away?"

"You could come with me," I said. I wanted to be with her, but worried about how the distance would affect our relationship. It was strong, I thought, but how long could it survive with us so far apart? I knew it was a long shot, but I wanted her to know living together was an option, and one I wanted.

"I can't pick up and move. I have nothing there. No job, no family or friends. Just you."

"Would that be so bad?" I asked. "I can take care of you until you find something, if you want a job."

"I don't need to be taken care of, Ryan." She crossed her arms. "But that's not the point."

"Brooke, come on."

She turned away.

"You said you'd support my decision, but you're upset."

"That's before you said you were taking it."

"Listen, I understand if you don't want to go. We can work something out later. I'll come down as much as I can, and I'll buy you plane tickets. I want to be with you. This could actually be a good thing for us. At least think about it."

"I just..." She sighed. "Okay. I'll think about it."

I opened my arms, and she leaned into me and wrapped her arms around my waist. She wasn't thrilled, but I hoped despite everything, we would work it out. But really? I wasn't so sure anymore.

I had to tell only one person, and I didn't know how she would react. So far, the reactions had been mixed. I considered what Scott had said and finally admitted to myself the reason I was taking the promotion.

It was because of Angie.

I still hadn't fully gotten over her, and I realized I might never be. I would do nothing to harm the life she built for herself, but despite this, I still wanted to be close to her.

It was stupid. I knew I was risking my chance at happiness, but I felt compelled to follow this path, though I knew it risked my losing Brooke. I thought maybe I should save myself the trouble and turn down the promotion. There was still time for me to change my mind. Again, I felt torn.

I called Angie's number. It rang several times before Bill picked up.

"Hello?"

"Hey, Bill," I said, both disappointed and relieved. "It's me, Ryan."

"Ryan! It's great to hear from you. How you doing?" He sounded genuinely glad to hear from me, and somehow, it made it harder.

"I'm fine. Is Angie around?"

"No, 'fraid not. Her mother came by and kidnapped her and the kids. They went to the city for the day."

"Sounds fun."

He laughed heartily. "Yep. I get a break. I don't expect them back until later. You want to leave a message?"

"No, it's something I'd like to say in person."

"Something the matter?" His voice grew concerned.

"No, no. Nothing like that. I just got a bit of news."

"Not bad, I hope."

"Well, it's nothing you won't find out anyway," I said.

"Don't leave me hanging, my friend."

"I got an offer at work. A promotion, raise, everything."

"That's great."

"If I take it, I'll be moving up that way."

"What, to Iowa?"

"Yeah, I'll be running the office in Des Moines. I'll have to find a place to live there."

"That's quite a surprise. Are you taking it?"

"I think I will, but it's a change. Kind of scary, if you ask me."

"I understand, but you can handle it. You know it's cheaper outside the city, and it's just a short drive from here."

"I know."

"It's a good area. If you come here, I think you'll like it. If you don't mind my asking, what are they gonna pay you?"

"Sixty grand," I answered.

Bill gave a low whistle. "Not too bad."

"I have to let them know my decision tomorrow," I said. "I wanted to let you guys know first and see what you thought."

"You do what you think is best, Ryan."

"Seems to be the running sentiment."

"If you decide to take it, we'll help you get settled in. In Chester, Des Moines, wherever. You won't have to worry."

"I appreciate it, but you don't have to do anything."

"I know, but that's what friends do."

"Thanks." His sincerity awed me. "Listen, I want to tell Angie myself, so could you keep it hush for now? Have her call me when she gets back."

"Sure," he said. "She'll be happy to hear it."

"Thanks, Bill. We'll talk later."

I hung up and thought about my future. One in Iowa, of all places. What would become of my life? What chaos might it bring?

Only time would give the answer.

⊚

Angie called me later in the evening, and we talked for an hour. I told her almost everything, including Brooke's reaction. She assured me Brooke would come around if our relationship was for real. The only thing I kept from Angie was that she was the main reason for my decision.

I lay in bed that night and decided that accepting the promotion would be best. If Brooke and I didn't work out because of it, it would be better for it to happen now.

It was the consensus, and everyone was right. I wondered what might have been if I had taken the same advice twenty years ago.

CHAPTER FOURTEEN

On Monday morning, the office had a tension you could almost taste. In less than a week, it would be closed, and everyone was well aware of it. Three people didn't bother to come back after the weekend, but the rest of us, most of whom were taking the work-from-home offer, had stuck it out. Some of us thought that if we performed well that week, they would change their minds, but they had already decided.

Joe rolled his chair over to my desk and, in his Scooby-Doo voice, said, "Say, Ryan, do you have any Scooby Snacks?"

"Don't know, Scoob. Let's see." I grinned, reached into my drawer, and grabbed a couple of butterscotch candies. "Fresh out of Scooby Snacks, so this'll have to do."

"Good enough," Joe said normally and popped one into his mouth. "I'm gonna work at home for a while. At least until the wife can't handle me being there all day."

"She'll love it, Joe."

He shrugged. "What about you? You stayed behind a while Friday. What did they tell you?"

I glanced around, then said quietly, "They want me to manage an office in Iowa."

"Huh." Joe considered it. "You taking it?"

I nodded.

"You'll have to move."

"Yeah, but I have friends there, so it'll be okay."

"I think you'll do well, but if it doesn't work out, you can grow corn."

I laughed. "I'm not much of a farmer, so I'd better."

"We should throw a party. Have pizza. Beer too."

I shook my head. "No, it's just a job."

"Yeah, but this is a new path. You've lived in Tulsa for how long?"

"I don't actually live in Tulsa, but I've been around here all my life," I said. "I feel good about it, though."

Joe slapped me on the back. "I wish you the best of luck."

"Thanks," I said as he rolled back to his desk. He looked over at me and smiled with a touch of sadness.

I wondered if we would still be friends, or merely become a footnote in each other's lives. The chance of any relationship with my coworkers, even after so many years, was almost nil. Many people had come and gone in my life, and there would probably be many more. If I made a list, it would be long, but most would have been forgotten. But I couldn't forget Joe.

I picked up my phone and punched in Mr. Beyer's number. Suddenly I doubted my decision, but I chalked it up to nerves. His secretary patched me through, and I let him know I accepted. After preliminary paperwork and training, I would be the new manager of the Des Moines office.

I hung up, and doubt plagued me again. I hoped I had made the right decision. If I didn't, I would be stuck or have to come home in shame.

By the end of the week, I had packed everything. I stored what I couldn't take until I found a place, or I donated it to Goodwill. The rest went in my car.

Angie and Bill had looked around and kept me apprised of places available. They had little luck, but it was really a job I needed to do myself. I had decided to find a place in Chester. I was used to living in a small town, and I liked it. Living there would give me an air of familiarity. Until I found a place, I would use my per diem to stay at Ms. Kenyon's motel. I had told her I would stay whenever I came back up, so I felt obligated.

I spent my last evening in Tulsa with Brooke. I didn't know what would happen to us, but I knew I didn't want us to end. We went out to dinner, and afterward took a walk and held hands like we were still in high school. Later, we lay in bed where, in the darkness, the soft light through the window highlighted her features. I held her close and breathed her in.

"I wish you didn't have to go." Her finger traced lazy circles down my arm.

"I know," I said. "Don't worry, it'll work out."

"Think so?"

"Tesla said it best when they said, 'Love will find a way.'"

I felt her grin against my chest. "You're quoting hair-metal lyrics to me?"

"There's a lot of wisdom in hair metal."

"Oh god." Her grin turned into a laugh.

"It's true," I said. "I want it to work."

"Me too." She brushed her lips against mine.

We kissed and made love as if the slightest wrong move would break us, like fragile glass. I committed her smell and touch to memory as if it might be forever. We fell asleep holding on to each other and blended into dreams.

The next morning was bittersweet. We had breakfast together and tried not to think about the fact I'd be leaving shortly, without knowing when we'd see each other again.

"You'll call?" She had walked me to the car and stood close, her fingers in my belt loops, like we were teenagers.

I nodded. "I wish you would come with me."

"I can't. Not now."

"Why not?"

"This isn't the best time to say this." She sighed. "I love you, Ryan."

I don't know why her words affected me the way they did. We seemed to understand how we felt about each other, though we hadn't said it out loud. I loved her too, but hadn't found the courage to say it. She gave me courage.

"I love you too, Brooke."

I knew then we could make it. If we were apart for a while, maybe we would appreciate each other more. I wanted her to go, yes, but I understood why she stayed behind. They were the same reasons I had struggled with over the past week. Those three words made it okay to wait.

"I need to go," I said. I kissed her and held onto it like a talisman.

"Okay," she whispered. "Drive careful, and call me."

"I will," I said, and let her go.

"I'll miss you," she said as she stepped back, her arms crossed under her breasts. She bit her lip, and I knew she was trying not to cry.

I rolled down my window. "I'll call as soon as I get there." As I drove away, I watched her in the rearview and waved until I could no longer see her.

On the highway, I settled in. My thoughts bounced around, and I wondered when I would see her again. Did I make the right decision? Would I be okay, so far from the people and places I knew by heart? Would I be successful, or was their faith in me misplaced? My biggest fear was that I would be a major disappointment to everyone.

I had a friend there, true, but I was leaving my support system behind. If I failed here, I would have enough familiarity and people to fall back on. I wouldn't have the same there. Already, I wanted to forget it and turn around, but I couldn't. I had agreed, and I couldn't go back on my word.

Trepidation was normal, especially when venturing into the unknown. Unlike many others, I had someone on the other end to help. I was fortunate.

The passing scenery lulled me as I drove, and I imagined different scenarios my future might hold. Foremost was whether I could truly have a friendship with both Angie and Bill when old feelings had never truly died. They lay dormant and sparked when I found her again. I had never mentioned it; it would have accomplished nothing.

I had caught up with Aaron again. While he worked construction for money, he put his focus on his band, Schist, who had been together for five years and were working on their first album. We had reminisced about old times and, of course, talked about Angie. Being able to voice what I felt to someone who was there from the beginning helped. Though he was her brother, he was surprisingly sympathetic.

I worried my old emotions were working their way between me and Brooke. I loved her deeply, but I felt I hadn't been giving her what she deserved. It might dissipate eventually, but I didn't want to waste time. Angie's happiness was what I told myself I wanted, and she was happy.

Though it was difficult, I needed to truly let go. It was time for my happiness, and it was within my grasp. The only thing that held it back was me.

I took breaks to fuel up and ate meals of deep-fried pizza pockets and chicken tenders in the convenience stores. Sure, it was bad for me, but it tasted fine. I blasted the radio and sang along to keep myself from growing bored. The trip this time felt longer, and I assumed it was because I had a lot more to think about. The main thing was whether the move would come back to bite me in the ass.

It was late evening when I got to Chester. I stopped at Ms. Kenyon's motel and expected the vacancy sign to be on. It was. The sudden quiet surprised me when I turned off the engine. In a way, it felt like I was coming home, but I knew it was only the familiarity.

Though our relationship was business and cultivated over the phone, we developed a kind of friendship. I knew about her daughter, who served in the army, and her son, in college on a football scholarship and majoring in physical education. In turn, she knew about my mother and Scott.

There was no one in the lobby, so I pressed the buzzer and waited. The place was the same, except for a new potted plant near the window. It was still orderly and plain. I could smell a hint of the supplies I had sold her.

I heard the dog bark. Ms. Kenyon snapped at it as a frustrated parent would to an unruly child. The door opened, and Ms. Kenyon turned, her finger pointed toward a spot beyond it.

"Stay back now, you stay back." She shook her head. "That damn dog," she muttered as she moved to the desk.

She beamed when she saw me. "Why, funny seeing you here again."

"Couldn't keep away." I returned her smile.

"What brings you back this way?"

"Business. How are you doing, Ms. Kenyon?"

"Oh, fair to middlin'. Keeping busy. How long are you staying with us? Just the weekend?" she asked as she took out a registration card.

"Afraid it'll be longer this time," I said. "I'm planning on staying here for a week or so until I can find a place."

"Oh? You're moving up here?"

I nodded.

"Now, why on earth would you do something as silly as that?"

"I took a new position managing the office in Des Moines," I said. "Thought the change would be good, so here I am."

"Why, that's wonderful. I had no idea your company had a place around here."

"Don't feel bad. I didn't either, and I've been with them for seven years."

"I just love the things you send me."

"Thanks," I said and signed the card. I looked forward to getting some sleep. "You wouldn't happen to know of any places for rent around here, would you?"

"What did you have in mind?" she asked.

"A decent neighborhood. Other than that, I'm not too picky," I said with a yawn.

"If I think of something, I'll let you know. In the meantime, you get some rest." She handed over a key, and I took it, slipping it into my pocket. "I have you in room 212."

"You plan that?"

"What do you know?" She laughed. "Funny how things work out. You let me know right away if you need anything. Don't be shy."

"I won't, Ms. Kenyon. Thanks, but I think I'll be fine."

"Welcome to Iowa!"

I thanked her again, and she went back to her rooms, the dog barking again. I drove my car around to the back and parked in front of the room. After I let myself in, I tossed my bag onto the table by the window and fell into the bed without bothering to turn on the lights or undress.

I began to doze off before I remembered I had promised to call Brooke.

She answered sleepily, so I kept the call short. We told each other, "I love you," and I said I'd call her the next day when we both weren't so tired. After I hung up, I fell asleep and was with her in my dreams.

For the first week, I acclimated to the job and got to know the employees. Though everyone was focused on their work, they also had camaraderie. It was the same stuff we did in Tulsa, so it didn't take long to get the hang of it. The only difference was that here, it seemed to be more efficient. Still, I thought of ways to improve and watched everyone work their accounts, noting the ones who might need help.

After work, I wandered aimlessly around Chester and got to know the layout of the town. When people learned I had just moved, they were friendly. It was a big change, but I knew I would quickly fall into a routine.

Finding a place to live was a different matter. Angie and Bill found a few, but they all had something I didn't like. I scanned the classifieds in the mornings, but didn't have luck there either. I wanted a house rather than an apartment. Something to grow into and be happy without being overwhelmed. I still hoped Brooke would move here and searched with that in mind. I needed to find something quick, because before long, my motel bill would come out of my pocket. As much as I enjoyed Ms. Kenyon, I didn't want to live in a motel. I had everything I needed, but in the long term, it was too small. I longed for rooms, and space for a home office.

Saturday morning I awoke at dawn and made a pot of coffee. I turned on the TV for background noise and settled by the window to drink my coffee and watch cars pass by. It had been a hectic week. I needed to pay my motel bill and thought, since I'm going to be out, I might as well have breakfast at the diner and check the listings in the paper.

I stepped out into the brisk morning and walked to the front office. Several cars were parked in front of the rooms, and I was glad to see the motel was busy. I said hello to Maria, the head housekeeper. She liked to practice her English with me, and I had noticed an improvement. I enjoyed talking to her and always left a tip in the room whenever she cleaned.

I rang the bell in the lobby and listened for the dog as I waited for Ms. Kenyon. She came through the door and commanded the dog to stay inside. She looked up at me and smiled.

"How are you, Ms. Kenyon?" I asked.

"Just fine." She shuffled to the counter. "What can I do for you?"

"Thought I'd settle up for the week," I said.

"Have you found a place yet?"

I shook my head and handed her my credit card. "Not yet. I bet you're tired of seeing me around, huh?"

"No, I enjoy having you here, but know you'd like to settle." She frowned thoughtfully. "I have a little place outside town, just sitting empty. If you'd like, you can take a look and if you like it, we might be able to work something out."

"Wow, that'd be great." I imagined it would be a ramshackle place that needed work, since she'd only now brought it up. "It won't hurt to look. When would be a good time?".

"Now, if you have the time," she said.

"I planned on checking out some places after breakfast," I said. "So whenever you're ready, we can go."

"Oh, I can't leave here today," she said. "Hold on, I'll get you a key." She opened her door and pushed the dog back with her foot. She came back and handed me the keys. "Here you go. Take your time, and if you're interested, we'll talk. If not, you won't hurt my feelings none."

"Thanks." I pocketed the keys while she jotted in a notepad and ripped the page off.

"That's the address. You can't miss it."

"Okay," I said. "I'll bring the keys back and let you know. I appreciate this."

"It's no problem," she said. "I'm glad to help."

After I had breakfast, I drove out to a ranch-style house, painted a light beige with russet-colored trim. It stood on a large lot off the highway, with another house on one side fifty yards away, and an empty field on the other. Across from it was a gated subdivision. It looked like a decent neighborhood, with well-maintained homes and yards.

I parked in front of an attached two-car garage and got out. I walked around and checked out the exterior. The wide porch with a wooden swing painted to match the trim was a nice touch. The house looked solid, and though I thought it might be more house than I needed, I reserved judgment until I looked inside.

I unlocked the door and entered a large living room that opened into a dining area with a set of French doors leading onto the back deck. Between the living room and the kitchen, which was big enough to cook anything I could dream up, was a stairway that led down to a basement.

Two bedrooms and a bathroom were off a hallway, and a master bedroom and bath were at the end. I liked the layout, saw potential, and being move-in ready didn't hurt.

I checked out the large finished basement and saw where I could set up a home office, and a place to relax and watch TV. The idea to buy another drum kit and set it up here crossed my mind. I had sold my set a while back, but missed it. Playing again would be fun, even if it just served as a stress reliever.

Overall, I liked the house and the location was perfect. But I worried it might be out of my range. Out of all the places I'd seen, I liked this one the best. I could see myself on the back deck with a drink and a cigar as the sun set behind the trees. I left and locked the door behind me before I got too excited and hoped Ms. Kenyon might offer rent I could manage.

↩ↄ

"Would you like some coffee?" Ms. Kenyon asked while she poured herself a cup.

I shook my head. "No, thanks."

She sat down carefully in her chair and let out a sigh. "Did you go by the house?"

"I did." I wished I had taken some coffee so I could have something to hold. "It's a good-looking house, and the property's nice."

"We enjoyed it for many years," she said with a wistful smile. "After my husband died, I thought I'd move here and let it out, but haven't had a lot of takers. I guess people don't like the idea of living next to the highway."

"I don't think it'd be too bad," I said.

"No, but it's too much house for me, being alone and all. My kids are both gone, and I didn't want to have to keep up with it." She looked at me over the rim of her cup. "Do you think you'd be interested?"

I leaned back in my chair and pretended to think, but already knew the answer. I nodded. "What would you ask for it?"

"I think five hundred a month sounds fair," she said after a moment.

Five hundred sounded cheap. I had expected more. "Isn't that a little low?"

She shrugged. "It's just sitting there, and you seem like you'd take care of it."

"I would," I said.

"What would I do with it, anyway?" She took a sip of her coffee. "I thought of selling and being done with it."

She was fishing, but I was willing to bite. "What would you sell it for?"

"Oh, I don't know." She smiled. "If the right person came along, maybe one-fifty."

"Thousand?" I asked. Though I knew little about real estate, it seemed low. I had seen the number often for comparable places, so it was probably right.

She got up and took her cup to the sink. "You wouldn't be interested in buying that old place."

"I might be," I said. "But I would like to at least rent it, if that would suit you."

"Well, a young man needs a real home, not some little motel room." She leaned against the back of her chair. "You could move in now, and pay me rent on the first of the month." She paused for a moment. "You'll have to put the utilities in your name, but you can do that from here."

"Sure," I said while a hundred things ran through my head. "Where do I sign?"

"There's no rush." She waved it off. "You go on and get your things moved in. I think I can trust you. Anyway, I know where you live."

"Okay," I laughed. "I appreciate this so much. My things will have to be sent up. I'll stay here for a couple more days, so I at least have a bed."

"That'll be fine," she said.

"Thanks, Ms. Kenyon. If there's anything I can do to make up for it, just ask."

"How about a discount on my supplies?" she asked without hesitation.

"You're a shrewd businesswoman, Ms. Kenyon," I said with a chuckle. "I think we can arrange it."

She gave me a satisfied grin as we sealed the deal with a handshake.

CHAPTER FIFTEEN

A few days later, the movers arrived and got everything into my new home. After they left, I unpacked and soon realized my stuff wouldn't even fill up half the house. It was more house than I was used to.

I cleaned and put everything away for a few hours, then fell exhausted into my bed. I called Brooke as I rested my head on the pillow and listened to the phone ring.

"What are you doing?" I said after she picked up. "I'm in my bed all by my lonesome."

"We're not having phone sex," she said with a stifled yawn.

"Too bad," I said. "Maybe you can come up and we could have the real thing."

She laughed. "Is that all you think about?"

"No, I think about other things. Food. Beer," I answered. "But mostly about you. I miss you."

"I miss you too."

"So, how about it? I can fly you up for the weekend."

"We'll see," she said. "How are you liking it there?"

"It's not bad," I said. "It still feels weird, but I'll get used to it."

We talked for a few more minutes about irrelevant things, but hearing her voice made me miss her even more. I wanted her here with me, and thought if I could get her to come up for a weekend, I might convince her to move in with me. I would probably need to do a little more to get the place ready, but it wasn't anything I couldn't handle.

I tuned the radio to a jazz station, turned the volume low and let the music lull me to sleep.

☺

I went into town to pick up some things for a barbecue I planned for the afternoon; Angie, Bill, and their kids were coming. I had invited Ms. Kenyon, but she said she couldn't leave the motel. After I finished setting up the house and put a home office in the basement, I decided there was plenty of room for a drum kit, so I put shopping for one on my agenda.

At about four o'clock, they showed up. Bill helped grill the steaks, and we put on some burgers and hot dogs for the kids. I was happy to have friends already with whom to celebrate. After we ate, we sat on the deck with glasses of iced tea and let the food settle while we watched Eva and Lily play and chase each other around the yard.

"Got to hand it to you, Ryan. It's quite a place you found here," Bill said. "Plenty of room, good view. A decent place to raise a family."

"Don't have any plans for that yet," I said, though it was something I had thought about.

"You gonna buy it?"

"Oh, Bill, stop asking personal questions," Angie interjected. "Let him get settled first."

"He's settled just fine from the looks of it," Bill said.

"No, it's okay," I said. "It's a legitimate question."

173

"It's not very polite." Angie shot Bill a disapproving look.

"We're friends," I said with a shrug. "I'm thinking about it. I want to see how it goes first."

"Yeah, good idea to think on it," Bill said.

"But it would be a good investment," I said.

"True." Bill took a sip of his tea.

"I'll probably buy it if I'm going to stick around. I like the layout."

"It's a solid place," Bill said.

I nodded and watched a hawk circle the sky. "I've always wanted a place out in the open. When I was a kid, my friend Scott and I would wander the fields by his house. It's not the same, but I think it's the best of both worlds."

"So, Ryan," Angie said. "What's going on with the girl you're seeing? Is she moving up here?"

"Leave it to a woman to talk relationships." Bill laughed. "And she said real estate was too personal."

Angie ignored Bill and looked at me expectantly.

"I don't know, but she might come up for a weekend," I said. "We talk on the phone all the time, but it's not the same."

"A long-distance relationship can't be easy," Angie said.

"It's been tough," I said with a sigh. It felt strange talking to her about Brooke.

"If it's meant to be," Angie said softly, "it'll work out."

Bill didn't stifle his yawn.

Angie ignored her husband. "I can't wait to meet her. She sounds nice."

"She is," I said.

"I don't know if I could do it. Having my girl so far away?" Bill said. "But then, it might be a blessing."

Angie narrowed her eyes. "What's that supposed to mean?"

Bill held up his hands. "Nothing, dear. I couldn't stand it if you were even an hour away."

"You watch it." Angie shook her fist playfully, and we all laughed.

"You know what they say, Bill," I said. "A woman scorned."

"I do, but Angela's a good woman."

"Don't butter me up now," Angie said.

"Oh well, I tried." Bill stood with a grunt. "Ryan, thanks for having us, but we should get going. The kids are worn out, and we still got to clean them up and all."

"Sure," I said. "Thanks for coming and helping with the food."

"No problem. You come out and see us anytime you get bored in this big house," Bill said, then yelled to the kids, "Come on girls, let's go."

Eva and Lily ran to the deck, their faces streaked with dirt.

"We saw a frog!" Lily squealed.

"You did?" Angie said, matching their excitement. "Did you catch it?"

Lily shook her head. "No, Eva was too scared."

"Was not!" Eva cried.

Lily giggled. "Uh-huh."

"That's enough now," Bill said. "You girls are going to get in the bathtub as soon as we get home. Say thank you, and goodbye to Ryan."

"Bye, Ryan! Thank you!" the girls sang in unison.

"You're welcome. I'm glad you came over," I said. "I hope you had fun."

They plodded along while Bill herded them to their car. Angie and I were alone for a moment.

"Your kids are great," I said, and felt a little envious.

"They can be." She smiled tiredly. "You'll have your turn. There's no hurry."

"I hope so."

As we went inside and walked to the front door, I said, "I just thought, what if—"

Angie stopped and turned to me. "No, Ryan, keep the past there and look forward."

"You know, I've always had feelings for you, Angie," I admitted. "They've never really gone away."

"Ryan," she whispered sadly.

"No, don't get me wrong." I took a breath. "I'm not saying...I'm not trying to come between you and your family."

"I know."

"I could never do that to you."

She looked at me with an understanding smile.

"Bill's great. He loves you and the girls with all his heart," I said. "I like him, and I'm happy you found him. I want us all to be friends, so..."

"He likes you," Angie said. "The girls, too."

"I don't think I'll find another one like you." I turned with my hands shoved in my pockets and found something to look at in the corner.

"You have someone now, Ryan." She rested a hand on my shoulder. "Better, I think."

I just nodded.

"You probably don't realize it, but you get goofy when you talk about her."

I snorted. "I don't get goofy."

"You do."

"Okay, maybe I do," I conceded. "I do like her a lot."

"I have a good feeling about it," she said. "I'll always be your friend,

Ryan. You're a good guy. What we had, that was another time. We've grown up."

"I'm just being stupid."

"No." She glanced out the window by the door. Bill shut the back door and got into the driver's seat. "I gotta go."

"Yeah," I said. "Hey, thanks for coming, and tell Bill I said so. Maybe we can all do it again soon."

"Of course." She smiled and went to their car.

I stood alone and waved to the kids as she got in. I watched them long after they disappeared.

What am I doing here? I thought as I walked back to the kitchen and made myself a drink. I wasn't sure what I expected, but I wasn't unhappy. Angie was right, along with everyone else. I didn't know why I had to keep being told to move on, and I don't know why I seemed to always do the opposite.

I felt lonely for home, for my friends and family. I thought of Brooke. Though we spoke almost every day, I missed her physical presence, and wanted her to come up for at least a weekend. Though I made my admission to Angie, the truth was, I had the same feelings, though more immediate, for Brooke. Being away from her only made me realize it more. Could I truly have a committed relationship when I still had these old feelings, which had lingered for twenty years? I couldn't get rid of them easily, not after having them for so long. It was a risk, but a worthwhile one. I could only hope it wouldn't become a wedge, like it had several times before.

☙

I called Scott out of boredom after a grueling day at work. I thought about not calling, but I needed the respite he could give me. It wasn't the same as hanging out with him, but the phone was better than nothing.

"Hey man, how's life in Iowa?" Scott asked as soon as he picked up. "You eating enough corn?"

"Oh Hell," I said, and rolled my eyes. "Oklahoma's got its cowboys and Indians; Iowa's got corn. That's all people seem to ask."

"What can I say? It's what we know," Scott said with a grin.

"Things aren't so bad," I said. "Believe it or not, I like it. It's not really much different from my life in Tulsa."

"Yeah? Well, everyone misses you here, man. They're always asking me, 'How's Ryan?'"

"Right. My mom and who else? If they gave a shit, they'd call." I heard the bitterness in my tone and immediately regretted it. "Sorry. I guess I could call them just the same."

"Yeah, buddy. You became a big shot and forgot about us little guys. Up there in your castle," Scott said. His easy dismissal made me feel a little better.

"Nothing near a castle, but it is comfortable," I said. "Come up sometime, check the place out. I think you'll like it. They've got minor league hockey, and the Cubs have their farm team in Des Moines."

"I might, but I'd have to find the time," he said. "But it sounds like fun. When I do, I'll bring beer."

"Dude, there's breweries and all kinds of places here," I said. "You don't have to."

"I'll buy some when I get there then."

"I'm gonna hold you to that," I said. "Hey, guess what? Brooke's coming up this weekend."

"Yeah? Don't I know how to pick them or what?" he said. "Tell me I don't."

"It's not like you don't know," I said. "She's probably told you."

"She did," he affirmed. "She's excited, but probably trying to hide it from you."

"I am too," I said. "It's hard being apart, but we're still together."

"So she's flying up?"

"Yeah, I'll pick her up Friday afternoon, and she'll be flying back Sunday."

"Crazy to fly up just to spend a weekend."

"Maybe, but it's worth it. It'll give us more time together."

"True."

"Don't want her to get here tired and lose time with her."

"No, I get it, man."

"I think I'm going to ask her to move up here."

"Does this mean that you're finally over Angie and ready to get on with life?"

I didn't say anything, but it was a question I had asked myself.

"Oh, bloody Hell, Ryan," Scott said. "When are you going to give it up?"

"I've given it up," I answered.

"Brooke's a great girl. Are you really going to risk losing her over this bullshit? Again?"

I sighed. "No, you're right. She's what I want. I love Brooke."

"For real?"

"Yeah, don't worry about me."

"If I don't worry about you, bro, who will?" Scott said with a laugh.

"Whatever, man. Listen, whenever you want to come up, let me know and I'll get you a ticket."

"Maybe I want to drive," Scott said. "Take in the scenery."

"Not much to see, but you do you. Think about it, okay?"

"Sure, I will," Scott assured me. "We'll do it soon."

I hung up the phone and felt homesick. While I had made some friends, it just wasn't the same. I wanted familiarity. I was excited about Brooke coming for the weekend and looked forward to being able to hold her after what seemed an eternity of separation. Seeing her would ease the homesickness, at least for the weekend.

I grabbed a beer out of the fridge and went to sit on the back deck. The air had grown cooler, and the dark clouds across the horizon promised rain. I thought about my life now, and how it seemed to fall into place by a series of coincidences. I had never been a big believer in coincidence, so I wondered what it meant, and what it might lead to.

The first drops of the rain began to fall, so I went back inside and turned on the TV. I contemplated calling Brooke, but couldn't think of what to talk about. Calling just to say "I love you" was great for Stevie Wonder, but for me, it seemed silly. She'd be here in a couple of days, so I figured it could wait. I flipped through the channels, but there wasn't anything I wanted to see. I turned it off and picked up the phone. Silly or not, Stevie had the right idea.

CHAPTER SIXTEEN

At the airport terminal, I stood near the gate and waited for Brooke. Nervousness clenched my stomach, and I tried to ignore it by watching people come out of the gate and meet their friends and loved ones with hugs and kisses. They acted as if it had been ages. I understood how they felt and couldn't help but think of how long it had been since I'd felt her touch, and how in a short time, she'd be gone. A weekend just wasn't long enough.

The crowds dwindled. I glanced at my watch, and it occurred to me I might not even be at the right gate. Then I worried Brooke had decided not to come and hadn't told me. Before I could get myself into a panic, I saw her walking toward me. She had her red hair pulled back in a loose ponytail and was dressed in worn jeans and an oversized sweatshirt that made her look ten years younger. She spotted me and beamed as she waved enthusiastically, like an excited schoolgirl. I felt my grin helplessly stretch across my face.

"Hey you!" she shouted without embarrassment and walked quickly toward me, her large bag bouncing on her hip.

She jumped into my arms with such force, I stumbled backward. I caught myself and held her tight.

"I missed you," she said, her voice muffled through my shirt.

"I missed you too," I said. "I almost forgot how beautiful you are."

"You're crazy." She laughed. "I look a mess."

"You look great," I said. "How was the flight?"

"Scary, but I handled it." She pulled away and looked me over. "You've lost some weight."

"Have I?"

"Yeah, I can tell."

"I've been busy, but I eat okay."

"It looks good on you."

"You hungry? Want to grab something?"

"No, I couldn't eat now. I need to let my stomach settle."

"You look pretty good too."

"You think so?"

I nodded. "Hey, we should get moving before the traffic picks up. Did you bring any luggage?"

"Nope, this is it." She patted the shoulder bag.

"A woman who packs light. I like it," I said. "Knew there was a reason I picked you."

"I thought you picked me because of my good looks."

"There are many reasons," I said, and I kissed her.

She moaned and reluctantly pushed me away. "I thought we had to go?"

"You're right," I said. "We can continue later." I took her hand and led her through the terminal to the parking lot.

Brooke was quiet during the drive to my place. She looked out the window at the passing landscape under an azure sky with billowy clouds that promised a mild weekend. I had driven this highway often enough that it had become routine. The novelty of an unfamiliar landscape had worn off, though it was still pleasant.

"It's pretty here," Brooke said as she stretched in her seat and stifled a yawn. "I thought it wouldn't be any different, but it is."

"It is," I said. Her yawn was contagious.

"How much longer will it be?"

"Maybe another ten minutes."

"I'm so tired. I could hardly sleep last night." She reached for my hand. "All I could think about was seeing you again."

I intertwined my fingers in hers and smiled. "I'm glad you're finally here."

"Me too."

"Sorry you're tired," I said. "Maybe when we get there, we can take a little nap."

"That sounds good," she said with a happy moan. "Unless you had plans."

"No plans except to be with you."

"So I get you to myself all weekend?"

"Most of it," I said. "I sort of planned a get-together tomorrow. I wanted to show you off to my friends."

"I'm not impressive enough to show off," she said with a snort.

"I think you are," I said. "They'll adore you, especially Ms. Kenyon."

"Isn't she your landlady?"

"Yeah, so what?"

"Don't you think it's a little weird hanging out with your landlady?"

"No, Ms. Kenyon's good people." I dismissed her comment. "If it weren't for her, I'd have had a harder time starting out here."

"You befriend the strangest people."

"Anyway, she won't be my landlady for long."

She sat up and looked at me. "Oh?"

"I'm buying her house."

"You've said nothing about buying a house."

"I wanted to be sure first," I said. "Before too long, you'll be looking at a full-fledged homeowner."

"Wow, that's great," she said, but she didn't sound enthusiastic.

"Hopefully not alone," I said as I pulled into my driveway. "We're here."

She got out of the car and stretched. "It's not as big as I thought, but it's nice."

"It's roomier than it looks." We held hands as we walked to the front door. "It's got a finished basement."

I was happy Brooke was here and hoped I could plant the seed for her to move up here so we could be together. For now, I was content to have her for the weekend. I made us a light dinner, and then we cuddled in bed and watched an old movie on TV. I wanted it to last forever.

"This is nice," Brooke murmured as I ran my fingers through her hair and let the strands fall against her pale shoulder.

"I think so," I said. "About tomorrow, I hope you don't mind. I've talked about you so much, everyone's curious to meet you."

"It's okay," she said. "I want to meet them, but they'll be disappointed."

"Stop." I kissed her forehead. "They're going to love you. Anyway, I'm not, and that's what matters."

"Flatterer," she giggled and lightly pushed me away. "So who do you have coming to gawk at me besides your landlady? Your boss?"

"I am the boss."

"Oh, Mr. Big Shot." She tapped her chin thoughtfully. "An old girl-friend?"

I hesitated. Though I knew she was joking, I didn't want her to find out later and think there was anything untoward. I was honest. "Actually, yeah."

"Really, Ryan?" She pushed herself upright and glared at me.

"It was a long time ago. When we were in school."

She crossed her arms and looked away. "That's just great."

"Come on, Brooke." I put my hand on her shoulder. She shrugged it off. "She's married with kids. Her husband's been a big help to me."

She got out of bed and stood at the window. "Do you still love her?"

"I love you." I got up, went to her and wrapped my arms around her waist. She tensed, but didn't stop me. "They're friends. I think you'll like them."

She sniffed. "Do you love me?"

"I just said I did."

She let out a long sigh. "Any more surprises?"

"Nope," I said. "Everyone coming is happily married."

"Not everyone." She relaxed and turned around.

"Yeah, there's Ms. Kenyon. You might have to worry about her. She's widowed and smokin' hot."

She narrowed her eyes. "Oh, yeah?"

"Yeah," I said with a lascivious grin. "How do you think I got this house?"

"You're crazy," Brooke said with a laugh.

"Crazy for you." I growled, nipped her neck, and we fumbled our way back to bed and showed just how much we missed each other.

Brooke had fallen asleep two hours ago after we had made love, but sleep eluded me. I sat up in bed and watched her sleep. She looked beautiful, pure, and innocent. Her hair fanned across the pillow like a halo. The pale light of the full moon sifted through the window and gave her skin an iridescent glow. Her lips were parted slightly, and her chest rose gently in rhythm as she breathed. She looked as if we were living in a perfect world where nothing bad could ever happen.

While it probably wasn't a good idea to have mentioned my past with Angie, I knew she would have found out eventually. I loved her, but hadn't been completely honest about my feelings, and understood her sting of jealousy. At least she seemed placated when I mentioned Bill and the kids, and how happy they were. I also needed to be honest with myself and admit I was jealous of Angie's relationship with Bill. For so long, it was what I wanted, but it was never really within my reach.

I had talked to Brooke about her moving up here already, but didn't push it. Though I wanted to be with her, I also realized I wasn't completely sure I wanted her to move. I felt conflicted. True, I loved Brooke, but would it be the best thing for us? Would we really be happy? I thought we could be, but only if I allowed it. When we finally saw each other again, I was disappointed because there were no fireworks and no immediate feelings of unbridled passion. Maybe there was a problem.

The thought was stupid. There were no problems.

I needed to stop having unrealistic expectations of our relationship. Fireworks and passion are fantasies, much like happiness. They exist, but only in short bursts. It's like the first taste of ice cream on a summer day, or an orgasm.

I kissed Brooke gently on the forehead and rested my head on my pillow. I felt her warmth next to me, and as I closed my eyes, my thoughts turned into dreams. My dreams weren't of the possible, of things within reach and could give me the happiness I was seeking.

They were of Angie.

☺

"When is everyone supposed to get here?" Brooke said as she put all the ingredients into the bowl for potato salad. She was thoroughly enjoying making a mess.

"I said we'd eat around five or six." I glanced at the clock while I put the marinated steaks in the fridge. "It's three now, so we have a couple of hours."

"I'm nervous," she admitted.

"Why? They're all normal folks. Well, maybe except for Chuck. He's a little weird, but harmless," I said. "You'll like them. They'll like you. Don't worry about it."

"Do you think so?"

I took her in my arms and kissed the cute furrow that appeared on her forehead whenever she was nervous. "Why do I have to tell you this? You're going to make all the guys jealous."

"Am not." She pushed me away. "No one is going to be jealous."

"Yeah, they will. You're sexy, smart, funny, sexy—"

"You already said sexy."

"It bears repeating. You wanna go dancing?" I asked as I nipped at her earlobe.

"Mmm, no, no, they might show up any minute."

"Only takes a minute," I suggested.

She rolled her eyes. "That's it? It wouldn't even be worth the effort."

"Make it worth the effort later," I said.

"Then we'll wait for later," she replied and went back to her work.

"Waiting's not easy."

"Maybe you should take matters into your own hand," she suggested.

"See? Funny." I left it at that and went to the back deck.

Ms. Kenyon arrived first and brought a big bowl of coleslaw. I introduced Brooke, and she immediately peppered her with questions. They found they had people in common and left me out of the conversation. I put the coleslaw in the fridge and got the grill ready for the meat.

Then, Chuck and his family showed shortly after. Chuck was a serious man and wore thick, horn-rimmed glasses. He looked like an accountant right out of the 1950s, but we had things in common and had become friends. Normally, I didn't fraternize with employees, but Chuck was an exception. He was intelligent and had a dry sense of humor most people didn't get. He was my top seller, and his dependable work ethic made him kind of my right-hand man around the office.

Chuck introduced his wife, Kay, a bubbly woman who was the opposite side of the clock from Chuck in every way. She was not unattractive, despite being on the plump side. Her blueberry pie looked like perfection, and I directed her to put it on the counter in the kitchen.

Chuck's twin girls, Amber and Abbie, favored their mother, but his son, C.J., was his clone, only shorter. Even their dispositions matched their parents. The kids appeared well-adjusted and respectful. Chuck's family was exactly the kind I expected him to have.

The kids stood shyly behind their mother. I promised them there would be other kids coming along to play with. They thought about it for a while and then went to play in the yard.

Bill, Angie, and the girls came half an hour later. Eva and Lily ran up to me. Eva held a yellow-colored puppy in front of her.

"We got a puppy!" she yelled happily.

The puppy squirmed, his tail wagging frantically as he tried to escape Eva's grasp. Lily stood to the side quietly and chewed her fingers.

"I see," I said. "What did you name it?"

"Puppy," Lily said and giggled. "Because he's a puppy."

"He is, and cute too," I said and pointed toward Chuck's kids, involved in some game. "I bet those kids'll love to meet him."

The girls brightened. Eva put Puppy down, and they ran toward the others. Puppy yipped and chased them. Not yet sure-footed, he stumbled every few steps.

The play stopped when Eva and Lily got there, and they eyed each other a moment before silently deciding it was okay to play together. I thought of how easy it was for kids to fall into friendship and wondered at what point in our lives we get away from the simple camaraderie and become suspicious of each other. Society would profit if our attitudes reverted to childhood.

"Hey, Ryan," Bill called.

I looked up from the grill and waved at him and Angie.

"Hope you don't mind us bringing the dog." He clapped me on the shoulder. "The girls insisted, and I couldn't say no."

"It's fine, I like dogs," I said. "He's got a lot of energy."

Bill blew out a gust of air. "You said it, but the kids'll wear him out. Poor thing can't keep up yet."

"Give him some time," I said.

Brooke came out carrying a tray stacked with meat. "Ready to put the food on?"

"Yep," I said as I took the tray and set it next to the grill. I nodded toward Bill and Angie. "Brooke, this is Bill, and his wife, Angie."

"Hi," Brooke said.

I put my arm around her waist. "This is my girlfriend, Brooke."

"A pleasure," Bill said and shook her hand. "Boy, Ryan wasn't kidding when he said you were a looker."

"Stop that, Bill. You're embarrassing her," Angie chided, then said to Brooke, "Never mind my husband. Ryan's said only good things."

"I'm sure he has. It's one of his bad habits." Brooke smiled and looked at me. "I think I'll finish up, so we can eat."

"Okay, thanks," I said and pecked her on the cheek. I could tell she was nervous, but she handled it well. It felt weird introducing them, but I was the only one who seemed to think so.

"Would you like some help?" Angie offered.

"Sure," Brooke answered. "That'd be nice."

We watched them go inside. Bill smiled and nodded. "She seems like a nice girl."

"I like her okay." I said casually.

"Hey guys." Chuck approached the grill.

"What's happening, Chuck?" I asked.

"Estrogen fest over there," Chuck said. "I needed to get away for a bit."

"Join our club," I said with a laugh and introduced him to Bill.

We chatted about barbecue techniques as I worked the meat. We segued into sports and things that made us feel distinctly male while the girls got the table ready. Occasionally I'd look over to see how Brooke was getting along. She was doing fine and having a good time. I loved to see her smile and laugh; it made her more beautiful.

After we prepared everything, we assembled plates for the kids.

Puppy looked up at me and whimpered, so I tossed him a few pieces of hamburger. He wolfed it down as fast as I could give it to him.

The kids sat on a blanket spread on the deck and chattered away as if they'd known each other their whole lives. Around the picnic table, the adults did the same, and the afternoon passed quickly. The sun set on the party and gave us a brilliant, beautiful display of colors. I thought I'd see nothing like it again. I looked at my small group of friends, the women I loved, then and now, and thought again of where life would lead me.

We wrapped up as the kids lost their energy. Puppy had plopped down on the deck long before. His head rested on his paws, but his eyes were still alert and watching everything around him.

"Ryan, thanks for having us tonight," Angie said after she had gathered the kids. "I think they've had it."

"Thanks for coming," I said. "It's been fun."

Angie gave Brooke a hug. "It was great to finally meet you. I'm glad Ryan found you."

Brooke returned the hug, but she seemed uncomfortable. I wondered if it was because I had told her about our past relationship. I couldn't imagine why Brooke would let it get to her, especially after meeting them, and seeing how much they loved each other.

When the last guest left, Brooke and I did a quick cleanup and sat on the back deck. We sat quietly as we looked at the moon and listened to the sounds of the cool Iowa night.

"Did you have a good time?" I asked. She didn't answer right away, so I looked over at her.

She shrugged. "It was okay. I liked Mrs. Kenyon. She was sweet."

"Yeah," I agreed. "She's the first person I met. Funny, she's from Tulsa. Small world, I guess."

I could tell she had something on her mind, but she wasn't saying anything. I resisted the urge to ask what was the matter. "Everyone liked you. I told you there was nothing to worry about."

"I know." She took a deep breath. "Ryan, what's going on here?"

"What do you mean?"

"You know. With us."

"I'm not sure what you're asking."

"Why did you move?"

"It was for my job," I said.

"Did you think of what would happen?"

I nodded. "Yeah, but I thought we could work around it."

She didn't answer, and I could tell I had said the wrong thing.

"Do you love me?"

"That's a silly question." I tried to hold her hand, but she pulled away.

"No, it's not."

"I never expected to find someone like you, Brooke. Someone I would fall in love with and want to be with," I said. "I thought maybe you might move up here so we could be together, not so far apart."

I understood. I tried not to be bothered by it, but it was hard. "You know I love you. I keep telling you I do. I wouldn't have brought you here, just for a weekend, if I didn't."

I tried to hold her hand again. She let me, but I could feel her reluctance.

"I just need to know where we're going. I don't want to move here and find out we won't work."

"What makes you think we won't?"

"I don't want to be stuck," she whispered.

"You won't be," I said. "I know it hasn't been easy, but we're working out, right?"

"I guess."

"What's really going on, Brooke?"

She looked at me, and I could see the sadness and fear in her eyes. "You're in love with her, aren't you?"

"What are you talking about?"

"Angie," she said. "I can see it."

I wanted to laugh, but held back. "She's a married woman, Brooke. Happily. With kids. And a dog."

"You do." She was on the verge of tears. "She said you used to be together."

"I told you the same thing," I said. "We were kids. The fact we had a past is irrelevant. We're just friends."

"But you had one."

"Let me tell you about it sometime," I said with a laugh.

"It's not funny."

"No, but if you only knew," I said, and felt her relax slightly. "I understand how you feel, but I love you and want us to be together. I want to have a life with you. It drives me crazy, you being so far away."

She sighed. "Me too."

"You make me happy now," I said. "I wouldn't do anything to hurt you, or make you doubt me."

"I know. I'm just not used to it." She snuggled against my shoulder. "They're nice people. I do like her."

"I knew you would."

"It's just the way she talked about you. I thought that...but it's stupid. I'm being stupid."

"No, you're not." I took her head in my hands and brushed away a stray tear. "I am lucky to have you. The best decision I ever made was to be with you."

We kissed under the night sky, then went inside. We made love as if it were the first time. It was bittersweet, knowing she would be gone the next afternoon. We had only spent one full day together, which was but a blink considering how long we had spent apart. I held her close as she slept, but felt like we were already miles away. I knew the statistics said we wouldn't make it, but I would do my damndest to make us an exception.

I stroked her hair and memorized the texture and smell. I loved her, but she was right; I still loved Angie. A part of me always would. If things were different, if she weren't married, I might try to pursue her, but she was.

I had to admit, Bill was a perfect match for her.

With Brooke, I had someone I could be with. Someone to love, without constantly comparing her to an ideal. I felt Brooke wanted us to work too and believed that with me, we could change the odds.

At the airport, we waited for her flight to be called and held hands. We had stayed in bed most of the morning and made plans to see each other again. Her insecurities of the night before had seemed forgotten. I broached the subject of her moving to Iowa again. She said she would need a more serious commitment before she considered moving.

To me, "serious commitment" meant marriage. I didn't think I was ready for such a big step, but I loved her. Though the idea made me nervous, I knew it would be the next logical thing to do.

"I don't want you to go," I said.

"I know, but I have to."

"You'll call me as soon as you get home?"

She nodded. "Yes, I'll call."

A minute later, her flight was called. I pulled her into an embrace and whispered, "I love you," in her ear, and kissed her gently.

She reluctantly broke the kiss. "I don't want to miss my flight."

"Would it be so bad?" I asked.

"Ryan, I need to go." She smiled. "I'll call you."

"Okay," I said. I let her go and watched her until she disappeared through the gate.

I left the airport with a heavy heart. Though we were secure in our relationship, I wasn't sure what was going to happen. Do I ask her to marry me? Do I let it keep going on like this, a long-distance relationship where we only see each other occasionally? The drive home felt as if it took days. When I walked through my front door, I could still smell her presence, and my heart filled with longing. I locked the door behind me and went down to the basement to do some work and try to take my mind off of it. I settled into my chair and checked my email before I began with work.

I glanced at my watch after a while and was surprised that several hours had passed. I went to the kitchen to make a cup of herbal tea and checked my phone to make sure it was on. It was. I thought about watching some TV, but decided to just drink my tea in my breakfast nook and try to enjoy the view outside my window. I had grown fond of the house, and knew if Brooke shared it with me, it would feel more like a home.

The phone rang, and I nearly knocked over my tea to answer it. I expected it to be Brooke, but it was only a wrong number. Disappointed, I hung up and considered calling myself, but I didn't want to seem needy. I had worried myself silly when it rang again.

I jerked the phone up. "Hello?"

"Hey you." Brooke's voice sounded breathless. "Sorry it took so long. I got stuck in traffic, and then my mother called. She talks forever. How are you?"

"I'm fine," I said. "What about you? I wondered if your plane crashed."

"Too bad for you it didn't," she said.

"Don't say that; I'd hate it if anything happened to you." I knew she was just joking, but it wasn't funny. "I'm glad you called."

"I told you I would, but I didn't expect the delay."

I knew she was tired, so I cut our conversation short. After we said "I love you" a few times, we finally hung up. I realized how tired I was, so instead of doing anything else, I went to bed. When I lay down, the emptiness was profound. I held her pillow close to me and considered my future. In my life, I had often sabotaged myself, and it was always my unrequited feelings for Angie that did it. I knew it was time to stop the pattern and begin anew with Brooke.

CHAPTER SEVENTEEN

Business was going well, with our sales increasing over the past quarter. The home office called to say we were the highest-grossing office for the period, with two top-producing account managers. With bonuses coming our way, I felt my work was paying off and planned for a catered lunch on Friday to celebrate. I thought I'd use the news as an excuse to call Brooke, though none was needed.

"Good job today, Chuck," I said as he closed his third sale in an hour. "Don't start slacking off now."

Chuck laughed. "I'll try not to. What's up?"

"Thought we'd grab some lunch, if you don't have plans."

"None," he said. "Kay packed me an apple and granola. Anything else would be better."

"She on another diet?"

"Indeed," Chuck lamented. "I tell you, if you ever get married, you do whatever your wife does."

"Yeah?"

"Yeah. Before, they let you think you can do your own thing. When that ring goes on, the rules change." He clicked his tongue. "Does it look like I need to diet?"

"Honestly?"

"No, lie to me." He patted his paunch.

"You're a regular stud, Chuck."

Chuck laughed loudly. "Sure. Where do you wanna go?"

"Was in the mood for a sub. Sound okay?"

"Sounds great. Kay'll probably have rabbit food for dinner," he said. "I could use some meaty, cheesy goodness."

"I can meet you there."

"No problem. You buying?"

"Sure, I got a two for one coupon," I said, and thought of Joe.

"I'll just be a few minutes."

"Okay," I said. I took a quick walk around and checked on everyone before grabbing the keys off my desk and headed out.

Chuck found me in the crowded sandwich shop and sat down across from me. "Pretty busy today, huh?"

I nodded. "Seems it's everyone's favorite place."

"So, what's going on?"

"Didn't feel like having lunch alone," I said with a shrug. "How's the family?

I saw that Chuck's sandwich was loaded with meat and cheese, completely ignoring any dietary restrictions Kay might have set for him.

"They're good," Chuck said. "Kay's mom's hinting at a visit. She and the kids are excited."

"You're not?" I asked.

"Not so much," he admitted, and bit into his overloaded sandwich, which was already falling apart.

"Ah, stereotypical mother-in-law."

He grunted. "You said it. If the threat's real, I might crash at your place for the duration."

"Sure, Chuck," I said. "We'll grill up steaks, pig out on chips and greasy crap while watching football and action flicks on the big screen. Explosions and big titties never looked better."

Chuck laughed. "I hope she visits."

"You don't need an excuse," I said.

"Yeah, I do. I'm married."

"Well, that sucks."

"It's not all bad," he said. "Hey, you let your buddy Bill know next time I see him, I'm gonna kick his ass."

I scoffed. "I'd like to see you try. What did he do?"

"Let his kids bring that damn dog to your get-together," he said. "Now my kids won't shut up about it. They want one too."

"All kids want dogs, Chuck."

"The man should've known better, bringing that mutt."

"I'm sure it wasn't his intention to plant a seed. Anyway, Puppy's a good dog."

"Well, I already take care of a hamster. I don't want another animal they'll forget about in a week. Especially a dog."

"How can you forget about a dog?"

"Don't ask me."

"Anyway, Bill didn't know," I said. "But I kind of liked having it around."

Chuck looked at me and shook his head as he picked at the leavings of his sandwich on the wrapper.

I changed the subject. "What do you think about the new scripts?"

"I don't use them, but they're fine," Chuck said.

"I know, I'm just asking," I said. "George uses them, and Debbie reads them word for word. They do well, but aren't good at talking off the cuff. I thought different scripts would help."

"Well, they haven't been there long."

"I just wondered if I need to make changes."

"Patience, my friend," Chuck said with a grin. "Give them another week or two before you bring out the big guns."

"Yeah, okay."

"Stop worrying. We're doing good."

"I just want to do better." I glanced at the drink station and contemplated a refill.

"Again, give it time."

"If we had more like you..."

"Nah." He waved it off. "I just do my job."

I leaned in. "Listen, Chuck. I'm thinking of expanding a little. Maybe give you a promotion. Office supervisor or something."

"That's not necessary."

"Why not? There's plenty of business to be had. I'd like to hire more people."

"I don't know." He picked up some of his leftover meat and popped it in his mouth.

"It'd have to go through the home office," I said. "I just wanted to run it by you."

"I'll think about it, all right?"

"All right," I said. I looked at the remainder of my meatball sub and regretted getting it. I had spent most of the lunch trying, without success, to keep the sauce off my clothes.

"Your girlfriend, she's quite a looker." He gave a low whistle and grinned. "They grow them all like that in Oklahoma?"

I chuckled. "We grow all kinds. Some you wouldn't want to touch with a stolen pecker. But they only grew one of Brooke."

"Hard though, her there; you here," Chuck said.

"Yeah, but I'm angling to get her to move."

He nodded thoughtfully. "Think she will?"

"Who knows?" I sighed and thought about what Brooke had said. "It sucks, because we have to find time in our schedules and then spend money for a trip."

"Yeah, it does suck. What does she do?"

"She's a receptionist," I said. "It's a job that translates well wherever she is."

"Sure," Chuck said. "She could work with us."

"I don't know." I widened my eyes in mock terror.

Chuck laughed. "Yeah, you're right. If I worked with Kay? It might be cool at first, but then I'd probably get sick of her."

"Can't have that," I said.

"Nope," he agreed. "So, you gonna marry her?"

I paused. That refill sounded good about now. "It's crossed my mind. I think she wants to, but I'm not sure."

"You're the only unmarried person I know," Chuck said. "Personally, I mean. There's a couple in the office, but I don't hang out with them."

"You think it's a bad idea?" I felt I could trust Chuck's opinion.

He leaned back in his chair. "Not necessarily. It's a commitment, to be sure. I mean, you're promising someone you'll be there, no matter what, for the rest of your life."

"True," I said.

"I just met her once, but I like her. And I know you well enough. But it's not all wine and roses."

"I know."

"People expect it to be, but it's not, even if you're madly in love."

"You still in love with Kay?"

"Ever since we were in high school," he said with a wiggle of his brow. "We don't look like our prom picture anymore, but I still love her like I did then."

"Must be nice." I ate the rest of my sandwich and didn't care anymore about the sauce dripping on my shirt.

Everyone I knew seemed to be married. And mostly, they were happy. I was in my mid-thirties, had a career, a house, and a woman I loved. I wasn't rich, but I had no debts. Nothing was stopping me except myself. I decided then that I should ask her to marry me.

I looked at my watch. "You ready?"

"Back to the ol' grindstone," Chuck said with a sigh and got up.

"The grindstone's making you rich, my friend. Don't forget it."

"I wouldn't say rich, but I do okay," he said.

"Well, don't forget about the expansion idea."

Chuck grinned. "I won't if you won't."

Later in the evening, I was still feeling the rush from work. I wandered through the house looking for projects to keep myself occupied. While I found a few, I was really trying not to think of Brooke. I wished she were here, so we could go out and celebrate, but the best I could do was to hear her voice, so I sat down and called her.

The phone rang a few times, and I started to hang up when she finally answered.

"Hey you," she said brightly. "I was just thinking about you."

"I wanted to hear your voice."

"Here it is," she said.

"I just missed you."

"I miss you too. Everything okay?"

"Sure," I said. "I got a call this morning. We're the top office, and I'll get a bonus."

"Wow, that's great."

"I guess, but it's not the same without you here."

"Yeah, I know."

I thought I sensed something different in her voice, though I didn't know what to make of it. "I could come down next week."

"Special occasion?"

"I want to see you, even if it's just for an hour."

"Well, I hope it's longer," she said. "An hour's just a tease."

"It'll be longer," I assured her. "I'll let you know in case you have a date."

"I'll cancel." She laughed.

I didn't hint at a proposal. It wasn't something I wanted to blurt out over the phone. I wanted it to be special, so I stayed quiet and simply savored the sound of her voice. I was thankful technology narrowed the distance, but I was lonely for her presence.

"Hey, I got another call," she said.

"Okay, tell him I said hi."

"Stop that," she said. "It's my sister."

"I love you," I said.

"Love you too, gotta go."

I reluctantly set the phone down and consoled myself with the thought I'd talk to her again. Soon, I hoped, it would be as my fiancée.

In Bill's backyard, we worked on a doghouse for Puppy, who was happily getting in the way. Bill picked up a scrap of wood, threw it, and Puppy gave chase.

"He's already getting big," I said. "They should have thought of a better name."

"He's a big pain in my rear. Hold this." Bill put a plank of wood on the roof frame, and I held it flush while he nailed it into place.

"The house isn't turning out half bad," I said. "Kind of plain, though."

"The girls wanted windows, a porch, and other fancy things."

"They're very thoughtful," I said. "Where are we going to put the windows?"

"Dogs don't need windows."

I shrugged. "Maybe he would like one."

"And what's he going to do with a porch?"

"Oh, I don't know. Sit with a fresh cup of coffee?" I answered.

"You're a funny guy. He's not getting a porch, much less his own coffee mug."

I nailed the other side, then put on another plank. "Hey Bill, can I ask you something?"

"Sure."

"Are you happy being married?"

Bill drove in a nail, then looked at me. "Thinking about stealing my wife?"

I shook my head. "No!"

Bill laughed at my horrified expression. "Relax, I'm only kidding. I can't say I'm unhappy. Why?"

"Just asking."

"Oh, I get it." He chuckled as he placed another nail. "You're thinking of taking the plunge, huh?"

"How do you know?"

"Just do. Are you?"

"I think she wants to," I said.

"Look, Ryan, it should be what you want. You serious about her?"

"Yeah." It felt good to say it out loud to someone else.

"When will you ask?"

"I figure I'll do it when I go down there next week."

"Hope you know what you're getting into." He took off his tool belt and laid it on a sawhorse. "Let's take a break. Grab a drink."

"Sounds good."

Inside the house, Angie was making lunch for the girls while they busied themselves coloring at the table. Bill grabbed a couple of glasses from the cabinet.

"How's the doghouse coming?" Angie asked.

"No windows, but I don't think he'll notice."

"If you're thirsty, there's tea in the fridge," Angie said.

"Did you finish, Daddy?" Eva asked.

"Almost, baby," Bill said while he pulled a couple of glasses from the cabinet.

"Is there windows?" Lily asked.

"There's a door," Bill answered.

Satisfied, the girls dug into the sandwiches Angie set down in front of them.

"Guess what, Honey?" Bill said with a mischievous grin. "Ryan's giving up his manhood."

"I didn't say that," I muttered.

Angie rolled her eyes. "What are you talking about?"

"That little girl of his."

Angie glanced at me, then smiled. "Truly?"

I shrugged. "Not about me giving up my manhood, but yeah."

The girls glanced up, but stayed quiet.

"Do you have a ring?" Angie asked.

"No," I said. "Honestly, I don't know what to get."

"Something unique," Angie said. "But she'll love anything you pick out."

"Maybe. Do you think maybe you might help me find one?"

"Of course."

Bill handed me a glass of iced tea. "Watch out, Ryan. Women like shiny, expensive things."

"That's not true," Angie said. "I would've been happy with a Ring Pop."

"You say that now." Bill laughed.

"Ignore him," Angie said. "I'd be happy to help you."

"Thanks. I'd appreciate a woman's perspective. I have no idea what I'm doing."

"We can go look this weekend." She turned to Bill. "Would that be okay with you?"

"Hey, as long as I don't have to go. Me and the girls will find something to do."

"This weekend would be great," I said. "I appreciate it."

"Are you gonna get married, Uncle Ryan?" Eva asked, Disneyesque fantasies of happily ever after already running through her mind.

"Maybe," I answered.

"Will we get to watch?"

"We'll see what happens." I enjoyed her enthusiasm and wondered if maybe we could let her be a flower girl.

"You finished?" Bill asked.

I looked at my glass and nodded. "Guess I was thirsty."

"It happens." He set the glasses in the sink and heaved a sigh. "Better get back out and finish up."

We spent the rest of the afternoon finishing up the doghouse. We stood and admired our effort while Puppy sniffed around inside. He came out and gave a bark of approval.

"Told you he wouldn't care if there weren't any windows," Bill said.

"Not now, but he might want you to add a porch later."

Bill huffed. "You want to build a porch, be my guest. You want to stick around for dinner?"

"No, but thanks. I better get home," I said. "I'll call Angie later and set up a time to go look at rings."

Bill walked with me to my car. "She'll find the right one, I guarantee."

"I hope so," I said.

Bill shook his head. "You know, life won't be the same after."

"Yeah, I know."

"But worth it."

"I think it will be," I said, then got in my car. "Tell Angie I'll call."

"Will do," Bill said. He tapped the roof of my car, and I headed home.

Later that night, I lay in bed and thought about the future. I wondered if this was what I wanted to do, but really, I was afraid. Even so, I wasn't going to back out. While a life with Brooke would finally close a door, it also opened a on the precipice for far too long already.

Saturday morning, Angie and I headed into the city. Bill had promised the girls a trip to the park and cheeseburgers after, so they didn't mind us going without them. We spent the first part of the drive in silence. I had a lot on my mind, and I guessed she did too.

We had gotten close again after I had moved. We never really talked about our past, or about us now. It didn't feel like twenty years had gone by. I felt like I had become part of their family. Bill and I had become good friends, and I was enchanted with the girls, who had taken to calling me "Uncle Ryan." Most people would not have been as welcoming to a past love, and I felt privileged to have been included in their lives.

While things were good, I still had lingering thoughts that had not completely gone away. Occasionally, I would comment on things, sort of feeling around to see if Angie might still have some feelings for me. It was a curiosity I couldn't help but explore. I never got anything out of her, but I didn't expect to. It was a kind of self-torture, but a part of me still wanted to know.

Angie broke the silence.

"What are you thinking about?"

"Life and all it entails," I answered. I kept my eyes on the road, though traffic was almost nonexistent. "You?"

"The same thing, actually," she said.

Silence filled the car again briefly. It was almost uncomfortable.

"It's weird, you showing up again," she said. "There was such a long gap, but it feels like it's always been."

"Except you're married, have children, a career, and live much farther away," I pointed out.

"True, but you also have a career. And you're getting married."

"She hasn't said yes yet."

"She will."

"You sound confident."

"Because I am. And when she does, it will inevitably lead to kids."

"Perhaps even a dog," I said, and she laughed. "Is it everything you expected?"

"What do you mean?"

"Your life. Everything."

She thought for a moment. "No. Some things, maybe. My job. I always thought I'd have kids. But it's different. I didn't imagine I'd have Bill, or that I'd be teaching fourth graders."

"What did you expect?"

"I thought I'd teach kindergarten." She paused and reflected. "I used to think we'd get married."

"Did you?"

"Didn't you?"

I just shrugged.

"It was a classic case," she said. "We weren't supposed to be together, but we were."

I continued to stare at the road. "There were too many things working against us."

"Are you disappointed?"

"Maybe at first," I said. I had to think of my answer, so I wouldn't end up saying something stupid. "But now I see how happy you are, and successful. I'm not disappointed."

"I wouldn't say I'm successful," she said. "It's not always easy."

"I'm not saying you never had problems, but you have something most never get in a lifetime. I don't think I could have ever given what you deserve."

"You shouldn't be so hard on yourself."

"I know, but it's not easy." I shot her a grin. "Truth is, for the past twenty years, I hoped you were happy, and had reason to smile. Now I'm here, and I see you are."

"I am," she said with a serene smile. "I'm glad that we can do this."

"Me too," I said, but didn't mention that it still made me sad sometimes.

I imagined doing something like this with Brooke. Just going out and enjoying the weekend, and the thought didn't make me uncomfortable.

"You're thinking about her, aren't you?" she asked.

"How do you know?"

"I can tell," she said. "I'm really excited for you."

"Oh yeah? You don't think it's a bad idea?" I asked.

"No. I like Brooke. She's good for you. I'm surprised it took you this long, though."

"I was waiting for the right one," I said.

"It's a long time to wait."

"After you, nobody came close."

She rolled her eyes. "Come on now."

"I'm glad I waited. If it were anyone else, I think it would have been a mistake."

"She comes close, then?" she asked.

"Not at all," I admitted. "But I love her. She makes me happy, and I'd like a family of my own before I'm too old to enjoy it."

She patted my shoulder. "Don't worry, Ryan. We'll find the perfect way to tell her."

We shopped around the city for a couple of hours to find a ring. We looked in several jewelry shops, but I wasn't feeling any of it, and thought maybe I should try later.

"Let's check out this place," Angie said and pointed toward a ramshackle building.

"A pawnshop?" I asked. "I am not giving her an engagement ring from a pawnshop."

"Don't be so pretentious," she said. "You'd be surprised what you might find, and she'll never need to know where it came from."

"All right, we'll look." I sighed and pulled into the parking lot. Everywhere else, the rings were too plain, or too expensive. Brooke wouldn't have been comfortable with something extravagant, but I didn't want something that looked cheap. I was sure we wouldn't find anything here either.

A bell rang as we walked into the shop. A large man sat on a stool behind the counter.

"Can I help you?" he asked.

"We're looking for an engagement ring," Angie said.

The man beamed. "Congratulations."

"We're not—" I started, but Angie nudged me. "What?"

"Just shush," she whispered.

"We've got some nice ones right here." The man went to a counter and pulled out a tray with a selection of rings.

We looked them over as the man hovered. I spotted a simple white-gold band with a small diamond. I knew it was the one.

"What do you think of that one?" I asked Angie.

"I like it," she said.

"Good choice," the man said. "Since you look like a nice couple, I'll give you a discount, yes?"

I nodded. "Thank you."

"Good luck to you two," the man said while he rang it up.

I slipped the box into my pocket. I couldn't wait to give it to Brooke.

"Why did you let him think we were engaged?" I asked after we got in the car.

"So he'd give you a discount," she answered matter-of-factly.

"Good call," I said. "Want to get some lunch?"

"That'd be great," she said. "If you don't mind, I'd also like to do a little shopping while we're here."

"No problem." I was too excited to object to any shopping, even though normally it isn't my favorite thing to do.

At the last store, I found a couple of stuffed animals: a tiger for Eva and a monkey for Lily.

"What do you have there?" Angie asked.

"Just some presents for the kids."

"Oh, Ryan. You're just spoiling them."

"I didn't want them to feel left out."

"Left out of what?"

"I don't know. Hanging out in the city?"

"I don't think they'd care," she said. "They're having fun with their father."

"Well, it's still a necessary expense. Gotta keep them on my side."

She laughed. "Don't worry, you're a success already."

"I'd like to keep it that way," I said.

We paid for our purchases and then went to find my car. The sky moved toward dusk, and I was suddenly tired. The ring in my pocket felt heavier.

"How are you going to ask her?" she asked as we began the drive back to her house.

"I don't know. Just ask and give her the ring, I guess."

"You can't do that!" she said. "You should be more romantic."

"I don't know how."

"Oh, bull, Ryan. You should find a special way to do it without being cheesy. At least make her dinner."

"Not a good enough cook to make a romantic dinner," I said. "Anyway, that's cliché."

"Who cares? What's her favorite food?"

"She's fond of pizza."

"Be serious."

"What's wrong with pizza? It's a lot of people's favorite. She's a girl with simple tastes."

"There's nothing wrong with it, but I said special. Pizza's a kid's favorite food."

"I would think it's hot dogs," I said. "What's your favorite food?" I asked.

"We're not talking about me," she said defensively.

"I bet it's still pizza, huh? With extra cheese and mushrooms." I grinned. "Admit it."

"So what if it is?" she huffed.

"Maybe I could have one made in the shape of a heart and delivered by a guy in a tuxedo," I said. "I'll ask her while we have cinnamon sticks in the candlelight."

She glared at me. "Now you're making fun."

"Not at all." I resisted the urge to laugh. "I'm just thinking about my options."

"And now you've had your laugh."

I gave in and laughed. "Okay, so I did. How did Bill ask you?"

She groaned. "You don't want to hear it."

"Sure I do."

"If you insist." She looked over at me.

"Well?"

She sighed heavily. "We were at a stoplight. He looks over at me and says, 'Hey, you wanna get married?' I didn't know what to say. The light turned green, and he started driving. Didn't wait for an answer. No romance."

"Doesn't surprise me." I grinned. I could picture Bill doing it that way. "But what does it matter? You said yes, didn't you?"

"I did."

"So why does there have to be romance? That junk's for the movies. It's not real life."

"It's important to a girl, even if she doesn't say it," she said. "He took me to pick out a ring. That was romantic."

"Maybe," I said. "I don't see why you just can't ask."

"You can. Just don't ask her in the car."

"I'll keep it in mind. Do you wish he had done it differently?" I asked.

She thought before answering. "No, not at all. Now, it's a funny story. If he did it differently, it wouldn't be as good, I think."

"I enjoyed it. Bill seems the unromantic type. If he tried, it would have been cliché."

"He can be, but yeah." She sighed and looked out the window. "I think sometimes, what it might be like. If it were different. But I wouldn't change anything."

She gave me a look, and I understood. I turned the radio on low and let the music fill the car.

I had loved, lost, and found it again. It was different, but I also wouldn't change anything. I felt the ring's box in my pocket and anticipated seeing Brooke. I thought maybe I would follow through on the heart-shaped pizza and propose over cinnamon sticks. Maybe it was me being a man, but I thought it would be romantic. I still had time to think about it.

I glanced at Angie, who was looking out the window, her head nodding slightly to the music's rhythm. Though I still thought about what could have been, the ache was no longer there. She had her life, and I was happy she was once again in mine. The Universe seemed to smile as it put the pieces into place.

As soon as we pulled into Angie's driveway, Eva and Lily burst through the door, with Puppy tripping along behind them.

"Mama! You're home!" they squealed in unison.

Puppy barked, infected by their joy, while the girls threw themselves at their mother and hugged her as if it had been days instead of a few hours.

"I missed you too, sweeties." Angie kissed the tops of their heads. "Let Mama go, so I can see your daddy. What have you been doing all day?"

"We went to the park, and we had a picnic in the park!" Lily's words tumbled together. She jumped up and down, unable to contain her excitement.

"And we had ice cream," Eva added.

"With candy on it!" Lily finished.

"That explains a lot," Angie said and glanced back at me.

I laughed.

Eva placed her hands on her hips and scowled. "What's so funny?"

"You're funny," I answered. "I found something for you."

"What?" She perked up. The thought of a present forgave my indiscretion. "What did you bring me?"

Lily's eyes grew wide. "Did you bring us candy?"

"You don't need any more candy," Angie said.

"Sorry, no candy." I reached into the car, grabbed the stuffed animals, and handed them to the girls. "This'll last longer than candy."

Both the girls squealed and hugged the animals tightly. They started to run back into the house with their new treasures.

"What do you say?" Angie's voice brought them to a halt.

The girls turned and said sweetly, "Thank you, Uncle Ryan."

"You're welcome," I said, but they had already taken off.

Bill came out the front door with a mock stagger. "Oh, thank God you're home."

"It's your fault for feeding them a bunch of sugar," Angie said.

"I thought it would keep them quiet."

"Sugar? Keep them quiet?" Angie said and kissed him. "I should've let Ryan talk me into running away with him."

"I'd have let him if he took the kids too. Bachelorhood sounds pretty sweet about now." He wrapped an arm around Angie's waist and looked at me. "Don't suppose I could talk you into it?"

"Not on your life," I said. "You're stuck with them, I'm afraid."

"The dog too?" he asked.

"I'll take the dog," I answered, "but the wife and kids are yours."

Bill sighed and shook his head. "A shame. Did you accomplish anything?"

"Found a ring." I took out the ring and showed it to him.

"Nice," Bill said. "You want to stay and have dinner with us?"

"No thanks. I need to get home and do some work. Get ready for the week."

"You sure? We have plenty. You don't want to work too hard."

I nodded. "Thanks for asking. Maybe another time."

"Sure," Bill said, then kissed Angie's cheek. "Guess I'm stuck alone with the wife and kids."

"Too bad," I said, and Angie shot both of us dirty looks.

I drove away and watched them go into the house together through my rearview mirror. I felt the weight of the ring in my pocket as nervousness set in.

⊚

Our numbers at the end of Friday weren't as high as I wanted, but they were still good. There was too much on my mind to let it bother me. In less than a week, I would see Brooke, and ask her to be my wife. I had already arranged for Chuck to cover me Thursday and Friday, so I could have a couple extra days with her. It was hard not to let my plan slip when I talked to her, but I managed it. I didn't tell anyone about my plans; besides Angie and Bill, I told only Scott. He was happy; I feared he would give it away, but I also felt I could trust him not to.

I put some music on low, sat at my kitchen table, and looked at the ring for the hundredth time. The diamond glinted in the sunlight through the window, and I imagined how it would look on Brooke's finger. I rolled the ring in my hand and dialed her number. It went to her voicemail, but I didn't leave a message. I figured I'd try later and went downstairs to tinker with some design ideas for a workshop I hoped to build in the backyard.

I was absorbed in my work when the phone rang and brought me back. I glanced at the clock. It was a little after ten. I had been at it for hours without realizing it.

"Who'd be calling now?" I muttered, then thought it would be Brooke. I hurried to find my phone, which was buried under a pile of clutter on my desk.

"Ryan?"

"Yeah?" It took a moment to recognize Brooke's sister's voice. "Erin? What's up? It's late."

"Are you driving?"

"No, I'm at home."

"Ryan?" I could hear the shake in her voice. "I don't know how to say this."

"Say what?"

"Brooke's been in an accident."

"What?" My voice cracked. "Is she okay?"

"I don't think so," she said in a strained whisper.

"What do you mean?"

"She's..." Erin took a shuddering breath. "She's dead."

My fist clenched the phone. I felt it give. "Don't screw with me, Erin. It's not funny."

"I'm not, Ryan. I wish I didn't have to tell you."

The silence seemed to go on for eternity as I tried to fathom it. Erin said nothing and allowed me to digest it. "What happened?" I asked.

"She left my house. Another car hit her head-on." She sniffled between words.

"What about... was the other guy drunk or something?" I sank into my chair. I felt dizzy and nauseous.

"No. Just a freak accident." She sobbed. "The other driver's dead too. And his son."

I didn't want to talk. I just wanted to be left alone, but I also didn't want to let her go. The ring I had set on my desk looked dull now. "I'll drive down tonight."

"No, Ryan. I don't want anything to happen to you too."

"I'll be fine."

"Ryan?"

"Yes?"

"There's something else I should tell you."

I took a heavy breath and leaned back in my chair. "Okay?"

"She was pregnant."

"She... pregnant?"

"Yeah. She came over here to tell me."

"When? Why didn't she tell me?" The news cut through my heart like a hot knife.

"She just found out," she said. "She was really nervous about telling you."

"Why?"

"She was going to tell you when you came."

"Oh, Hell, I don't know, Erin. Maybe I should come now."

"There's nothing you can do."

"I guess not." I choked on the words. She was right. "I'll try to get the earliest flight I can."

"Okay."

"Is there anything I can do for you?"

"No, there's nothing. I'm sorry, Ryan."

"I'm sorry too."

"I know she meant a lot to you," she said.

"You have no idea," I whispered, and hung up the phone.

I continued to stare at the phone for several minutes. I hoped I would wake up, or Brooke would call back, laugh, and say it was just a joke, but it never came.

I picked up the box holding my shattered future and took out the ring. I clutched it and laid my head on the desk. The reality of it hit me. I gave in to emotion and cried myself to sleep.

CHAPTER EIGHTEEN

I booked the earliest flight I could and arrived in Tulsa a couple of days later. I spotted Scott waving as I got off the plane.

"Hey, man. Want me to take your bag?" he asked.

I shook my head. "No, thanks."

"How are you doing?"

"Doing? Tired, confused, sad, angry. I'm a regular mixed bag of emotions."

"I hear ya." He squeezed my shoulder.

"I keep expecting to wake up and tell her about the crazy dream I had."

"I know," he said. "Whatever you need, man, I'm here for you."

I stopped. "Do you think maybe I could see her? Before?"

I wanted a chance to spend some time with her alone before the funeral. To look at her one last time.

"Sure. We can go now, if you want."

"Okay."

We got into Scott's truck and left the airport. We didn't speak; I watched the familiar, yet foreign, world pass by. The feeling that a piece of me had been ripped away hadn't faded, and I wondered how long it would take me to recover, or if I ever would. I knew I already had the inclination not to let things go easily.

Scott coughed. "Didn't think you wanted to go back to my place just to come back, so I got you a room. We can stop by there first."

"No, I'd rather..." I couldn't bring myself to finish.

Scott nodded and said nothing else until we got to the funeral home.

He stopped the truck next to a Victorian-style house. It looked more like someone's grandmother's home than a place of mourning. "We're here," he whispered.

"Okay." It took a lot of effort to get out of the truck.

"You want me to go in with you?"

"No, but if you want to, I won't stop you." I hoped he'd at least walk to the door with me, because I felt a little scared. I had only been in a funeral home once, when I was nine years old and my grandfather had died.

Scott got out of the truck and put his hand on my shoulder. "Come on. I'll walk you in."

"Thanks." I let him lead me up the sidewalk and through the door.

A silver-gray-headed man in a dark suit greeted us. When he shook my hand, I noticed it was baby-soft, but firm. He offered condolences and led us to the viewing room. He and Scott stopped at the door, and I went in alone.

The room was softly lit, and the flowers surrounding the casket emanated a thick, sickly-sweet scent.

I approached carefully, as if she might awaken, and looked down at her. She looked different. The vibrancy that had been her true beauty was gone. All that remained was a shell, painted to resemble Brooke, but it was not her.

"Hey," I whispered and reached out to stroke her cheek. Her cool skin under my fingers was unforgiving. I felt the tears start to fall, and I let them, without bothering to wipe them away.

"You know, you could've told me. I would've been happy. Maybe if you'd known, you'd still be here, and I'd be able to see you. We could've shared our surprises together. You were always a surprise. When I first saw you, I knew I'd love you, but I never knew I could feel for anyone the way I do for you. I'm sorry that we didn't get to spend more time together. I feel like this was my fault somehow. I wanted to have a life with you. Forever. I love you, Brooke."

I leaned in, kissed her softly, and took the ring out of my pocket. I slipped it onto her finger and kept talking to her as if she could hear me. I tried to say goodbye, but couldn't wrap my mind around the fact she was truly gone. The life I wanted for us, the one I placed so much hope in, could never begin.

I wiped my eyes and took one last look at her, and locked the memory of her face and her smile in my heart. I knew she would've given me an enthusiastic *yes* if she'd been able to hear my proposal, and I let that thought console me. When I got to the door, I stopped and took a look back, but still could not say goodbye.

Outside, Scott stood by his truck with his hands in his pockets and watched the passing traffic.

"You okay?" he asked.

"Fine."

"Ready to go?" he asked. He walked around and opened the door for me. I didn't object and accepted the small kindness without a word. "You want to get something to eat?"

"No."

"You sure?"

"Yes."

"You wanna talk?"

"No."

"Okay, buddy," he said quietly.

He drove to the motel and opened the door. We went in, and I immediately fell onto one of the double beds and stared up at the ceiling. Scott didn't talk. He simply left me alone with my thoughts until I was ready to speak. I was grateful to him.

"Why?" I asked after a long silence. It was the same clichéd question everyone asked, and it had no right answer. Any given would be nothing but a worn-out platitude.

"Who is John Galt?" Scott replied.

I smiled faintly. I knew he understood and wouldn't say something for the sake of comfort.

"I was going to come up here this weekend and ask her to marry me. Got a ring, planned it out and everything."

Scott nodded but said nothing.

"I was going to have a family of my own. Everything was good. I finally found someone I want to be with, was getting my shit together, and the goddamn Universe throws this at me."

"It wasn't anybody's fault, Ryan. It's not something that was meant to hurt you. It just happened."

"But it happened to me. To us."

"I wish there were something I could do for you, but I know there isn't."

"No, you're doing it. By being my friend. It's one of the few constants I have in my life."

"I'll always be your friend, no matter what."

"Thanks." I lay back on the stiff pillow that smelled faintly of bleach and closed my eyes to a film of memories in my mind.

☺

The weather for the graveside service was mild and bright. Birds twittered songs of joy in the purest blue sky. The scene contrasted with the occasion's solemnity. I couldn't help but smile a little. I allowed myself to imagine that Brooke had planned it that way. She sent a secret message specifically for me.

Scott stood beside me as the minister from her childhood church spoke briefly about heaven and how the brevity of life should inspire us to follow Brooke's example, to live fully, with love and kindness toward those around us.

I looked around at the people. Some I recognized; most I didn't. Though it wasn't a large crowd, everyone there meant something to Brooke, and she to them.

Her mother and sister stood near the casket, close together. I had met both of them not long after Brooke and I started dating. We had dinner at her mother's and went on a few double dates with Erin. I hadn't known them very well, but I'd thought they were decent people.

Brooke's mother was a handsome woman, and I saw the resemblance immediately. She held herself with quiet dignity as she listened to the minister.

Her sister looked up and offered me a sad smile. She was a few years younger than Brooke, but taller, with auburn hair and a fuller figure.

I nodded to them in acknowledgment. After the service was over, I walked over to speak with them.

"Ryan." Her mother clasped my hand in both of hers. "I'm glad you could come."

"Thank you, Ms. Daly. How are you, Erin?"

"Fine, thanks," Erin said, and I gave her a brief hug.

"I'm glad I could make it," I said, "but sorry it wasn't under better circumstances."

"Ah well, our loss is the Lord's gain," her mother replied softly. "Brooke always spoke well of you."

"That's good to know. I loved her very much. She was special."

"Yes, she was." She turned her attention briefly to the small crowd, many of whom were drifting away.

"I'm going to go speak to some people, Mom. Thanks for coming, Ryan," Erin said.

"You're welcome," I answered.

"I'll be back in a few minutes, Mom."

"Okay, dear." She watched Erin walk away before turning back to me. "You were going to propose to her, weren't you?"

"Yes," I said quietly. I realized she must have noticed the ring I had placed on Brooke's finger.

"It may not mean much, but I'd still like to think of you as part of the family."

"No, it means a lot. Thank you. Is there anything I can do for you?"

She shook her head and turned her gaze toward the open grave.

"If there's anything, I'd be more than happy to do it. For you or for Erin."

"That's sweet of you, Ryan. You being here is enough." She grasped my arm. "We're going to be okay. Sad, missing my special baby, but she's in a better place now."

"I'm family," I said gently. "Anytime you need me, call. I mean it."

"Bless you, Ryan," she whispered. She embraced me and gave me a motherly kiss on the cheek. "You made her happy."

"Thank you."

She only nodded, and I said nothing more. I excused myself, spoke briefly with a few others before I found Scott and returned to the motel to rest for a few hours. Soon, Scott would drive me to the airport, and I would go back to Iowa. Back to my quiet house and the life that suddenly felt smaller. Emptier. It seemed I was destined to spend it alone.

CHAPTER NINETEEN

Everything had gone without incident with Chuck in charge. I hadn't told him my intentions, but I wanted to see how he would handle things. I had hoped to promote him if I had the chance to expand our office. When I returned, I threw myself into work, just to keep my mind occupied. Bill and Angie were supportive, but they didn't understand. Even though it hurt, I kept reminders of Brooke around me. On my desk at work, I had my favorite photo, a candid shot I had taken of her when we had spent the day at an amusement park. It was exactly how I wanted to remember her. The setting sun created a halo through the loose strands of her hair, and her face was pink from being out all day. She wore her beautiful smile, with a bit of cotton candy stuck to her chin. The people and the lights from the booths were unfocused, and she looked as if she could walk out of the picture. I looked at it often and missed her. I resolved to move on, though I knew it wouldn't be easy. It would be what she wanted.

At home, I took on several projects. I built a swing set in the backyard. I said it was for the kids to play on, but really, I just wanted one for myself. The work, the home projects: it was all just an excuse. At night, when I lay in bed, too tired to move, I always thought of Brooke. I hoped for a life beyond this one, so we could be together again. I had lost Angie, and now, I had lost Brooke. Different circumstances, but I couldn't see a difference. I didn't want to fall in love again. It was safer not to. I didn't think I could handle a third loss. I was empty. Lost. Alone.

A couple of weeks later, Bill came by. I had finished the swing set and had drawn up plans for a workshop. He found me at the picnic table with my notes and drawings.

He slid onto the bench across from me. "Thought I'd find you here."

"Hey, Bill. How'd you know I'd be here?"

"Your car's in the drive, and you didn't answer the door."

"Good giveaway," I said. "I'm just taking advantage of the weather. Want some coffee?"

Bill shook his head. "No, just wanted to check on you."

"I'm fine," I said. "There's already a pot made, and I could use a break."

"Yeah, okay. I'll have one." He thumbed toward the notebook. "What're you working on?"

"I'm going to build a workshop so I can have a place to build some stuff," I said. "I might have to buy a pickup truck."

"Ambitious."

I shrugged. "Got nothing better to do."

"You haven't been around," Bill said. "Thought you might need to talk."

"Just been busy." I pushed myself up from the bench. "I'll get the coffee."

"Sure," Bill said and pulled my notebook over and looked it over while I went to get the coffee.

"Thanks," he said after I set his mug down. He took a sip. "Better than the sludge they have at the station."

"I'll take it as a compliment."

He grinned. "It's not. Anything is better."

"At least it's not the worst."

"Indeed." He wrapped his hands around the mug. "I'll be honest. Angela sent me to check on you."

I rolled my eyes. "I'm fine, really."

"Well, she's worried about you. Frankly, I am too." He looked up at me and sighed. "You've been working too hard. You need to relax a bit."

"I am relaxed."

"Look, I know you've had a loss," he said. "It's no reason to ignore people who are still here and care about you."

"Come on, Bill," I scoffed. "I'm not ignoring anybody."

"You are," he said. "We're here for you. There's no reason for you to stay away."

"Yeah, I know. I just need to figure things out myself." I held out my hands. "You can see I'm okay, so don't worry."

He nodded. I closed my notebook and slipped the pencil back into my pocket.

"You should let her know too," he said.

"I know. Just needed some time by myself to figure things out. I'll talk to her."

"You know I'm your friend, right?" Bill asked.

"Sure," I said. "Most guys wouldn't be under the circumstances."

He laughed. "You're probably right. I'm going to tell you something, as friends, but don't tell Angela I told you."

His expression was so serious, I could only nod.

"I've known about you, pretty much from the day I met her."

"Yeah, you've mentioned it," I said.

Bill ignored my comment. "I admit I was jealous at first. I got over it pretty quick."

"Yeah?" I didn't expect the conversation to go this route.

"You know how she is."

"I do."

"I thought about looking you up myself, but never got around to it." He shrugged apologetically.

"She's talked about me?" I asked. "I mean, more than you've said before?"

"A few times. Usually, if something reminded her. I don't think she realized it half the time."

"I'm surprised," I said.

"Why? We all do it from time to time. You don't forget a first love. It sticks and doesn't go away."

"I guess you're right."

"I had one. Nancy." His expression grew wistful when he said her name. "We were just kids, but I can't remember when I didn't know her. We were neighbors. Best friends. Did everything together. Maybe I was too young, but I loved her just the same."

I didn't know what to say.

"When I was twelve, we moved. She became nothing more than a memory, but she's still there."

"You still think about her?"

"Sure," he said. "Something will make me think of her, and I wonder what she's doing. Like you did. But I never had the guts to find out. I guess I was afraid of what I'd find."

"I understand," I said, but wondered where he was going with this.

"Angela's not Nancy, but sometimes, she does something that reminds me of her."

I played with my empty mug and simply listened.

"We always look for that first. The rest of our lives, though we don't admit it. But usually, what we find is better."

"You're a better man than me, Bill," I said.

"I didn't mean it like that."

"I know, but I don't understand what you're getting at."

"Ah, I'm just rambling." He picked up his mug, then set it back down. "I didn't know Brooke well. Just what you've said, and meeting her once."

"She was a good girl."

"Don't doubt it at all, but I'll say this." He leaned in. "I could see a bit of Angela in her."

"Me too," I admitted. "Do you know I'm still in love with her? Angie, I mean."

Bill folded his hands and looked across the field. The world seemed to join in the silence. I held my breath, afraid I had said the wrong thing.

"Yeah, Ryan. I know." He looked at me and frowned, though it was not unpleasant. "Suspect she's still in love with you too."

"It bothers you, doesn't it?" I knew if I were in his place, it would bother me.

"It should, huh?"

"Probably," I said.

"But it doesn't." He sighed. "I've gotten to know you. Like I said, you can't help who you fall in love with, and you can't help who you stay in love with. Life's funny that way."

I hoped he had a point.

"You know, I consider myself a Christian man."

"Yeah."

"1 Corinthians 13 gives a description of true love. Patient, kind, not jealous, doesn't act unbecomingly."

"I'm familiar," I said.

"I don't know where you stand religiously, but it doesn't matter. That's none of my business," he said. "What I'm saying is, I love my wife. With every quality in that chapter. I know she loves me. I also know you had something special, and love her too."

"True," I said.

"If it were anyone else, I'd question their motives," he said. "But I've seen you express the same true love in the passage. You wouldn't do anything to hurt her. You don't have it in you."

"Sure, Bill, but you've said it before."

"It bears repeating," he said. "I'm not perfect, but I try my best. And I trust her."

"You should." I swung my leg and straddled the bench. "It feels like whenever something good happens, it gets taken away. I'm a little jealous of you."

"Come on. There's nothing to be jealous of."

"Sure there is," I said. "You have a wife who loves you, beautiful kids. A nice home. I hoped to have something like it."

"You still can," he said.

I took a deep breath and cleared my throat. "Brooke was pregnant."

He frowned. "I'm sorry, Ryan."

I shrugged. "Way it goes. What hurts the most is, it was all within my grasp and in a blink it was gone."

"God, Ryan." He got up and moved to sit beside me. "You're not alone. I believe something good will still happen for you."

"No, I don't think so," I said. "Not sure I want it to."

"Look, I know you probably think it's easy for me to say, but just give it time. It will."

I felt the comforting weight of his hand on my shoulder. "Thanks for being my friend."

"No problem," he said.

I stood and took a few steps and turned to him. "I first came here on a whim, without knowing what to expect. When I left, I knew. You're the best thing to happen to her."

"Appreciate you saying it."

I sat back down and propped my elbows on the table. "When I got home, I found Brooke. But..."

I fell silent. Anything else I could have said would just be repeats. We sat together in the quiet for a while, our bond having grown stronger.

I nodded toward his mug. "So, you want another?"

"No, I should get home," he said and stood. "Just wanted to make sure you were okay."

"I am," I said. "I'll swing by soon so she can see for herself."

"You do that." He pulled his keys out and rattled them in his hand. "Everything will work out. Just have a little faith."

"I'll try," I said and watched him walk to his truck.

I returned to my plans and watched a flock of birds fly under the afternoon sky. I felt blessed to have friends who cared enough to offer themselves during a difficult time. It made it easier to call this place home. It was nice to sit in my own backyard and enjoy nature. Having lived in town all of my life, I never really had the opportunity. I continued to sit until the sun painted the sky with brilliant color. I imagined Brooke held the brush and was telling me not to worry. After twilight fell, I went inside and made a drink. I glanced out my window and saw my reflection. I resolved to move on again, and make the best of it.

CHAPTER TWENTY

The young woman sat across from me in a small conference room. She was plain, but not unattractive. She dressed modestly and folded her hands in her lap. Her dress was old-fashioned, and she wore no jewelry. Her manner reminded me of New Hope, and I wondered if she was religious, but didn't ask.

I scanned her résumé and pretended to be interested in it. The truth was, she was only the fourth person since I had started who had brought one to an interview. She had little work experience, but had volunteered at a few places, and had recently graduated from college.

I laid the résumé on the table and chatted with her a while to see how her voice sounded. It was confident and pleasant. I hired her. She was a good fit, and it didn't hurt that she wasn't bad to look at.

"Well," I said. "You're hired. Come in on Monday and we'll get you started."

"Thank you." She stood, shook my hand, and left.

I watched her walk to her car from the window. She wasted no time leaving, but didn't seem to hurry. I scooped up the paperwork and put it in a manila folder and headed back to the floor.

I stood at the doorway and took in the bustle of the employees. Everyone was busy, and I couldn't help but feel proud of what we had accomplished. The company had given the go-ahead with my expansion ideas and we had moved into the new building a few weeks ago. We had finally just settled in. The building had a large open space I called the Stage where I'd sometimes sit and watch the floor, and there was a decent break room with a kitchenette. Below the Stage, the floor had enough room for fifty cubicles, and offices were around the perimeter. I kept a couch in the office I claimed. It also had a private bathroom with a shower. Sometimes I slept there if I worked late, though I didn't make it a habit.

We had grown to thirty employees, and consistently had the best numbers in the company. I liked to think it was because I treated my people well and created a variety of scripts for different situations, but really, it was the people who deserved the credit.

I got Jamie's attention and motioned for her to come see me. She held up a finger, and I went to my office and checked on our stats while I waited for her to get off the phone. She came through my door a few minutes later with her usual bright smile.

"What's up, Boss?"

I pinched the bridge of my nose. "I really wish you guys wouldn't call me that."

Her grin widened. "I know, but it's fun to watch your reaction."

I let out a sigh. I knew that no matter how many times I asked, she'd keep doing it. She was one of my best account managers, so I tried to ignore it. "Anyway, I hired a new girl and would like you to get her set up and train her."

"Sure, no problem," she said. "Was it the girl who just left?"

"How did you know?" I asked.

"I thought you might interview today, so I had a peek."

I shook my head. "How do you manage to get any real work done?"

"I'm good," she said with a shrug.

"She's starting Monday," I said. "I think she'll catch on quick."

"She's cute too, huh?" She winked.

"You trying to get me sued?" I asked.

She laughed. "Relax, Boss. While I'm training, I can drop a word. You can't get sued then."

"No, Jamie, I'm sure she's not the type."

"Are you sure?"

"Yes," I said. "While I appreciate your concern, I'm not here to pick up dates."

"Just looking out for you, Boss."

I glared at her and sighed. "Just make sure she gets acclimated."

"Sure thing," she snapped a salute. "By the way, I got a deal with the hotel where my sister works. They're going to order for all their hotels."

"That's great," I said, glad for the change of subject. Hotels were lucrative. "How many?"

"Eight, but they're getting more," she said. "It's a pretty big deal."

I calculated the possibilities in my head. "Fantastic. You give them a break?"

"Ten percent for anything over a thousand," she said. "The smallest has about fifty rooms. I should clear at least five grand a month."

I nodded. "Ten percent's good."

The phone rang.

"Give me a second," I said, then picked it up.

"Ryan! What're you doing?" Scott shouted over a lot of background noise.

"I'm at work." I motioned for Jamie to hold on a little longer.

"Did you forget?" Scott asked.

"Forget what?" I glanced at my calendar and saw the note scrawled on today's date. "Oh shit, dude."

Jamie looked at me with surprise, and I mouthed, "I'm sorry."

"I can be there in...half an hour?" I said. "Hell, I can't believe I forgot."

"'S okay, bro. I can sit in the coffee shop and ogle the girls." He tried to sound nonchalant, but I could tell he was annoyed.

"I'll be there as soon as I can." I hung up the phone and looked at Jamie. "Jamie, I'm proud of you. All of you. Go make some more money. I've got to go right now."

"Everything okay?" she asked with a grin.

"Fine. We'll talk later."

"Sure thing, Boss," she said and left my office.

I shut down my system and glanced through my window onto the floor. Most of the people looked as if they were winding down for the weekend. I found Chuck and asked him to lock up, then rushed to the airport, angry with myself for forgetting Scott was coming today.

☙

We got to my place, and he grabbed his bag from the backseat. He stretched as he looked around. "Man, I hate flying. Nice place."

"Thanks," I said. "Look, I'm sorry for forgetting."

"You don't have to keep saying it. It's cool," he said. "I don't like flying, but I like to hang out at airports. Great place to pick up girls."

I laughed. "Did you pick up any?"

"Nah," he said. "I didn't want to hook up and leave you hanging."

"Sure. I bet you were beating them off."

I showed him around the place, and then we ordered in a pizza and found a mindless action flick on TV. It felt just as it did when we were kids.

"I never expected you to have a place like this, man," Scott said during a lull in the movie. "It's a little big for one guy though, don't you think?"

"I didn't intend to be here by myself forever."

"That's right. I wasn't thinking."

"It's okay."

"Hey, it's good to see you finally," he said. "You miss home at all?"

"Sometimes, but this is home now."

"It's different."

"A little. I'm glad I moved, though I wish it were different. I never expected all of this."

"All of what?"

"The house, the job, everything." I didn't say it, but he knew what I meant.

"You didn't get the job here. You moved after."

"I kind of did. If I hadn't found Angie, I wouldn't have considered it. Probably."

Scott rolled his eyes. "Come on."

"I know it's stupid. I'm happy for her, but honestly? Sometimes I still wish it were me."

Scott groaned. "Why doesn't this surprise me? But at least you're friends."

"I know."

"Look, Ryan. I know you've had a hard time losing Brooke."

I couldn't speak, so I just nodded.

"Don't be afraid to move on. You did it once and were happy."

"Look where it got me," I said.

"Hey, life's not always fair. Just don't wait another twenty years to be happy again. Life's too short."

"I have friends," I said. "I get out."

"That's good."

"Let's not talk about that shit. We'll have fun this weekend. I got tickets to a hockey game. We'll leave earlier so I can show you around."

Scott gasped. "Hockey? In Iowa? Places to go?"

"They're not the Panthers, but it's still hockey," I said. "And there's lots of things to do around here."

"I'm surprised," he said. "We going to hit a corn festival?"

"Hey, it's about perception. There's just as much to do here as in Tulsa. Maybe more."

I finished a beer, cracked open another, and turned back to the movie. We hadn't missed any important plot points.

❦

The next morning, Scott helped me with my workshop, which was very close to being finished. Later, we headed into the city, where I showed him a few places I had discovered before we went to the hockey game. I hadn't been to one here yet. It was a lot of fun, and we were surprised at how much we cared they won. The next day we ate a late breakfast at my favorite diner and then stopped by Angie and Bill's. I really didn't want to, but Scott insisted on saying hello. He reminisced with Angie, talked country music with Bill, and let Eva and Lily talk him into a tea party. He cracked a few jokes about me, which I ignored.

It was an interesting reunion, and I was thankful Scott said nothing inappropriate, though I didn't expect him to. We finally wrapped it up and said our goodbyes, and then I took him to the airport. It was bittersweet. I already missed my friend and didn't want the weekend to end.

Scott turned down the radio. "Thanks for having me down."

"Sure," I said. "We'll do it again whenever you want."

"You were right," he said after a moment.

"About?"

"She hasn't changed."

"Nope." I wondered where he was going with it.

"I don't know what drugs you put in their drinks, but they like you."

"What the Hell?" I said. "You doubt people can like me?"

"No, but..." He laughed.

"What's so funny?"

"Hell, you are," he said.

"Why?"

"Seriously, dude. Who picks up and moves across multiple states and becomes best friends with his old girlfriend and her husband?"

"I'm sure lots of people do."

"No way," he said. "Just you, but it doesn't matter. I'm just glad you're doing okay."

"Why wouldn't I be?"

He punched me on the arm. "I know you. Didn't want to see you get in a rut and become complacent. Life's not going to wait on you."

"You keep saying that."

Scott looked over at me, and I could tell he had something on his mind, but I kept quiet and waited for him to say it.

"Remember, she's a married woman."

"What are you talking about?" I asked, but I knew.

"Look, Ryan. I know you still feel for her," he said. "Even after all this other shit."

"We're just friends, Scott," I said.

"Sure, and I know you're not going to fuck things up. Just be careful."

"You got me wrong." I knew he was coming from a good place, but it still kind of irked me. "I'm not gonna do anything."

"Just saying."

"I'm not," I repeated and turned the radio back on.

At the airport, I went with him to see him off. We didn't bother with extended goodbyes. We never had to. They called his flight, and he started toward the gate. He stopped and turned to me.

"No hard feelings?" he said.

I shook my head. "It's good. No worries."

"All right," he said. "Catch you later."

I nodded and then headed home. I thought about our weekend together. It had been as familiar as when we were kids. He was right. Life was short, and I realized nothing in the past was very long ago. But I had already started trying to look ahead and forge a new life. Though I wasn't sure I had convinced him, he really had nothing to worry about.

CHAPTER TWENTY-ONE

The weather report on the radio said rain was inevitable. I looked out my workshop window to double-check. The clouds were thick and dark, so it looked like they might be right. I went back to my work, finishing up a set of shelves for the girls. They had a shelf made of cheap press-board, but I wanted them to have something nice to put their storybooks and toys in. I stepped back and looked over the shelves and felt the satisfaction of having a space to tinker around in. It reminded me of helping my father in his wood shop when I was a boy. I already had several projects going in anticipation of Christmas.

I switched off the radio, bored with the incessant chatter, and put on a Therapy? CD. I sang along while I sanded down the wood and prepped it for the vibrant pink paint I had already picked out. I glanced at my watch and wrapped up my work. It was Bill's birthday, and I planned to take them all out to lunch to celebrate. I covered the shelves and grabbed the oversized paddle I had made Bill as a joke and locked up.

On the way to their house, I noticed the weather had started to clear, and was relieved it might not rain after all. I pulled into their driveway and parked next to the space where Bill's truck should have been. I assumed he was on a call and hoped he would be back in time for lunch.

Angie opened the door. "What in the world do you have?"

I held up the paddle. "For Bill. Later, you can give him his birthday licks."

She shook her head and laughed. "He'll love it."

"Is it Daddy?" Eva yelled from the living room.

"No, sweetie, it's just Ryan."

"Just Ryan?" I huffed. "I'm hurt."

"Oh hush." She swatted at me. "Get in so I can close the door."

"Where's Bill?"

"He got called out early." She looked at the clock on the wall. "I thought he'd be home by now, but I haven't heard from him. It was probably a big one."

"Man, it must suck getting called to a fire on your birthday."

"Yeah, but he loves it," she said. "I'm used to it, but I still worry every time he's called."

"I'm sure he's fine."

"I'm sorry he's not here yet."

"There's no hurry," I said.

I sat down at the end of the couch with the girls. "What're you doing?"

"Lookin' at pictures," Lily said without looking up.

"Pictures of what?" I asked.

"Mommy and Daddy and when I was a little baby."

"And when I was a little kid," Eva added.

"You're still a little kid," I pointed out.

"Nuh-uh, I'm a big girl now."

"You're right." I tousled her hair. "Can I see some pictures with you?"

"Okay." Eva got up and made room for me to sit between them.

I held the album on my lap while they flipped through the pages and talked about each picture.

"I'm going to finish up in the kitchen," Angie said. "Don't let them annoy you."

The girls looked at her, and I smiled. "They don't annoy me. I love looking at pictures of people I don't know."

"Sure you do." She left me alone with the girls, who chattered happily about whatever flitted into their minds.

Fifteen minutes later, we had exhausted the album, and the girls argued about what to do next.

The doorbell rang.

Lily looked towards the door. "Is that Daddy?"

"Daddy don't push the doorbell," Eva explained with her mother's inflections. "He just comes in."

"I hope it's not those Mormons again," Angie muttered as she walked by.

I chuckled. "You have them here too?"

She ignored me. The girls gave me a "how should we know" look.

I heard the door open, and shortly after Angie gasped, "Oh God."

There were other voices, but I couldn't make out what they were saying.

Angie came back into the living room, her face emotionless. "Ryan, could you take the girls in the back and put on a video for them?"

I nodded and stood. "Come on, kiddos. Let's go find something to watch."

"But I wanna look at more pictures," Lily complained.

"Take them with you." Angie's voice was uncharacteristically harsh.

The girls huffed and trudged to the back. Lily clutched the photo album to her chest. I followed, but kept looking back at Angie and tried to discern what was the matter, but said nothing. I knew something wasn't right, but it wasn't my place, or the time, to ask.

"What's wrong with Mommy?" Eva asked as we reached the family room. She had seen what I had, but I didn't have any answers to give her.

"I'm sure she's okay. Do you want to watch something?"

She thought a moment. "I don't know."

I started to ask Lily, but she had already settled into a chair and was looking at pictures again, quietly talking to herself.

"Your sister's got something to do," I said to Eva.

"Okay." She sighed and went to pick something out.

I sat down while she found a video and put it in. She crawled into the chair with me and settled in to watch.

I tried to get comfortable, but it wasn't easy. Distracted with what might be going on, I kept looking back toward the living room. I worried about Angie and hoped it wasn't anything bad, but I feared it was.

"I'm hungry," Lily said after a few minutes.

"Me too," I said. "We'll eat soon, okay?"

"When my daddy gets home?" she asked.

"That's right," I said, but I wasn't sure.

"Be quiet," Eva growled. "I'm trying to hear TV."

"Yes, your majesty," I said, but she failed to recognize the sarcasm.

☙

"Ryan?"

Angie stood in the doorway. I turned to her. The rawness in her voice and puffy eyes told me something was wrong. Eva had nodded off, so I gently lifted her and got up.

"Where are you going?" Eva mumbled.

"Nowhere. I'll be back," I said, though her eyes had grown heavy again.

Lily slumped in her chair, her head cocked at an odd angle. The photo album had slipped off her lap and onto the floor.

"The girls are having a little nap," I whispered. "What's going on?"

She didn't answer, just turned and went back into the living room, and I followed her. There wasn't a trace of the visitors who had been here. She sat on the couch, placed her head in her hands and sobbed.

I sat down with her and placed my hand on her shoulder. "Angie, talk to me."

I felt her shake, and with each sob, she tried to stay quiet. She began to speak, but choked on the words. I didn't push, only waited until she was ready.

After a few minutes, she looked up at me. Her face was blotchy, and her eyes were red. "Ryan?"

"Yeah?"

"Bill…" She took a gasping breath. "Bill's…gone."

"Gone?" I said, but I understood.

She looked toward the room where her daughters slept peacefully, completely unaware their world had changed. "What am I going to tell them?"

"The truth," I said. "That's all you can do."

"But how?" she asked, but I had no answer.

"Did they tell you what happened?"

She nodded. She pulled a tissue from a box on the end table and dabbed her eyes.

"You don't have to talk about it," I said.

She crumbled the tissue in her hands, then straightened it. "He went back in the house. To save a little boy."

"Geez," I whispered.

"They couldn't get to him. It..." She blew her nose and let the tissue drop to the floor.

"I'm sorry, Angie."

She shook her head, grabbed another tissue, and fisted it in her hand. "He's thirty-nine today. We'll be married ten years next month."

I let her talk and simply listened. I had no idea what to do, or what to say.

Lily shuffled into the room and rubbed her eyes. "Mommy, I'm hungry."

Angie dabbed at her face quickly and sat up.

Lily leaned on Angie's shoulder and looked up at her. "Is Daddy home yet?"

Angie pulled Lily to her and held her tight.

She took a breath and kissed the top of her head. "Go tell your sister to come here."

"Okay." Lily slowly headed back to the family room.

She glanced back at her mother a couple of times, and Angie tried to smile at her. Lily's expression said she knew something was going on, but didn't understand what it was.

"I'm scared, Ryan," Angie whispered after Lily disappeared through the doorway.

"I know," I said. "You'll be okay."

"I'm not so sure."

I didn't answer. What could I have said to make it any better?

Lily returned, pulling Eva along behind her, and announced, "I brought my sister."

247

"Mommy, what's wrong?" Eva asked. The energy in the room had changed, and she had felt it.

Lily went back to her mother's side and tugged on her shirt. "Mommy, why isn't Daddy home yet?"

I realized then how strong a woman Angie had become as she sat there, able to hold back her emotions. She allowed only a single tear to fall as she prepared to give her little girls the first bit of tragic news they would get in their young lives.

Angie took both their hands and guided them in front of her. She looked at them and sighed.

"Mommy?" Eva's voice trembled.

"Girls, your daddy's not coming home," she said softly.

"Why come?" Lily whined. "Does he still love us?"

"Oh, honey, your daddy will always love you. He's..."

The girls waited for her to finish, but they had picked up on her emotions.

"Your daddy's gone to heaven," she said, then glanced at me as if for approval.

I just shrugged. I didn't know what I would have said. How do you explain death to a child? I wished there were an easier way, but one hadn't been invented yet.

Eva realized the implication first.

"Daddy died?" Her voice was small as it registered.

Lily looked at Eva, then at her mother. Angie closed her eyes and nodded almost imperceptibly.

"Nuh-uh, you're teasing!" Lily shouted and ran through the house, calling for her daddy.

I heard the door to the garage open. Eva chewed her lip and stared at her mother. Lily returned, out of breath. She thrust out her chin, put her fists on her hips, and scowled.

"Where is my daddy?" Lily shouted.

"He's gone, honey," Angie said in a hoarse whisper. She gathered her children to her and cried. She clutched at them as if she would lose them too if she dared to let go.

I felt helpless. I was an intruder into one of the most private moments of a family's life. Raw emotion filled the room, and the girls began to cry from the sheer intensity of it without understanding why, or what their future might be.

I wanted to say I understood, but I didn't. I had suffered loss, but this was wholly different.

"Maybe I should go now," I said.

Angie shook her head and mouthed, "Stay, please."

"Do you want me to get you some lunch?" I asked.

"I can't possibly eat."

"The girls should eat something," I said. "I could get something and bring it back."

"Yeah, okay. Are you hungry?" she asked the girls.

They both nodded.

"Can I have cookies?" Lily asked.

Angie smiled weakly and pushed Lily's hair from her eyes. "Maybe later."

"I'll get some burgers, or something," I said.

"Okay," Angie said.

"You want something?"

"No."

"You sure?"

She nodded.

I picked up my jacket.

"Be careful," she said.

"I will." I let myself out and wished it was all of us going for the lunch I had planned just a few short hours ago.

❦

I stayed with Angie and the girls all day until late evening. I had kept the girls occupied while Angie made phone calls to family and took care of a few things. The shock had not worn off, and there was almost an expectation Bill would show up and apologize for being late.

"I should go so you can get some rest," I said.

"You're fine," she said. "Thanks for being here, Ryan. It's been a big help."

"No problem."

"Okay, girls," she called to Eva and Lily. "Let's get ready for bed. Go brush your teeth, and I'll be there in a bit to tuck you in."

"I want Daddy to tuck me in." Lily pouted and sucked her thumb.

"He can't. He's at Jesus' house," Eva said and looked at Angie for confirmation.

Angie nodded and brushed a loose strand of hair behind her ear. It was a nervous habit I recognized. "Take your sister with you and make sure she brushes."

"Okay, Mommy," Eva said.

She took Lily's hand, and we watched them as they disappeared down the hallway.

"I wish there were more I could do," I said.

"You're doing enough, Ryan," she said. "Give me a moment to get them into bed."

"Sure."

I went into the kitchen and made a pot of coffee, then sat at the table to wait.

"You made coffee," Angie said as she came into the kitchen. She poured herself a cup and sat with me. "Sorry it took so long. They kept asking questions. How can I answer them if I can't answer my own?"

"You're doing fine," I said.

"I don't feel fine." She fell silent.

We sipped coffee together in the stillness. I was afraid to speak, worried I'd say the wrong thing.

"How do you handle this?" she asked.

"I don't know. I can't imagine what you're going through right now."

"You lost Brooke."

"It's different."

"It's not," she said.

"It is," I insisted. "We didn't live together for ten years. We didn't have a family. Not yet."

"I guess, but you still lost someone you love."

"Yeah, but..." I didn't finish. I understood what she was saying, but I couldn't see it as the same thing. "Anyway, whatever you need, I'm here for you."

"I need my husband. My kids need their father," she said without bitterness.

I got up and poured myself a cup of coffee.

"Don't think I'm taking it out on you," she said.

I turned to her. "I don't."

"This is...we were married for ten years," she said. "You get used to routine, and...and I don't know what to do now."

"I get it."

"Bill always thought of others before himself. He's..."

"You don't have to talk about it, Angie."

"No, I do," she whispered. "He gave his life to try to save someone else. I didn't even get to say goodbye."

"I don't think anyone does," I said.

She pushed her mug away. The coffee had grown cold. "He believed in God. I respected him for it. A lot of people say they do, but they don't live like it. Like those people when we were kids."

"Yeah," I said. I knew exactly who she was talking about. I could see their faces in my mind and remembered how they treated people when they thought no one was looking.

"I'm not sure I believe in God," she admitted.

"Why?" I asked.

We had never talked about God, or religion. Not even when we were in school. It had never come up. It was something we assumed and took for granted, almost like breathing. To hear her admit a lack of belief came as a surprise, but it didn't bother me. How could it, when I didn't believe myself?

"I don't know," she said. "You see beauty in the world. Mountains, the oceans. The stars in the sky. It's so big, you can't help but think there's something that made it all. It doesn't feel random."

She took a sip of the cold coffee and cringed.

"More?" I asked.

She shook her head. "Then there's war, hunger, disease. Then you wonder what kind of God would allow it."

"It's an age-old question," I said. "But a fair one."

She laughed shortly. "Bill would tell me not to be silly and change the subject."

I smiled. "I can see him doing that."

"I just worry about the girls. It hasn't sunk in for me, much less them," she said. "The girls loved their daddy with their whole hearts. He was Superman to them."

"They'll be okay, Angie. Kids are resilient," I said. "They'll follow your cue."

"It's scary."

"Sure, but you're a strong woman," I said. "You always were."

"I don't know how I'll repay you," she said.

"No, you've been there for me. Bill too. My move, Brooke. Everything. If anything, I owe you."

"Let's call it even," she said with a tired smile.

"Even. I'm going to head out," I said and got up. "Unless you need me to stay?"

"I think we'll be okay," she said.

"Okay. Call if you need anything. I'm here for you."

"Thank you." She got up and walked me to the door.

She hugged me warmly. "Thank you for being you. For being here."

CHAPTER TWENTY-TWO

A week later, the Episcopal Church held Bill's funeral. The church was large, but his family, friends, and a sea of firefighters in uniform filled it. I saw Angie and the girls in the front pew sitting with her mother and Aaron. Bill's mother and sister had flown in from Tennessee and sat with them.

Two firefighters stood on either side of Bill's casket, draped in an American flag. His portrait, in full uniform, had been set up behind the casket. Soft music played quietly as people found seats. I was aware of the snug fit of my suit as I sat down in a back pew, and the service began soon after. Several people spoke, including firefighters who spoke about Bill's kindness and courage. They shared some humorous stories, which brought a little laughter to the solemn occasion.

Bill's sister, Beth, sang his favorite hymn, then a minister spoke briefly about a life of service and Bill's example of a Christ-like attitude, which he implored others to follow.

After the minister spoke, a memorial video played. It showed Bill as a child and followed him as he grew and closed with him surrounded by his family. I learned about the man I had called a friend and felt a profound respect for him. Bill was a man who lived by his principles and did not compromise. I understood how Angie had fallen in love with him, and the devastation she must feel now that he was gone. I could see his qualities in his daughters, and knew that through them, he would live on.

"Hi, Uncle Ryan," the girls said when I found them after the service.

"Hi, girls," I said, then asked Angie, "How are you?"

"Fine," she said. "Thanks for coming."

She looked as if she hadn't slept all week.

"It was a nice service," I said. "They went all out."

"The department arranged everything. Bill would have liked it," she said. "Are you coming to the cemetery?"

"Yeah, I'll be there," I said.

I hugged her and the girls and watched them leave. A couple of firefighters escorted them to a limousine waiting at the front of the church.

I stopped by the casket before I left. Two firemen still stood at the casket. I looked at the portrait of Bill and said a quiet goodbye. I felt sad for his family, but also for myself. Bill was my very good friend, and I had lost him too.

The procession, led by a fire engine, drove to the cemetery where he would be laid to rest. The graveside service was an elaborate ceremony. The girls took it all in, but Angie's eyes never left the casket.

I looked over at them occasionally. I noted Angie had made another exception and wore a new dress. The girls seemed to hold together well and faced the tragedy bravely. It was a tough job for how young they were. Bill would have been proud of them.

After the last prayer, the honor guard folded the flag on the casket and presented it to Angie. She thanked them and held it against her chest.

Her tears fell freely as firefighters stood at attention and saluted while Bill's casket was lowered into the ground.

The firefighters dropped their salute and a crackle filled the air.

"Dispatch to Firefighter William Tidman..."

Silence.

"Dispatch to Firefighter William Tidman..."

Silence.

"Firefighter Tidman is not responding. Firefighter Tidman has answered his final alarm. He served the community with honor and dedication. We thank him for his service and sacrifice. May he rest in peace. Dispatch clear."

After a moment, two firefighters approached Angie and the girls, spoke briefly, and led them away from Bill's grave.

People went back to their cars, while some stayed and talked. Aaron walked toward me, stopping only to say a quick hello to a couple of people.

"Hey, Ryan," he said. "Glad you could be here."

"It was the least I could do."

He sighed and looked around. "I can't believe it. It doesn't seem real to me, so I can't imagine how Angie feels. Bill was a good guy."

"He was," I said.

"I wanted to say thanks for looking after them."

"It's no problem," I said. "Bill was my friend too."

"Yeah, he had that way with people." He tugged at his jacket. "You ought to come up and hang out sometime."

"Sure, Aaron. That'd be good."

"Cool," he said. "Angie asked me to come by for dinner later. Maybe I'll see you there."

"Maybe."

"Okay. See ya."

He went and stopped to talk to someone else, and I looked for Angie. I found her with someone and waited until they had finished before I approached.

"How you feeling?" I asked and gave her a quick hug.

"You asked that already."

"I know," I said. "I can't help it."

"It's going to take some getting used to, but I'll be okay."

"I didn't know we had that many firemen," I said.

"A lot of them are from other departments. They go to funerals for firemen who died on duty."

"Even volunteers?" I asked.

"Yeah. They treat them as if they're full-fledged firemen. They all came to pay their respects."

"That's nice."

"Yeah, but it doesn't bring him back, or answer the girls' questions," she said. "The church also offered to help. People are too, but..." she sighed and shook her head. "Here I am, blathering on like an idiot. I'm sorry."

"No, it's okay. You can blather all you want," I said. "I never thought you were an idiot."

"Thanks. Do you want to come by for dinner?"

"Sure, I can come," I said.

"People have brought so much food. The girls want to see you too."

"I'd like to see them too."

"You should know," Angie started, then lowered her voice to a whisper, "I think Eva's got a crush on you."

"Oh, Hell, the poor girl has no taste," I said with a laugh.

"She thinks her tastes are impeccable."

"I'm flattered, but it's just a phase."

"Indeed you should be, even if it is only a phase," she said. "So, you're coming?"

"Sure. I wouldn't want to disappoint anyone. I'd like to get out of this suit first, so about six?"

"Six is fine." She turned toward someone calling her name. "That's Beth. I should go talk to her, then rescue my mother from the kids. I'll see you later. Don't forget."

"I won't," I said.

I saw the girls with their grandmother. They stood quietly beside her while she spoke with some people. She didn't look like she needed rescuing. I looked at Bill's grave and said another goodbye, then got in my car and wove my way through the crowded cemetery. I was anxious to get out of my clothes and find something to distract me until dinner.

∞

Angie had invited several people to dinner. Her mother, Bill's sister and his mother, Aaron, and the minister. We all chatted while we ate, but I sensed Bill's sister and mother were uncomfortable with me there. I didn't know if they knew my relationship to the family, but they were civil.

The conversation moved to Bill, and we shared our memories of him. It was a good time, but also bittersweet. After everyone had their fill, there was still a lot of food left over, and everyone took some with them. Even then, Angie still had enough. She wouldn't have to cook for at least a few days.

Aaron stayed and played with Eva and Lily until their bedtime. They were thrilled when he tucked them in, strummed his guitar and sang to them until they fell asleep. I helped Angie clean up and let her talk. I thought it was important to let her get it out so she could start to heal, but I found it helped me heal as well.

Aaron walked into the kitchen and leaned his guitar against the pantry door. "Them two's gonna be groupies when they grow up."

"Watch your mouth," Angie snapped. "No daughter of mine is going to follow any band around. Even if it is yours."

"Just kidding, Sis," Aaron laughed and kissed her cheek.

She wiped it away with the back of her hand and left a streak of dish soap across her face.

"That's a good look for you." I handed her a towel.

She glared at us, swiped at her face and threw the towel back at me.

Aaron backed up to the entryway. "I think it's time for me to go."

"Perhaps I'll go with you," I said, then looked at Angie. "Do you mind?"

"I'm not your mother. Do what you want," she huffed, but quickly smiled.

"Thanks," I laid the towel on the counter next to the dish rack and went outside with Aaron.

"Thanks again for being there for her," he said after we got to his car.

"She's still my friend, you know. I want to be there for them."

"She's hurting really bad, man."

"I know, but she seems to handle it okay."

"She won't tell you," he said. "She'll just hide it away and act like it doesn't bother her. Don't let her fool you. Take it easy, okay?"

"I remember," I said. "Don't worry, I won't hurt her."

"You're a good dude." He slapped me on the back. "When are you going to come check us out?"

"Your band?"

"Yeah."

"When I get time," I said. "I've been busy with work."

"All right, man. Take care and don't be a stranger."

"I won't."

He drove off and I went back in to say goodbye to Angie.

"Take some of this with you." She handed me a bag of leftovers she had wrapped up.

"Thanks." I took them without argument, but didn't really want it. I had eaten so much of it already that the thought of another day or two more of it made me almost nauseous.

As I drove home, I realized that my world was in flux and I wasn't alone. It was a time when I needed to have friends and be a friend. If we could all get through this time intact, then we just might get through anything.

CHAPTER TWENTY-THREE

Chuck knocked and poked his head through my door. "Hey, you busy?"

I motioned for him to wait while I finished up a call, and he settled into a chair and flipped through a coffee-stained notebook.

I hung up the phone. "What can I do for you?"

"We got Heartland Hotels." He beamed. "They're the biggest chain in the region."

"I'm aware of who they are, Chuck," I said and poured a cup of coffee. "Who got it?"

"Corrine," he answered. "She's good."

"She is. I knew she was angling for it," I said. "It's what, her seventh big account?"

"Eighth, but who's counting?"

"Want coffee?" I asked.

He thought for a moment, then nodded. "Maybe a little. She's not shy about getting referrals. Most of these guys never ask."

I pushed a half-filled mug toward him. He slipped his notebook into his pocket and took the mug.

"Okay, Chuck. What's going on, really?" I asked. "You know I keep up with the floor. I'd have known about this whether or not you told me."

"Sure. She would have told you," he said. "By the way, how was your date?"

And there it was.

"It wasn't a date."

"You took her out, didn't you?"

"So?"

"So it's a date."

"I take you out too," I said. "Are those dates?"

"That's different."

"No, it isn't."

"Sure it is. You don't want to sleep with me."

I took a slow sip of my coffee and looked at him over the rim. "Yeah? Who says?"

He frowned. "I hope you're screwing with me."

I raised my eyebrows.

Chuck blushed and fumbled his mug. Some coffee sloshed out and spattered his shirt. "Oh, Christ, bad choice of words."

"You know better, Chuck. She's a nice girl, but nothing's gonna happen there. Don't get jealous."

"Yeah," he laughed. "I also wanted to check in on you. What with your friend and all."

"Time's passed since then, Chuck."

"I know, but—"

"I'm happy you're concerned, but it's not necessary."

"People still talk about it."

"They're going to," I said. "Worry about his wife and kids if you need to worry. Let's not talk about it anymore."

"Sure, okay." Chuck wiped at his shirt.

"What do you think about pizzas for lunch on Friday?" I asked.

"Sounds great," Chuck said. "You know, most of us only work as hard as we do because you've made it fun. Bringing in lunches and stuff."

"Fun?" I slapped the top of my desk. "You've got to be shitting me. Work can't be fun. I should rethink a few things."

Chuck laughed. "Admit it. You have fun too."

"Yeah, I have fun," I said. "Now get the hell out of my office and find out what everyone wants on the pies."

"Sure thing, Boss." Chuck snapped a salute and marched out.

I got up and went to my door and looked out at the floor. I listened to the hum of the chatter as they worked. They felt like family. I had met some of their families and listened to their problems. I didn't know all of them well, but my open-door policy let them know I would accommodate them, within reason. None of them took advantage of my kindness. Ones who did, didn't seem to last long. I missed Tulsa, but I had grown to love it here. If I went back, I would probably miss it here more.

I sat back down at my desk and tapped a few keys to monitor one of Corrine's calls. She had an easy rapport with people, and I understood why she did so well. I liked her voice. I had recorded a few of her calls and used them in training.

Chuck had read too much into the relationship between Corrine and me. I had taken her out a few times. She was a nice girl, but we were simply friends. I knew it could never work out, because she reminded me too much of Tina.

I glanced at the clock. It was only three o'clock. The day had seemed to drag. Probably because I skipped lunch, but I had to finish up a report the home office wanted on some new marketing I had been working on. Though it was tedious, I reminded myself the weekend was here, and I had made plans to hang out with Aaron. He wanted me to jam with him, and I had put him off long enough. Playing along with the stereo at home was fun, but it wasn't the same as doing it with other people. I looked forward to it. I took a break, grabbed a cup of coffee, and then sat down to finish the report. The office wanted it by the end of the day, but as long as I didn't get distracted, it wouldn't be impossible.

⌘

I met Aaron at a small dive, and we grabbed a bite to eat before I followed him to his place. We pulled into the back of a dilapidated building in the Sherman Hill section of Des Moines. It might have been nice. Once.

"Here we are," he shouted as I got out of my car.

I shoved my hands in my pockets and pulled my jacket tight against the chill. "It looks like a dump."

He didn't answer. He opened the large, heavy door with his key, and disarmed the alarm system before he let me inside.

"You have this thing armed?" I asked. "Who the Hell's going to break in?"

"Looks can deceive, my friend," he said.

We walked into a large room cluttered with furniture and band equipment, some of which looked like it had survived a tour with The Who.

"You live here?" I asked.

"I live upstairs with the other guys. We rehearse down here and record sometimes. I thought we might jam out a bit. See if you still have some chops."

I laughed. "Some. Let's do it."

He flicked a switch. The fluorescent bulbs flickered and filled the room with a low hum.

The room was set up with a drum kit behind a plexiglass shield, and several guitars hung on the walls and sat on stands. Amplifiers and cabinets were pushed against the walls. The floor was littered with pedals and cables leading to a large soundboard on one side of the room.

"Wow," I said. "Wouldn't expect this from the outside."

"Told ya," Aaron said.

"How'd you get this place?"

"Our bass player found it. He's buddies with the owner. He lets us stay. All we gotta do is pay utilities." Aaron picked up a beat-up Gibson and flicked on an amp. He tuned it up and played a few licks. "You still play drums?"

"I hadn't for a while," I admitted. "I bought another set after I moved here. Been playing along with the radio, mostly."

"Cool. What'd you get?"

"Found a set of Exports someone was selling. A five piece."

"Rock on. I remember you had some Ludwigs."

"Yeah. I had them since I was a kid. I wish I never let them go."

"Why I don't get rid of my guitars. Not even the crappy ones. No regrets," he said. "Get back there and bang on those and we'll jam."

"I probably shouldn't." I suddenly felt shy. Drummers could be particular about their kits, and it was a nice one.

"It's cool," Aaron said. "Tod won't mind."

"You sure?" I was reluctant, but I really wanted to play them.

"Sure, go on."

"All right then." I took a seat on the throne and picked up a set of well-worn sticks. They felt awkward, a little bigger than what I was used to. I tapped on the heads and worked the pedals. It sounded good.

"Pound the shit out of 'em," Aaron shouted and started the opening riff to Back in Black.

Aaron was in his element. He segued into different songs, and I tried to follow along. He never stopped. Fifteen minutes later, a man dressed in cut-off jeans and a ratty Grateful Dead T-shirt walked in. He looked to be about sixty, with a frizzy gray beard. He had a receding hairline, but wore a long, thin ponytail. We stopped playing.

"No man," he said. "Keep going."

"What's up, Smokey?" Aaron said. "Noise didn't bother you, did it?"

Smokey huffed. "No, man. Heard you start. Wanted to check it out. Ain't nothin' on TV." He looked over at me. "You get a new drummer? That's good. I didn't like the other one. He's an ass."

"No, Tod's still with us," Aaron said. "This guy's just messing around."

"Ah, that's good. I like Tod. Nice guy." Smokey pulled a joint from behind his ear and lighted it. He pulled deep, held it in, and blew it out in a heavy, gray cloud. He held the joint toward Aaron. "Want some?"

"No thanks," Aaron said.

Smokey waved the joint at me.

I shook my head.

"More for me." He took another drag and plopped onto a couch.

"Smokey's kind of our landlord," Aaron said. "He runs a head shop up front."

I'm not the least bit surprised, I thought, but said, "Hey, Smokey."

"This is my friend Ryan," Aaron said to Smokey. "He went to school with me and my sister in Oklahoma."

"Hey, where they got all the cowboys and indians. How's it hangin', man?"

"Good." I ignored the cowboy and indian comment.

"You play pretty good, man." Smokey swayed his head. "Say, where the other guys?"

"Don't know," Aaron said. "We just got back, and I wanted to show Ryan our setup. Haven't been up yet."

Aaron took the guitar off and put it back on the stand.

"Aw, you don't have to stop," Smokey said. "I was diggin' it."

"Maybe later, Smokey. I wanna catch up with my buddy."

"That's cool." Smokey pouted. "You do your thing. I could use the peace and quiet. You kids are too loud."

Aaron shook a finger at Smokey. "You're not fooling me."

"Another time." He grunted as he pushed himself up from the couch. He said to me, "You didn't sound bad."

"Thanks," I said.

Smokey disappeared, and I got out from behind the kit. I was a little disappointed we didn't play more, but it wasn't my place, or my kit.

Aaron leaned into the fridge and came up with two beers.

"Want a beer?" He tossed one to me without waiting for me to answer.

I caught it and cracked it open. Aaron took a long pull from his beer and sat down in a worn recliner. I followed his lead.

"Remember how we talked about starting a band?" he asked, and I nodded. "You ever do it?"

"A band?"

"Yeah."

"I played with some guys in college, but it didn't go anywhere," I said. "After, I just jammed with friends a few times, but didn't play much since."

"That sucks."

"Life got in the way, I guess," I said. "And I sold my Ludwig. But I got a good kit now."

"Tod has a monster," Aaron said.

I agreed.

"He uses them, though. Man, he's good." He slapped a rhythm on his leg. "You ought to come see us play. We're having an album release party at Jack's in a couple of weeks."

"An album, huh?" It didn't surprise me, but I was impressed. Hearing him play again after so many years, I noticed he had gotten really good.

"Yeah, man, but we're doing it ourselves," he said. "We don't want to give some label a chance to rip us off."

"I hear you, but don't disregard an opportunity if it comes."

"We had one already, but it seemed sleazy."

"I haven't checked out any bands," I said. "Might as well make yours the first."

"There's a lot of good bands here," Aaron said. "Jack's is a good place to start. Maybe you can drag my sister with you."

"I don't know." I tossed my empty beer into a nearby wastebasket.

"Why not? She should get out a little."

"She's not holing up, or anything," I said.

"Come on, Ryan. It doesn't have to be a date. Just listening to some music as friends."

"What about the girls?" I asked.

"She can get someone to watch them for a few hours," he countered.

"I guess it would do her some good."

Aaron leaned on his elbows. "She's good at hiding her feelings. There's a lot you don't know. We haven't seen you in a long time."

"I get it. People change."

I focused on the room. Behind all the equipment, I noticed water stains on the walls and cracks in the plaster. I couldn't help but wonder if the place was even up to code.

"At first, there was a part of me who expected things to go back the way they were. I know it's stupid."

He regarded me for a while. "You're still in love with her, huh?"

He already knew. He had always known. Though I had moved on, and had accepted how things were, there was always a part of me that loved her, and always would. I sighed and wished I had another beer.

"I guess I am."

Aaron just nodded.

"I guess she told you about how I showed up out of the blue one day."

He smiled. "She is my sister."

"I almost didn't take my job," I confessed.

"Why wouldn't you? Seems a pretty sweet gig," he said.

"I loved Tulsa. Things were okay there. If I stayed, I'd be doing the same work. I had a good relationship. I had nothing to lose."

"Why'd you take it?" he asked.

"Angie," I said. I knew, but never admitted it to anyone. I barely admitted it to myself. "The same job somewhere else? I would have turned it down."

"Even though you knew there was no chance?"

"Yeah, even though," I said. "I was going to get married. At least I hoped I was."

He winced. "I forgot. Sorry."

"It's okay," I said. "I wanted her friendship again. Everyone was happy. I still love her, true, but that doesn't mean we have to be together. Some things aren't meant to be. I'm okay with it."

I changed subjects.

"How long have you been with your band?"

"Schist's been together for five years."

I laughed. "Where'd you come up with Schist? It sounds like shit."

"Just take out two letters. I know." He shrugged. "But a schist is a metamorphic crystalline rock, not a turd. I thought it sounded cool."

"It's interesting."

"We did mostly covers until last year. Now we focus on original stuff. We've known each other for a long time." He stood, stretched out his arms and grinned widely. "I'm living my dream, man."

"Must be. This place is falling apart."

"Yeah, but the price is right."

"That's what matters." With a yawn, I stood up. "I'm happy to see you again, man, but I got to get going. I'll come to your party."

"Right on. Keep an eye on my sister. Not that she needs it, but you know..."

"Sure," I said. "Take care, man. We'll jam again another time."

"Absolutely." He walked me out. The sun had set a long time ago, and the air had grown considerably cooler.

On the way home, I thought about what Aaron had said. What were my intentions? Did I ever expect anything to happen? It was a thought, but I knew it wouldn't. Even knowing, I placed myself back in her life. She was content. What could I possibly have given her? Nothing. It came to mind that my actions might have brought on Bill's death. Maybe even Brooke's. My hidden desire to be with Angie had created a series of events to make it happen. I shuddered.

No, I thought. It's ridiculous. We have no control over what happens; it is just how life works. I will be Angie's friend. I'll be someone she can depend on, but I can't be her lover. Not now, or ever. It didn't matter how long I had dreamed of it.

CHAPTER TWENTY-FOUR

I slipped my favorite flannel over a black T-shirt and checked myself in the mirror. I had owned the flannel for such a long time. The hems were frayed, and it was worn thin, but I couldn't bring myself to get rid of it. It was my lucky shirt. The pair of jeans I had on were just as worn, with holes in the knees. My outfit wasn't something I'd consider wearing on an actual date, but this wasn't a date.

I fussed with my hair and tried to cover some of the thinness, but it proved to be too much effort. I wasn't a sixteen-year-old boy trying to impress some high school girl. It was just Angie and me going to see her brother's band play for a couple of hours as friends, but I still felt nervous.

I was making a big deal out of nothing, I thought. I ran my fingers through my hair, called it good, and picked up the keys on my way out the door.

☙

"Uncle Ryan!" Eva ran toward me. She slammed into me, and I

nearly fell over. She squeezed me as hard as she could.

I huffed. "Hello to you too, girlie. Let me go before you bust my spleen."

"What's a spleen?" she asked.

"It's a very important organ, and I want to keep it. Lemme go."

She looked up at me. "Do I have a spleen?"

"Yes," I said. "Come on now, let go."

"Okay."

She let me go, and I gave an exaggerated sigh. "I thank you, and my spleen thanks you." I patted her head.

"Where is you and Mommy going?" she asked.

"What makes you think we're going anywhere?"

I stepped inside and went to the living room while Eva trailed close behind.

"'Cause she's been getting pretty," she answered. "And Missy's coming over to babysit Lily."

"Is that so?" I smiled. It didn't escape my notice that she didn't include herself in Missy's babysitting gig.

She looked at me with doe eyes. "Can I go too?"

"Aw, you're breakin' my heart."

"Please? I like Shit too. Can I go?" She tried to bat her eyes.

It was all I could do to keep from laughing.

"'Fraid not. Maybe I'll take you in fifteen years."

"But that's forever away!" she cried. "I'll be old in that many years."

"You won't be old, just older," I said. "You don't think I'm old, do you?"

She answered with only a giggle and ran off to the back of the house.

"Is that you, Ryan?" Angie called from her bedroom.

"Yeah, it's me. I know I'm early."

"I'll be out in a minute."

"Okay," I said.

I went to the back of the house. Eva and Lily were playing on the floor with the television turned on. Nobody was paying attention to it.

"What are you doing?" I asked.

"Playing," Lily answered and went back to brushing her doll's hair.

"Sounds fun," I said. "Your doll looks pretty."

Lily nodded. "I know she is pretty."

"Missy should be here any minute," Angie said as she came into the room. "Then we can go."

"I'm not in a hurry," I said.

"Where are you going?" Eva asked. "Ryan won't tell me."

Lily looked up.

"We're going to see your Uncle Aaron play," Angie said with a sigh. She had probably told her a hundred times already.

"I want to see Uncle Aaron," Lily whined.

"Not tonight," Angie said.

"Ryan said I could go." Eva shot me a sly look.

Angie glanced over. "He did, did he?"

"Half truth," I said, and gave Eva a mock glare. "I made a date with your daughter. In fifteen years."

Eva stamped her feet. "But I'll be really old!"

"And old is the perfect time for your first date," Angie said as the doorbell rang. "That's probably Missy."

"You trying to get me in trouble, little girlie?" I grabbed her and tickled her ribs.

Eva laughed and tried to escape. Lily left her doll and jumped on my back. She wrapped her arms around my neck, and together they wrestled me to the floor.

"Who's the overgrown one?" I heard someone ask.

"Help," I shouted. "I'm being mauled by miniature cannibals!"

"I don't know..." Angie thought a moment. "Okay, girls, leave Ryan alone. I'd like to keep him in one piece."

The girls looked up and saw the chubby teenage girl with their mother. "Missy!"

They jumped up and ran to hug her.

Missy tried to pry them loose. "Don't hug me so hard."

"Am I hurting your organ?" Eva asked. "I hurted Ryan's organ."

Angie and Missy looked at me askance.

"It's not what it sounds like." I grinned and pushed myself off the floor. "I think I called it a spleen. How ya doin'?"

Missy smiled. Her braces glinted in the light. "I think my spleen's okay."

Angie shook her head. "Ryan, this is Missy. She babysits for me sometimes."

"Well, Missy," I said. "Your job should be easier. I think I wore them out."

"Thanks, but they're no trouble," she said.

"They can fool you," I said, but I could picture Missy growing up into a schoolmarm, able to handle any kid, no matter how unruly.

Angie grabbed her jacket. "Make sure they're in bed by nine and call if you need to."

"They won't be a problem." Missy looked at the girls. "We're going to have fun, aren't we?"

Eva and Lily nodded their heads enthusiastically.

"Can we play a game?" Lily asked.

"Whatever you want," Missy answered.

"Be careful what you promise them," Angie said. "Okay, girls, give your mama hugs and kisses."

She grabbed one in each arm. As they kissed her cheeks, she kissed them back and gave them a squeeze. "I love my girls so much!"

"Say hi to Uncle Aaron for me," Eva said.

"And bring us candy," Lily demanded.

"Boy, that girl is obsessed with candy," I said.

"She is," Angie said, and Missy nodded.

Angie pointed at Lily. "No candy."

"A cookie?" she asked hopefully.

"Maybe," Angie said. "If you're good."

"Okay!" Lily ran off to play with her doll again.

"The girl's relentless," I said and looked at my watch. "We should go."

"We should," Angie said, and blew the girls kisses.

I started up the car. "So you won't let her have candy, but a cookie's okay?"

"I'll give her an animal cracker," she said. "She'll be just as happy."

"I see. Doesn't take much then, does it?"

"Not for another few years," Angie said and adjusted the vent. "Eva did the same, though she wasn't as persistent as Lily."

The sky was already growing dark when we hit the highway. We didn't speak for a while and just enjoyed the quiet. The outside air was cool, and I had thrown a jacket in the back seat just in case. I still hadn't gotten used to how cold it could get here.

Angie looked out the window. She had dressed in a pair of jeans and a Schist T-shirt. It looked handmade.

"I like the shirt," I said.

She looked down at the shirt. "This? I've had it forever. A friend painted it. I thought I'd show a little support for the band."

"It's unique," I said.

"That's what I was going for." She returned to the window.

"You okay?"

"Yeah. Just thinking."

I wasn't convinced. "I'm excited to see the band. Live with an audience."

"You'll like them. They have good energy," she said. "I'm not fond of the album name, but oh well."

"You don't like 'Eat Schist?'" I asked.

"No, not really. It's crude."

"I think it's funny."

She snorted. "You would."

"I remember we talked about starting a band," I said. "Now he has, and is putting out an album."

"I'm proud of him," she said. "My dad wasn't happy, but he was always hard to please."

I agreed, but said nothing.

"Aaron's worked hard. He's happy, and the band is good."

"How come you haven't seen him play in so long?" I asked.

"Bill wasn't a fan. He's...was more of a country guy."

"He didn't let you go?" I asked.

"No, he would have, whenever I wanted," she said. "I'd rather he went with me."

I felt a little uncomfortable. Bill had been gone a few months, but he was still a big part of her life, and I knew he always would be. Her daughters were a continual reminder, especially Lily, who had his quiet seriousness. I still thought of Brooke, so I imagined it was more natural for her to think of him.

She talked about him sometimes, and I let her. It made her feel better. I still missed him too. I switched on the radio, and we kept the conversation light the rest of the way to the city.

We parked the car and walked down Court Avenue. We found a place to eat, then went to Jack's Place, where the party had already started. The band who had opened for Schist was finishing up their set, and we caught the last song. I thought they were pretty good. Their music had a classic rock sound.

We ordered drinks and sipped them while we waited for Schist to come on stage.

"I haven't had a chance to see live music yet," I shouted to Angie over the crowd.

"Wow, I thought you'd have by now," she said. "This will be a good first."

The crowd erupted as Schist came on stage.

Aaron walked up to the mike, his favorite Rickenbacker slung on his hip. He looked like the quintessential rocker in a worn leather jacket and torn jeans. He had planned his look, down to each strand of hair, but it seemed he had just rolled out of bed with a casual carelessness.

"What's up, Des Moines!" Aaron shouted, and the crowd roared. "We are Schist, and welcome to our party!"

The band started the intro to the title track.

Aaron growled into the mic, "Eat Schist!"

The band played for an hour and mixed covers, songs from their album, and a few that didn't make it on. They left the stage, and the crowd chanted for more.

Angie and I went backstage and found Aaron with the band.

"Great show," I said.

"Hey, thanks," Tod said.

"How'd you get my sister to come?" Aaron asked while he gave Angie a hug.

"Oh, God, you're all sweaty!" Angie pushed him away.

"It's rock star sweat." He chuckled. "You're lucky. Do you know how many girls would kill for this?"

"They don't want to be your sister," she said.

"Thank God!"

"You're such a pervert," she said. "I know the real you."

"You still love me." He tried to sling an arm around her shoulder.

She ducked away. "Don't count on it."

"If you guys are going to bicker, I'll go hook up with some groupies," I said. "Tell them I know the band."

"You guys are all the same," Angie muttered.

I shrugged.

We chatted with Aaron and the guys for a while. Aaron gave us a couple of CDs and T-shirts for Eva and Lily.

"We got to get going," I said. "We want to get back by midnight."

"Okay, Cinderella," Aaron said.

"Yeah, yeah," I said. "I'll come back sometime and hang out."

"Cool," Aaron said.

"Again, great show," I said to the band.

They gave a half-wave, but they were deep into their beer and conversation.

In the bar, the party was still going strong, and I suspected it wouldn't die down until early morning. We walked out into the crisp air and strolled back to the car.

"I had fun," Angie said.

"Me too," I said. "They seem to be popular. There were so many people there."

"They are."

We found the car and made it back to Chester right at midnight. I parked the car in her drive and let the motor run.

"Thanks for taking me," Angie said. "I was overloaded with work and the kids. I didn't realize I needed the break."

"You're welcome, but you went with me. I should thank you."

"We'll thank each other." She yawned. "I didn't know I was this tired."

"I'm glad you got to relax a little," I said. "I want to be here for you, Angie."

I wondered if she understood.

She looked toward the house. A lamp dimly lighted the window. "Do you want to come in?"

"It's late." I wanted to say yes, but something held me back.

"Yes, but I thought..." she looked into my eyes.

"Angie," I whispered.

Without thinking of the repercussions, I leaned in and kissed her. My lips brushed hers. Her scent filled me as she started to return the kiss.

She gasped and pushed me away. "No, Ryan. Stop."

"I...I wasn't thinking." Embarrassment colored my face.

"I can't. We can't do this."

"I'm sorry."

"I miss him, Ryan. He was everything I wanted." A tear fell as she added, "Almost."

"It was stupid...I wasn't...not thinking," I stammered, but the damage was already done.

She forced a smile. "It's okay."

She opened the door and got out.

"Tell the girls good night for me." I regretted what happened and desperately wanted to take it back. All I could do was hope I hadn't just ruined everything.

She stood there, her purse clutched against her chest. "They're asleep."

"I know."

"Good night, Ryan." She turned and hurried to her door.

"Good night," I said, though she couldn't hear me.

It didn't matter. I watched her until she got to the door. She turned and waved before going in, where her daughters were sleeping, and Missy was probably watching TV and waiting for her to get back. I sat there a minute longer, the sound of the engine much louder. I wanted to find hope in her wave. What I did was stupid and inappropriate. If she never spoke to me again, I would deserve it. I hoped she would.

My heart longed for her. The girl she once was. Pure, and untouched by pain and death. I longed for the boy I was twenty years ago, and what could have been. I pulled out of the driveway, slipped in the new CD and turned it up loud.

I thought, Would I be listening if things had been different?

CHAPTER TWENTY-FIVE

I couldn't keep my mind off the kiss, no matter what I did. I spent more hours at the office and started new projects, but it only worked until I was exhausted. Then I had nothing to do but think. I tried to go out on dates, but couldn't get interested. Every one of them made me think of Angie. I couldn't even make it thirty minutes without comparing them. It was exactly like my life had been before I found her. The only difference was that this time, she wasn't just an old fantasy.

I hadn't seen her much since that night. If I did, I didn't stay long. It felt too awkward. When I did ask to see her, she made excuses. Something going on with the girls, papers to grade. There was always something. I knew she was avoiding me out of guilt. She had a sense of loyalty to the man she had been with for a decade. What made it worse was, she knew I knew it.

I had taken to sleeping on my couch at the office. Sometimes, late at night, I would explore the city or check out some local bands. Often, I hung out with Aaron, and occasionally we'd jam. If he was out, I'd hang out with Smokey. He always seemed to be around.

Smokey walked in a perpetual cloud of hash smoke. He was an old hippie who had a lot of stories, and I would sit on the sagging couch and listen. He talked of protests and hitchhiking across the country, once to Canada during Vietnam. Smokey had also spent his fair share of time in jail, but never for anything serious.

"Want some?" He offered me his pipe.

"I don't know, Smokey," I said.

"C'mon, man. Live a little."

I shrugged and took the pipe. I inhaled and coughed.

Smokey slapped his thigh and laughed. "Try again, man. Slow. Hold it in."

I fared better the second time. I had little experience with any kind of drug, so I felt the effects almost immediately.

"No, man, get some more," Smokey said when I tried to hand back the pipe.

I shook my head and leaned back on the couch. Smokey plucked the pipe out of my hand before I could drop it.

Frank Zappa played on an ancient turntable, and we listened for a while. I had never really listened to him, but I was mesmerized. The music was complex and richly layered, contradicted by the often infantile lyrics. Under the influence, though, it sounded profound.

"Smokey, you ever been in love?" I asked after the side ended.

"Sure." Smokey took a long pull from his pipe and scratched his grizzled beard. "Or maybe it was lust."

"You don't know?"

"Nah, man. Lust is all it is," Smokey said. "Love's just a polite way of sayin' you like gettin' your dick wet."

"Don't know, man." I couldn't see it his way. "Kind of crude."

"I'm old. I earned the right."

"I guess you have," I said. "You ever had one you couldn't forget?"

"Had a lot I wish I could forget!" he said with a coarse laugh. "You need to get laid. I could make a couple of calls, you want."

"No thanks, Smokey," I said. "I think I can arrange my own liaisons."

"Don't sound like it."

"I don't think I can trust you."

"It's all the same in the dark, man."

"Says you," I said.

He offered me the pipe again, and I waved it off. He shrugged and took a long hit.

Aaron came in through the back, his hair still wet from a shower. "Hey, Smokey. You're not razzing my friend, are you?"

"Naw, man. We been listening to tunes and talking of peace, love and naked bunnies." He laughed until he coughed, then took another toke.

"You smoke too much. Crazy old man," Aaron muttered, then said to me, "What's going on, bro?"

"Same ol'," I said. "Just hanging."

"You're stoned, aren't you?" He sounded disappointed.

"Maybe a little," I admitted.

He heaved a sigh. "Damn it, Smokey. We already have to breathe it. You didn't have to feed it to him."

"I wanted to. Nobody made me," I said.

"It's cool, man," Smokey said. "We're just bein' mellow."

Aaron gave a dismissive wave. "None of my business. Do what you want."

"We're cool," I said.

"Actually, I wanted to talk to you," Aaron said to me. "Let's go up. I haven't eaten yet. I'll make us some sandwiches."

"Cool. I am a little hungry."

"I'll bet." He shot a glare at Smokey.

Smokey smiled and hit his pipe.

I tried to get out of the chair, but I felt like I had fallen into it. Aaron offered a hand and pulled me up.

"I hope you don't make this a habit," he said.

"Nah," I said.

"Hey, man, I'll see ya around," Smokey said, then settled back and closed his eyes. He was either meditating to the music, or taking a nap. I couldn't tell.

I followed Aaron outside. We climbed the wooden stairs, and I made my steps carefully. I always wondered if they were safe, but trusted Aaron would have said something if they weren't.

"Hey, Chris," Aaron said as we went in.

Chris glanced over and nodded, then returned to his war game. Gunfire and explosions blasted from the speakers.

We went to the kitchen. A breakfast bar separated it from the rest of the place. It could all use a fresh coat of paint, but it was surprisingly clean for the living space of three single musicians. I sat on a stool while Aaron grabbed sandwich stuff.

"Bologna and cheese," Aaron said as he tossed it on the counter. "Manna from heaven. You want mustard or mayo?"

"Both?" I said.

He tossed the bottle of mustard in the air, caught it, and gave it a twirl before he set it down.

"Fancy work," I said. "What did you want to talk about?"

"Remember we talked about being in a band together?" He spread mustard and mayo on slices of bread. He looked as if he enjoyed it.

"Yeah, I remember."

"You want to play with us?" he asked.

"With Schist?"

He nodded. "Yeah."

"What, to jam today, or something?"

"No man," he said. "Do some shows with us."

"What about Tod?"

"His mom's been sick," he said. "He wants to take care of her."

"That sucks." I hoped it wasn't anything too serious, but didn't ask.

Aaron slapped meat and cheese onto the bread and put them on paper plates. He searched the cabinets for some chips.

"It could be a month," he said. "A year. Maybe permanent."

"It'd be fun, but I have work. I'm not sure." I wanted to, but I didn't want to commit to something I couldn't follow through on.

"Just a thought," he said. "You said you have a kit?"

"Yeah, but I don't know if I want to do it full time," I said. "Maybe for a couple of months."

"All right, man." He found the chips and shook some onto each plate. "Look, Tod'll probably let you use his set. You don't have to cart yours around. We'll work around your schedule."

"I'm not sure." I hedged, but the idea of playing in a band again appealed to me. Doing it with Aaron just seemed right.

"Think about it, dude." Aaron slid a plate toward me. "I'd rather have you come in. Someone else, they might not like a temp gig."

"All right, but I'm not on Tod's level."

"It's not complicated. You can keep a beat, and that's the main thing." He took a bite of his sandwich.

The hash had made me ravenous. I tore into the sandwich.

Aaron laughed. "That's what happens when you let Smokey feed you."

My mouth full, I mumbled incoherently. He laughed harder.

"So, what's going on with my sister?" he asked after I began to eat normally.

"What do you mean?" I wondered if she had talked to him, and what she might have said.

He waggled his brows. "You guys getting together?"

I shook my head. "She's not interested."

"Yeah? How do you know?"

I set down the sandwich. "Dude, her husband just died. She has her kids. Work."

"Bill died months ago, Ryan."

Chris sauntered into the kitchen.

"Don't mind me. Just getting a pop." He cracked open a can of soda, took a long swallow and raised it in a salute. "Cheers."

Aaron waited until Chris had settled back on the floor with his game. An explosion came from the TV, and Chris cursed loudly.

"Want to know something?" Aaron asked.

I heard hesitation in his voice. Curiosity won over. "Sure. What?"

"I thought you and Angie would get married, despite everything."

"How did you think it would happen?" I asked, and remembered Angie had said the same thing once.

"There's a lot you don't know."

"You keep saying that."

"Honestly? I thought you would find each other quick, but it didn't happen." Aaron grabbed two cans of soda and set one in front of me. "If things had been different—"

"But they weren't different," I said.

"I liked Bill. He was good to her and loved her like crazy," Aaron said. "A lot like you did. I love my nieces, but I think I'd be okay with you guys being together."

287

I lowered my voice. "Can I ask you something?"

"Sure." Aaron leaned in.

"What happened? Why didn't either of you get in touch with me then?"

"That was a long time ago," Aaron said. "Does it really matter?"

"To me it does," I said. Angie had never said much, and I wanted to know, even if it didn't go anywhere. "I could have gotten letters and calls. My mom liked both of you. I wondered for twenty years."

"I get it," Aaron said. "My dad moved us here to work in construction with my uncle. We didn't really tell anyone. He made the choice. We were just kids."

"I understand his deal with Angie and me. Don't like it, but I understand. You could have written."

"I never did like to write."

"You write songs," I said.

"Letters are different. Anyway, my dad wouldn't have let me. You were a bad influence."

I laughed. "Man, I never thought I'd be called one."

"It was only because you have a dork."

"If that's the qualification, we're all in trouble," I said.

"I liked you and Angie together. I got in on a secret," Aaron said. "My dad knew I'd pass messages along if we stayed in touch, so nothing."

"I wrote letters. Did she get any?" I asked.

He shook his head, but I already knew.

"Your dad put me on call block. My friend, Scott too. But she..."

"Don't know what to tell you," he said. "No offense, but for me, most of it's been lost to the mists of time."

"None taken," I said.

"Here's something." Aaron sat up. "You know she kept her maiden name."

"Yeah. It was part of the reason her being married surprised me a little."

"You know why she kept it instead of taking Bill's?"

"Because she thought Tidman was silly?"

Aaron snorted. "It's not that silly, but be real."

"No, I don't know."

"If you asked her, she'd probably tell you it was for her career. By then, she had already taught for a year or two, and people knew her by her maiden name."

"Makes sense," I said.

"Yeah, but teachers change their names all the time after they marry. The next year's students would be different, and kids don't give a crap anyway."

"That makes sense too."

Aaron pointed at me. "I think she never changed it so you could find her."

"That's crap, Aaron."

"Is it?" Aaron arched a brow. "Tell me, how did you find her?"

"Finally looked up her name." I realized how valid his theory was.

"There you go." He crossed his arms and puffed up.

"I never stopped loving her, Aaron," I admitted. "Even now."

"I know, dude. She had a hard time at first. Girls are stupid about that stuff. She's kept herself busy, but I'm sure she's always felt the same way."

"Even after she married Bill?"

"She let it slip a long time ago," he said. "Bill reminded her of you. Really, you guys had a lot in common."

"I guess it's why I got along with him," I said. "I chalked it up to co-incidence."

"Bill knew it too, I think."

I nodded. "He told me once."

He placed his hands on the counter. "So tell me. Why aren't you dating, or whatever, yet?"

I hesitated. Should I tell him? He had answered my most pressing questions from our past, so it was only fair. I let out a sigh. "Remember your release party?"

"Yeah, what about it?"

"When I took her home, we talked a little."

"So?"

I took a deep breath. I couldn't bring myself to look at him. "And I tried to kiss her."

He laughed. "You did? That's rich."

"I misread the situation," I said. "It got awkward after, and things haven't been the same."

"Because she feels guilty," Aaron said.

"Why?"

He shrugged. "When you came back, I think it brought back feelings. When you moved for good, it sort of made it worse."

"Was it a mistake to come?" I asked. I didn't need him to say it. It was something I struggled with all along. I had injected myself into her life and never asked permission, and I did it in the guise of friendship. Could a man truly be friends with a woman? One that he had loved long ago, and still loved? I had convinced everyone, myself included, that I never wanted to hurt her. Maybe I had. Unwittingly, but still, I had.

"No, I don't think so," Aaron said. "I can't speak for Angie, but she's my sister. I know her better than most. You should talk to her."

"Yeah, okay." I had to believe there was a reason for it. Something had brought us back together; something beyond my decision to move here. Maybe I was too late, but it seemed fate brought me another chance. I hoped it wasn't just to laugh in my face.

After a moment, I said, "I think I'll play with you guys."

Aaron grinned. "And?"

"I'll talk to her," I answered. "But I'm going to take it slow."

"All you can do," he said and slapped my back.

CHAPTER TWENTY-SIX

After I started playing with Schist, I spent even more time practicing in my basement. It felt good to release my frustration on the drums after a particularly rough day. Now, I had a purpose for it. I still wished I had kept my old kit, but I had become attached to the one I had gotten. Tod let me use his kit in our rehearsal space, which kept me from having to schlep mine back and forth.

On the nights I practiced with the band, I crashed on my office couch and did a quick cleanup before everyone came in to work. Chuck knew I was doing it, but everyone else thought I had come in early.

I had worked up a sweat, so I put on a pot of coffee and took a shower, then slipped into some flannel pajama bottoms and an old T-shirt. I sat at the table with my coffee and watched the sunset through my French doors. Here, I could see some of the most beautiful sunsets, but it made me think of Oklahoma, and my friends. I had slowly found equivalents to the places we hung out, but it wasn't the same. There, it was my friends and the memories that made it breathe.

As the sky grew dark, I thought of Aaron's encouragement to reestablish a relationship with Angie, Scott's warnings when I came to find her, and my own doubts. All were valid, but ultimately it didn't matter what anyone thought. If I were honest with myself, what I wanted was her. I always had.

I contemplated calling her, but wasn't sure what to say. I picked up the phone, but canceled before I punched in the number. It was nine o'clock, a late hour when you had kids and a career. I didn't want to disturb her, but I knew I couldn't put it off much longer. We needed to talk. I debated it for twenty minutes before I finally called. I told myself it was just to check on her, but I knew it was a lie.

She picked up on the fourth ring. Her voice sounded so tired, I felt guilty. "Hey, it's me. Is it a bad time?"

"No, it's fine," she said.

"I wanted to check on you and the girls. It's been a while."

"I'd be great if I could get some sleep, but I need to finish up these papers."

"You're busy," I said, and I felt guiltier.

"I need a break," she said. "I just finally got the girls to bed."

"How are they?"

Her heavy sigh was exaggerated through the receiver. "Lily's developed a fear of monsters in the closet, and they both still ask about their daddy."

"It's normal, Angie," I said. "Most kids have a phase where they're scared of something, and they'll always ask about their dad."

"They ask about you too." The way she said it was sad. I didn't know how to interpret it.

"It's nice to know people think of me," I said.

"We do. Eva's still nuts about you."

"I feel sorry for her."

"She'll get over it," Angie said dismissively. "Are you okay, Ryan?"

I wanted to ask her if she got over it, but it would have been the wrong thing to say. "Angie, I just want to say I'm sorry. About that night. The last thing I want to do is ruin our friendship, and I feel like I have."

"It's okay." She said it, but I couldn't be sure she meant it.

"I'd like to see you," I said. "We can go for coffee and talk. Or you can come see me play with your brother's band."

"Is that this weekend?" she asked.

"Yeah."

"It'll be your first, won't it?"

"Yes," I said. "I'd like you to be there."

"I might. It would be fun. My mom's been after me to let the girls spend a weekend with her. I think I'll take her up on it."

"The girls will like that."

"They'd love it. She spoils them. Maybe I can write you into my schedule." I caught the smile in her voice and was relieved. It was the first time I started to believe it really would be okay.

"Super," I said. "I'll let you go so you can finish and get some rest."

"Thanks for calling, Ryan."

I set down the receiver and stared at it. I didn't know how to approach the subject of us, or if it would be the right thing to do. She was a different person now. Even though her essence was the same, she was not the girl I loved, what seemed ages ago. Despite our past, if anything were to come out of this, it would be like starting over. If we became serious, how would Eva and Lily take it? Right now, I was "Uncle Ryan," just a friend of the family. If Angie and I became more, would they resent me? Would they think I was trying to replace their daddy? Was I even ready for something like this? I wouldn't be in a relationship with a woman, but a family. Was it worth the risk of losing it all again?

If I tried, at least it would be fully my fault if it failed. There would be no one else to blame, and there would be no lingering questions. I decided there wouldn't be any harm in talking about it. If I brought it up, and she resented me, then perhaps it wasn't meant to be after all.

☺

"Let's take a break." Aaron took off his guitar and wiped the sweat from his brow as he went to the fridge to grab a bottle of water.

I laid my sticks on the snare and stretched before getting up. I was still trying to get used to the practice schedule. Sleeping on the couch a few nights a week wasn't doing my back any favors, but I was having fun.

Chris approached me with a can of beer. "Hey man, you want one?"

"Sure." I came around the kit and took the beer.

"You're sounding good," Chris said. "You'll do awesome this weekend."

"Thanks," I said and took a drink. The beer tasted like it had just come from the freezer.

"Aaron told me you guys go way back."

"I went to school with him and his sister."

"Rock on." He slapped me a high-five. "You'll have to come off with stories. I bet you got some that'll embarrass the shit out of him."

"Not really," I said with a shrug. "None off the top of my head."

"Bullshit." He elongated the word and punched me in the arm. "He's only told us the school was fucked up. I bet he was a hellraiser."

"Aaron's right, it was," I said. "But he didn't get in trouble. He's like he is now."

"Hey, Aaron," Chris shouted. "Ryan said you're a pussy."

Aaron gave me stink eye.

"I did not," I said to him.

"Can't take it back now." Chris turned to Aaron. "He said you're the same now, so you must've been a pussy then."

"I'll show you a pussy," Aaron said, and rushed him. He tackled him to the floor and playfully punched at him.

"Uncle! Uncle!" Chris laughed and pushed him off. "Fuck, man. I gotta play this weekend."

"Keep your mouth shut and I won't have to keep you in check." Aaron helped him back up and looked over at me. "Don't pay attention to him. He's the first in his family to walk upright."

"Well, congratulations," I said to Chris. "Look, guys, I should call it a night. I have to work tomorrow."

"All right," Aaron said. "I'll walk you out."

"Great," Chris said and opened another beer. "Give me a chance to heal. See ya, Ryan."

"Later," I said.

"You gonna be ready this weekend?" Aaron asked as we stepped into the night air.

"Yeah man," I said. "A little nervous, but nothing I can't handle."

"First gig, you're always nervous," he said. "Any gig, really. You ask Angie to come?"

"What, and embarrass myself?"

"Nah, she'll be happy. You got to work yourself in. Just hang out, help get her mind off things."

"She says she's coming," I said.

"So you did invite her," he said. "That's the stuff, bro."

"Do you realize how weird it is to have a girl's brother try to hook you up?" I asked. "Not sure what to make of it."

"We're not in high school anymore, Ryan. Everyone's an adult here."

"You sure?"

"Yeah." He laughed. "I know you, dude. I love my sister, and I want her happy."

"Me too," I said.

"I've only seen her truly happy three times in my life." He held up a hand and ticked off his fingers. "With Bill, with her kids, and then there was you. Honestly? I wish I had your magic."

"Magic doesn't have anything to do with it," I said, though I thought it might.

"Just don't wait too long, okay?"

I opened my car door. "I won't. Waiting sucks ass."

"Indeed it does, my friend."

I let my engine idle until he got back inside, then I went home. I had things to think about.

Since it was already so late, I headed toward the office and drove at a leisurely pace. I wasn't in any hurry. When I had arrived in Iowa, I had no idea my life would have taken the turns it did. I thought I had gotten over my feelings for Angie, but with everything that had happened, and with her so close, my old feelings surfaced again and were battling it out. It seemed to be too much, but for now, I was still standing and stronger for it. At least it was what I wanted to think.

I pulled into my parking space and let myself into the building. I walked through the darkness to my office, flipped on my desk lamp and poured myself a drink from the bottle I kept in my bottom drawer. I sat down and sipped my drink slowly. My mind began to drift.

After I finished the drink, I shut off the light and settled onto the couch. I quickly drifted off and carried with me a new hope, rising like the Phoenix from the ashes.

CHAPTER TWENTY-SEVEN

"Chuck, have you talked to Matt?" I had been looking over Matt's numbers, and they weren't getting any better. In fact, over the past couple of weeks, they had gotten worse.

"A couple of times." Chuck leaned back in his chair. He held his coffee mug in both hands and drank from it as if he were afraid he'd spill it. "Isn't he showing any improvement?"

"Nope," I said. "Not even plateauing. Just keeps going down. He's been collecting base pay for almost three months."

Chuck clicked his tongue. "Not good."

"What did he tell you?" I hoped it would be something I could work with.

Matt had been with us for six months, and had done very well. He had quickly become one of our best and had a few dozen regular accounts. Then suddenly, he flattened out and started to fall. He had even lost some of his accounts.

He was a decent guy, but if things didn't get better soon, I'd have to let him go. I have had to let people go before, but if I had to fire Matt, it would be the first time I cared.

"I don't know, Ryan," Chuck said. "He made excuses. Things going on at home. Same crap they always say."

"Maybe there is. He's not a bad guy, and he's proven he's capable."

Chuck shrugged and sipped his coffee. "He said he'd do better, but that was two weeks ago."

"I've listened to his pitches. It sounds like his heart's not in it," I said. "He's got the right words, but no oomph."

"What do you want to do?" Chuck asked.

I shook my head. "Don't know. I'm trying to think of something."

"We can work with him," he suggested.

"I already have some. I'd hate to let him go, but I may have to."

Chuck nodded sympathetically. "It could be a phase. Maybe you can talk to him again."

"In this business, we can't afford phases," I said. "That shit's best left to the moon and toddlers."

Chuck looked out my window, and I followed his gaze to Matt. He sat slumped in his chair and looked exactly like he had been sounding.

"Look at him. He can do it, but not like that." I sighed. "I'll talk to him again. Man, I friggin' hate this. Going into the weekend with this kind of trouble."

"Part of the job description, buddy," Chuck said. He tossed back the rest of his coffee and got up. "I gotta take care of some business."

"Before you do, could you ask him to come see me?"

"Anything else?" he asked.

"No, that's all."

He nodded and closed the door behind him. I watched as he walked over to Matt's workspace and spoke to him. Matt glanced toward my office. I could tell what he was thinking. He said something to Chuck, and after Chuck left, Matt went back to what he was doing. I wondered if he was doing work, or was just ignoring Chuck's message. I didn't want him to make this more difficult than it already was.

I glanced at my watch. It was close to two. Scott should have already been on the road for a while. I didn't know what time he left, but it didn't matter. I couldn't wait to see him again, and still found it weird we didn't hang out several times a week. It was something we had done since we were kids. I was excited he was going to see me play with Schist. I had done a few gigs with the band already, so thought he'd get a better show.

Matt finally got up and shuffled his way to my office. A big guy, he was six-five and easily weighed three hundred pounds. He was built like a football player and had a boxer's nose. He didn't look like he would fit in a place like this, but he had a gentle disposition and was friendly. Everyone in the office liked him. I hoped we could work something out.

He looked nervous, but tried to carry himself as if he weren't. Like he was just going to pop in to ask a question.

"Come in," I said when he knocked.

"Chuck said you wanted to see me?" he said.

"Have a seat, Matt," I motioned to the chair in front of my desk. He sat down in it gently. "How are you doing?"

"Okay. What's up?" I appreciated his wanting to get to the point, but I could tell he expected the worst.

"Just a chat," I said. "You seem to be having some trouble. Just wondering what's going on."

He looked down at his feet. "I know. I'll try to do better."

"Look, Matt. It's not that you can't do it. I know you can. I don't want you to tell me you're going to try to do better."

He glanced up quickly and then picked at his fingernails.

"I'm not mad at you. I want to help you get back to where you were,"

301

I said. "But I can't help you until you decide to help yourself. Maybe you can tell me what's going on, so we can try to fix it."

"I just got stuff going on at home, is all," he mumbled.

"I'll be honest with you, Matt," I said.

"Okay." He avoided my eyes. Instead, he focused on something above my shoulder.

"When someone's performance drops over a period of time, we're supposed to let them go."

"You're firing me?" he asked.

I tapped my fingers on my desk. "I'd like to avoid that."

"Sorry, Mr. Logan. I've got a lot on my mind." He waited for me to say something. I didn't. "My mom, she's sick, and with school, I guess I've been overwhelmed."

"I'm sorry to hear about your mom," I said.

"Thanks." He looked a little relieved.

"But do you see where I'm coming from?"

He nodded.

"I want you to hear something." I pulled up an audio file and played it.

It was one of Matt's early calls, a solid pitch I had used in training. His voice was confident, and you could hear his enthusiasm. Matt listened.

"Now, I want you to listen to this one," I said.

I started another of his calls from a few days ago. The difference was profound. He sounded almost bored, like it was a chore, and it had an obvious effect on the client.

I stopped the file. "Hear the difference?"

Matt squirmed. "Yes."

"You've done a good job, but it's obvious you hit a slump," I said.

"You can do this. There's no reason for you to make base pay."

"I don't want to either," Matt said.

"I understand things happen, and we get distracted. We've all been there." I leaned in and held out my hands. "If it were anyone else, Matt, I would have let them go two months ago."

He sat up and finally met my eyes. "I appreciate this, Sir. I really do."

"I'm giving you a chance because I know you can do it," I said. "Do you need to go part-time for a while?"

"No, Mr. Logan. I'll be okay. I promise I'll do better," he said.

"We like having you here, but if you don't get your numbers up, I can't keep you," I said. "There's only so much I can do."

"I understand."

"We'll do this. I'll give you another month," I said. "Don't be afraid to ask me, or Chuck, for help. If you need to talk, my door's always open. Okay?"

"Yes, sir, I'll do my best. I give you my word, I'll get better." I heard the confidence come back into his voice.

"Great." I stood and shook his hand. "Go make some money."

He went back to his desk with a different step. I hoped he was serious and that our talk did some good. I never liked to let anyone go, especially with people in Matt's circumstances. But, as Chuck said, it was part of the job description.

By the end of the day, Matt had put some numbers on the board. He had gotten a couple of new accounts and had good contact with older ones. It seemed he had taken our talk to heart and was already coming out of his slump. I was glad. He was a good kid and a hard worker when he put in some effort. All my people were good. The ones who weren't never lasted more than a month before they quit, or I had to let them go. I tried to be fair, but expected everyone to do their part. In this business, you didn't get far unless you did.

I stopped by Matt's desk. I glanced at a photo on his desk of an older woman, his mother, I assumed.

"Good job today, Matt," I said when he finished up his call.

"Thanks, Mr. Logan," he said. "I guess I needed the pep talk."

"Sometimes it's all we need." I gave his shoulder a friendly squeeze. "Let's keep it up. You need anything, let me know."

"I just need to leave outside stuff outside."

"All right, Matt," I said. "Have a good weekend, and I'll see you Monday, ready to kick ass."

"You got it, Mr. Logan." He got up and grabbed his Iowa Cubs jacket. "Have a good weekend."

I was glad I had the talk with him. I went to Chuck's desk. "See that?"

"Yep," Chuck smiled. "Just needed some encouragement. It should always be as easy."

"Hope it sticks," I said. "I gave him another month to get his numbers up."

"That was generous."

"Not really. You see his numbers since our talk?" I pointed at the board. "It would be generous only if he were worthless."

"I see." Chuck slipped a file into his drawer. "What are you getting up to this weekend?"

"My best friend, Scott, is coming up," I said.

"I thought I was your best friend?" He tried to look hurt, but failed.

"Not this weekend, Chuck."

"I'll remember that."

"Hey, I'm playing this weekend with the band at Jack's. You ought to come."

"I would, but Kay doesn't like going out to those places. Don't think we could get anyone to watch the kids anyway."

"Oh well. Maybe next time," I said.

"You heading out now?"

"No, I'm going to do a couple more things here, but I'll be out in a few. Scott will be here in a few hours. If you want to go, you can."

"All right." Chuck shut down his computer and got up. "See you Monday?"

"Monday," I said. "Hey, Chuck?"

"Yeah?"

"Keep an eye on Matt. Encourage him. I'd like to keep him around."

"Sure, Boss. Good luck this weekend."

On the way home, I stopped off at a convenience store for a case of beer and some snacks. I had just got in and put the beer in the fridge when Scott called and said he'd be another hour. I made up the guest room and cleaned up. After I finished, I couldn't stay still. Seeing Scott again after what seemed forever was too much. Like a kid, I went out to sit on my porch and wait for him.

"Dude!" I shouted when he finally pulled into my driveway.

He jumped out of his truck. "Dude!"

We skipped toward each other like a couple of little girls and crashed into an embrace.

"You live in the middle of nowhere, you know," he said.

"It's far enough from town to seem like it."

"I almost missed it," he said with a yawn. "I'm worn out. That was a helluva long drive."

He looked around. "You're keeping this place up nice."

"Thanks." We headed to the house. "Got a room set up for you."

"What, I don't get to sleep with you?" He made his bottom lip quiver.

"Shut the Hell up," I said and punched him.

He smirked. "You hit like a girl. Maybe you do other things like one."

I shook my fist at him.

He laughed. "I got all night to sleep, so I'd rather hang out."

"I hoped you'd say that," I said.

Scott filled me in on the news from home, and I ordered a pizza. We found a favorite movie on the TV.

"So, good back home then?" I asked.

"Yep," he said. "You're playing music again, so not bad for you here."

"The band's a temp thing," I said. "Tod's gonna come back eventually."

Scott shook his head. "They never come back."

"Sure they do. Vince Neil, C.C. DeVille, Joey Belladonna," I counted them off on my fingers. "A lot do."

"Drummers don't," Scott said. "Keith Moon, John Bonham, Razzle—"

"Because they're dead," I shouted. "Tod's not dead."

"Good point, but I think this one'll stick."

"I don't know if I want it to, but who knows?"

"You seeing anyone?"

"Nothing serious," I said.

"Anyone from work?"

"You want a beer?" I got up and started toward the kitchen.

Scott jumped up and followed me. "Well?"

"Yeah, so?"

"You dirty dog!" He grinned lasciviously.

"Shut up," I said. "It was just a couple of dates. She reminded me of Tina."

"Damn dude. Oh well, there's more out there."

"I guess, but I'm not looking. All I do is work and practice with the band," I said. "I hang out with Angie sometimes, but other than that..."

"How's she doing?" He asked. I waited for some smart-ass comment.

"She's okay," I said when one didn't come.

"Good."

"Pizza's here," I said when the doorbell rang.

I brought the pizza back and tossed it onto the coffee table.

"I thought I blew our friendship," I said. "But we're working it out."

Scott reached for a slice. "I can't believe you tried to kiss her. That was a stupid thing to do."

"Why say that?" I asked, but it was true. It was stupid. I had put us in a precarious situation when emotions were in flux.

"She's still getting over her husband, that's why."

"Maybe I wasn't tactful."

"An understatement," he said through a mouthful of pizza.

"It can't last forever," I said. "I'm still in love with her."

"Yeah, yeah. If I ever forgot, you'd remind me." He yawned and then finished his beer. "I hate to do this, but you mind if I crash?"

"No, we've got all weekend."

Scott went to the guest room, and I went to the fridge to get another beer and drank it there. Having Scott here was just like old times. I was glad he was going to see me play, this time with a popular local band rather than a couple of other guys in someone's garage. Even though we were both older now, and we lived far apart, it felt like home.

CHAPTER TWENTY-EIGHT

I went into Jack's Place, where Chris and Aaron were getting things set on the stage. Lonnie, our unofficial roadie, was putting together the drum kit.

"Hey guys," I said.

"Hey man, thought you wouldn't make it," Aaron said.

"No man, I wouldn't leave you hanging," I said. "Hey Lonnie. You remember how I like it?"

He tightened a crash cymbal into place. "Trying to."

From where I stood, it looked right. I hopped onto the stage and helped Aaron move a speaker. "You remember my buddy Scott?"

"Yeah," Aaron said. "Been a while. How's he doing?"

"Good. He's in town."

"Cool. He coming tonight?"

"Yeah. He's riding with Angie."

"Here's good." We set down the speaker. "Letting another guy make a play on your sister, are you? I'm disappointed."

"They're not remotely interested in each other," I said. "They're probably talking about me."

"You bet they are." He hopped off the stage and motioned for Lonnie to follow him to the soundboard. He adjusted some faders, then said to me, "Get up there and let's check the levels."

We all got on the stage and ran through a sound check. I looked out across the floor and imagined it was full of people with my best friends up front. I was excited for Scott to share this moment with me. When everything sounded good, we went to the back. Aaron brought some sandwiches and beer, and we sat on empty kegs to eat.

"When are they supposed to be here?" Aaron asked.

"Probably not until just before we start," I said. "I hope they don't tell each other crap that'll embarrass me."

"They probably will, dude," Chris said, then sang, "That's what friends are for."

Aaron grinned. "He's right. They both know you. Prepare for it."

"Makes me more nervous than the show," I said.

"Why?"

"Because my best friend's here. I don't wanna screw up."

"No biggie." Aaron took a long draw of his beer. "Just jump back in if you do. Nobody'll notice."

"You're right," I said. "Any word on Tod?"

"Don't know. If he doesn't come back, you want to stay?"

"It depends. Let's see what happens."

We heard our introduction, and we started toward the stage. I took a few deep breaths and told myself there was no reason to be nervous.

Aaron slapped me on the back. "In the immortal words of AC/DC, 'Rock your little heart out.'"

The cheers of the crowd energized me as I sat behind the kit. We started our first song, and I saw Scott in the audience, standing next to Angie. He gave me a thumbs up. I twirled a stick and pointed it at him without missing a beat.

ↄ⦿ↄ

"That was a kick-ass show, man," Scott said. "Much better than your crappy band in college."

"We weren't that bad," I said. We were, but I wouldn't have said crappy. "Glad you had fun."

He smirked. "Had fun with your girlfriend too."

"You wish. And she's not my girlfriend."

"Whatever, dude."

"You can be such an ass," I said. "Glad you came for the show."

"I came to see my best friend. The show was a bonus." He banged an off-rhythm beat on the dash. "You looked like you were having fun. I haven't seen that in a long time."

"I wish Brooke could have seen it," I said.

"You still think about her?"

"Of course," I said. "A lot of crap's happened. It's hard to have fun."

"Yeah, but you're doing it."

"You know, I'm still sad about her, but I'm glad for what we had. It was like I discovered life, and I didn't miss out on it. You made it happen."

"Forget about it. You going to stay with the band?"

I shook my head. "I don't think so. Maybe I'm getting old."

"You're not sixty, dude. You just have different priorities."

I thought about what those priorities might be. Despite the energy I had felt, I was tired.

"We should get some rest. I'm beat, and you have to start out early tomorrow," I said.

"Yeah," Scott said. "I wish I could hang out longer."

"Me too. We'll figure something out."

Scott slathered strawberry jam on some toast and made a sandwich of his bacon and eggs. A glob of jam fell out and landed on the table.

"Too bad you have to go soon," I said. "But at least I'll be able to keep the place clean."

"If you hadn't moved, we could hang out more."

"Yeah, I know. Sometimes I wonder if I made the wrong decision. If I had stayed there, maybe none of this bad shit would have happened."

"None of the good would either," he said. "And maybe the bad stuff would have happened anyway. You don't control fate."

"True." I hated it when he was right. He usually was.

"It's annoying as Hell." He set down his sandwich. "You make progress and then you fall back. When you stopped that shit, things happened. Life happened."

"I'm stupid sometimes."

He regarded me for a moment. "Sometimes?"

I ignored him and focused on my food. Scott gulped down the rest of his orange juice and set the glass down with a loud thud.

"I'm going to tell you something, Ryan," he said. "I thought I'd never say it."

He had my interest. "What?"

"Hook up with Angie."

I looked at him slack-jawed. "You're kidding."

"No, I'm serious."

"Funny. Aaron is saying the same crap."

"For good reason."

I got up and poured myself a cup of coffee. "You know what Lily asked me last week?"

"I can only imagine."

"She asked if I was going to be her daddy."

Scott leaned back in his chair. "Shit. What did you say?"

"No, of course." I sat back down. "I can be there for her, and Eva, but I can't replace Bill."

"Kids know," Scott said. "They're smarter than people give them credit for."

"Yeah, and they're great kids."

"Ryan, you still love her. She loves you too."

"She's a married woman."

"Was, my friend. She was. It may sound harsh, but fate does strange things. It's not always pretty."

"It doesn't mean I have to start a relationship."

He shook his head and laughed. "You already have. Put it into motion when you came up here the first time. Listen, I'm not saying you should propose, or sleep with her. I'm just saying it deserves a shot. You're good for each other."

"Sounds funny coming from you," I said.

"I watched you two together. I got to spend a lot of time this weekend talking to her. Alone. The funny thing?" He rested his elbows on the table and leaned toward me.

"Go on," I said.

"It's almost like the last twenty years never happened."

I got up and took our plates to the sink and rinsed them off.

"I honestly believe you two are meant to be together," he said.

"Maybe I was the one who was wrong all this time."

"Come on, Scott. We had separate lives. Twenty years is still twenty years. Things happened and had nothing to do with us."

"Well, maybe it all happened to prepare you for now."

"Did you take a job with Dial-A-Psychic or something?"

"Stop fucking around, dude."

I knew when Scott got that tone, he was not joking. I just shut up and listened.

"I'm trying to help you, Ryan. You and I both know this is what you want. Talk to her. Take it slow, but get off your ass and do something."

"Whatever you say, Scott," I said sincerely.

He stood up and patted his stomach. "My friend, it's time for me to shovel along."

I walked with him to his truck.

"Well, Ryan, thanks for the show and breakfast. Now come give me some sugar." He held out his arms and made a kissy face.

"You're such a fag." I laughed and hugged him. "I love you any-way."

"Now who's the fag?" He smacked me wetly on the cheek and slapped my ass before he quickly jumped into the truck and slammed the door.

I wiped my face and grimaced. "You are such an ass."

Scott leaned out the window. "Did that make you randy, baby?"

I shook my head and smiled. "Damn it, Scott. You're a moron."

"I know. I'll call you when I get back. Love ya, brother."

"Yeah, me too, I guess. Drive safe."

I watched him pull out of my driveway and begin the long drive back to Oklahoma. Before he was out of sight, I had already begun to miss him.

CHAPTER TWENTY-NINE

I sat in the parking lot outside the office with my engine running. I wanted to organize my thoughts before I went to see Angie. Normally, I'd just go, but this time it was different. I had stayed at the office an hour longer than normal, at my desk and toyed with the idea of resigning. I had even drafted a letter. The way things had been going frustrated me and I had begun to doubt being here was in anyone's best interest. Especially mine.

Everyone seemed to act as if I should move forward with Angie. Aaron, who probably had the best perspective, thought I should. Scott surprised me. For two decades he had tried to get me to forget her, and now he had told me to take a chance. Even Lily had asked questions in such a way, it seemed she was, though unwittingly, for it. They all nudged me forward; everyone except for Angie.

Angie and I had recovered from the night of Aaron's release party. I spent more time with her and the girls. Sometimes we'd go out, but mostly we'd stay in and I'd play with the girls while she graded papers, or something. Our friendship was closer than ever. I had to admit, the next step would feel like the most natural thing in the world. By all appearances to everyone else, we were a couple, but whenever the subject came up between us, she shied away from it. I had been content to be friends, to hold on to our pasts, and the people we had loved and lost.

I wasn't content anymore.

I was tired of pretending my feelings didn't exist. I was tired of pretending she didn't feel the same way. What was she so afraid of? I was scared too. Would we end up hating each other? Could something that had held on like a leech for so long truly die when it finally came to fruition?

They were all right. It was time we had a talk. I needed to lay it all out and see what happened. The best case scenario was she would throw herself in my arms and we'd live happily ever after. But what if she rejected me? Could we stay friends? Maybe, but we couldn't continue the way we are right now. Something had to give. No matter the outcome, I couldn't keep doing this to myself. If she really did not want to move forward, then I needed to make other plans. Maybe even move back to Oklahoma. I just couldn't sidestep the issues anymore and keep making excuses. Not for myself, and not for her.

I pulled out of the parking lot and drove to her house. I didn't bother calling ahead. It was time to come to terms with our past and do something about our future, or move on. Even though it would break my heart.

∞

"Ryan? What are you doing here?" Angie stood at the door, her cheek streaked with tomato sauce.

"I wanted to drop by. Talk," I said. "Are you having spaghetti?"

"Yeah, how did you know?"

"You have sauce on your face." I pointed at her cheek.

She quickly swiped it off.

"It was cute. You should have left it," I said.

She rolled her eyes. "It's a mess, but come on in. What did you want to talk about?"

"Just stuff," I said. I didn't think it was time to get into it. Not yet.

I followed her to the kitchen. Eva and Lily were at the counter attempting to make pasta dough. Angie wasn't kidding. Flour and bits of dough covered everything, especially the girls. Puppy scrambled around the kitchen looking for stray bits. He lapped at some flour and sneezed.

Angie nudged him with her foot. "Get out of my kitchen."

Puppy looked up at her, sneezed again, and ran off into the family room and plopped down in his doggie bed and stared at us.

"Hi, Uncle Ryan!" Eva cried.

Both girls hopped off their step stools and ran over to me. Inevitably, I got covered with flour too.

"Hey girlies, are we having dinner?" I asked, and they nodded. "We'd better hurry and get you in the oven. I'm hungry."

"No!" Eva giggled. "You can't eat people."

"You can't eat people." Lily mimicked her sister. "We makin' 'paghetti."

"I see that," I said.

"Are you going to eat with us?" Lily asked.

"Please?" Eva added.

"Maybe Ryan has other plans," Angie said.

"For them, I'll change my plans," I said.

"You don't have to."

"It's no big deal. I just had a date with some model."

She huffed. "I'm sure she wouldn't mind. Do you want to stay for dinner?"

"Yeah, okay," I said. "But Olga will be disappointed."

"Olga?"

"She models kitchenware," I said.

She laughed. "Since you're here, you can help the girls make the noodles. They haven't quite got the hang of it yet."

"I'll say," I said. "Come on girls, since I can't have you for dinner, help me finish up these noodles."

The girls got back on their stools and I let them run the dough through the pasta maker. I knew I was delaying the conversation I meant to have with Angie, but I wanted this moment. It would be better to talk to her alone. I didn't want to discuss it in front of the girls. For the time being, I enjoyed being with the girls. If I failed, I wouldn't have the opportunity again.

⊚

"Do you want to have a cup of coffee outside?" Angie asked.

"Yeah, sure," I said.

She poured two cups of coffee, and we took them out to the deck. We watched the girls through the window as they sprawled on the floor and played a board game.

"Thanks for dinner," I said.

"You're not a guest anymore, Ryan."

"Yeah, I know." I didn't know how to start. Or maybe I did, but I was afraid to.

Puppy bounded over to me and waited to be petted. Relieved by the distraction, I rubbed him between the ears.

"I think this guy has fully outgrown his name," I said.

"I know. He's gotten big."

Puppy panted happily while I patted him. Angie's chair creaked as it rocked. I couldn't put this off any longer. I picked up a ball and tossed it into the yard. Puppy barked and gave chase.

I let out a sigh. "So..."

Angie looked over at me.

"I was thinking about us."

She turned her attention back to the girls. I knew she understood what I was talking about.

"I know things are different now," I said. "We're not the same people."

I gave her an opportunity to say something. She didn't.

"I think you know how I feel about you," I said. "How I've always felt."

She stiffened slightly. "I know."

I hoped it wasn't a bad sign, but I had to keep going. "I care about you."

She hugged her arms and whispered, "Me too, but it's not a good idea."

"I can't say if it is or not, but I'm tired of waiting. Of wondering."

"What do you want?" she asked.

When I looked at her, I saw a woman, but I still saw the girl she was twenty years ago. Time had honed, but had not erased her. Why was this so hard?

"I want to be with you," I said.

She kept silent.

"Angie, just listen. When you left back then, my heart broke. I broke. I've spent most of twenty years alone because nobody compared to you."

"Ryan..."

"I'm not blaming you. It's on me. But I couldn't help but wonder if it had been different, if I had met you at the mall, or in college. If we had the same chance as normal people did."

"You don't know how I feel," she said.

"I do. You loved Bill." I motioned to the girls through the window. "He was their father. I don't want to be a replacement."

She spun toward me. "What else would you be, Ryan?"

"Please, Angie. Don't be upset."

"I'm not upset."

"I never stopped loving you. From the moment I first saw you. All this time, if I heard your name, or saw someone who looked like you, even a little, my heart jumped. In every girl, I looked for you. When I finally found you again, I knew it couldn't be the same."

She bit her lip and pushed a strand of hair behind her ear.

"I won't say it didn't hurt. It did," I said. "You were happy, though. I wasn't going to try. But I did want to be your friend."

"What do you want from me, Ryan?"

"I just want you to be honest with me. With yourself."

"I have never been dishonest."

I stood and walked to the edge of the deck and looked into the dark sky. "I just can't forget my feelings, Angie. If I could, I would have, believe me."

This wasn't going the way I expected. I was going to lose her. Again. I faced her. "I just want to know how you feel."

"I don't know what I feel, Ryan."

"Do you still love me?"

She sucked in her breath. "Don't ask me that."

"Why not?"

"I can't answer."

"It's a simple yes or no."

Her eyes were moist. "It's not simple. It's not."

It was too hard to look at her; I had to turn away. "I get it, but I can't do this anymore. I've tried, but it's impossible. I'll be content to just be your friend. Or, I'll go away and never bother you again, if that's what you want. But I can't do it with some hope hanging there. Just be straight with me."

I chanced a look at her and waited for an answer.

She didn't give one.

I lowered my head. My eyes burned, and I didn't want her to see me like this.

"I'll go home," I said, and added under my breath, "Maybe back to Oklahoma."

I walked down the steps and headed to my car. I didn't want to walk through the house and have the girls see me. Then I might have to explain, and I didn't want to lose my resolve.

I rounded the corner and wiped my eyes with my sleeve.

"Ryan," Angie shouted. "Wait!"

I swallowed and turned around. She ran toward me. I went to her.

She threw her arms around me and sobbed. "I don't want you to go. I don't want to lose you too."

"You will not lose me, Angie."

"Come back?" Her voice hitched. "Please?"

"Okay."

We walked back to the deck. She held onto my hand as if I were going to turn back around. I wasn't.

"What are you afraid of?" I asked.

"I...I don't want to be hurt. I don't want my girls to be hurt."

I looked into her eyes. They shimmered in the dim light. "I would never hurt you. Or them."

"That scares me too," she whispered.

"Why?"

I took her hands in mine and pulled her close. "I love you, and I don't care if you don't love me back. If you never do. Even if you hate me, just to have known you is the best thing to ever happen to me."

"I do love you, Ryan."

I felt I could see into her very soul. "Do you?"

"I do. My heart broke too when we left, and they wouldn't let me tell you. Tonight, when you walked away, I realized I don't want it to happen again. I don't—"

"It doesn't have to."

"I hope not."

I lifted her face to mine. "Always and forever?"

"Always and forever."

We kissed under the twilight sky as two little faces smiled and watched from the window.

AE
AAA

Acknowledgments

This novel, like life, was a long journey. Along the way, I have had the privilege of meeting people who have made mine better.

My friend, Sarah, who has continually offered encouragement and support, even when she didn't care for something I had written.

The team at AZ Literary Press. They worked very hard to bring this novel to life.

My fellow Astro Zombies: Keven and Joe. We'll get that ficus yet!

For the readers of the early drafts, especially Jimmy the Pirate, who pointed out the ending wasn't good enough.

To all the Ryans and Angies out there, and those who find a little of themselves in them.

And a special thank you to the brave men and women who serve on fire departments across the country, both regular and volunteer. You are appreciated.

About the Author

Richard Leighland is the author of House of Fate. Finding Angie is his second novel. He lives in the woods of Minnesota, where he continues to work on stories and novels in various genres. When not writing, he enjoys playing music and creating art. He can be reached through the publisher.

www.ingramcontent.com/pod-product-compliance
Lightning Source LLC
Chambersburg PA
CBHW011507170626
46812CB00009B/3011